Ian C Douglas wanted to be a writer
ambition that earned disapproval fro
not until teaching English at a Thai university, in the ... ...,
plucked up the courage to share his writing. After working as a golfing
correspondent, he returned to the UK and graduated with an MA in
Creative Writing (distinction). Today, he focusses on speculative
fiction. He also writes for the press, as well as for apps and the odd
radio play. Workshops, school visits, and mentoring are all part of his
writing practice. Ian lives in Robin Hood country with his wife and
children.

Ian is also an artist, a teacher and a counsellor. Sci-fi is his first love
and his passion for the genre inspired him to create the world of Zeke
Hailey.

Follow Ian at facebook.com/ian.douglas.3994
And Twitter @Iandougie

Also By Ian C Douglas in the Zeke Hailey series:

The Infinity Trap (Book 1)
Gravity's Eye (Book 2)
The Particle Beast (Book 3)
Electron's Blade (Book 4)
The Paradox War (Book 5 - forthcoming)

Zeke Hailey Series: Book 4

Electron's Blade

by
Ian C. Douglas

Electron's Blade

All Rights Reserved

ISBN-13: 978-1-925956-34-4

Printed in Garamond and Signo typefaces.

IFWG Publishing International
Melbourne

www.ifwgpublishing.com

Geoffrey Paul Douglas
1953 - 2018
Together, we walked the golden beaches of our childhood.

Prologue

Onboard the Televator,
Above the Himalayas
AD 2260

Most of the screamers stopped screaming after the first forty miles. By that time, the Televator was halfway up. Only another forty to Hyperbola Spaceport and from there to all known points in the galaxy. The passengers were comforted knowing they had less distance ahead than behind. After all, rotating up a magnetic pole into outer space could give anyone the heebie-jeebies.

Stella Gates, Stewardess-in-Chief, dimmed the cabin lights with a flick of her magnopad. The passengers settled down. Some read iMags, some enjoyed the in-flight holo-movie, and others simply snored into their pillows.

"I've had worse shifts," she remarked.

With any luck the passengers would doze through the final hours. And Stella could enjoy some coffee and cheese in the galley.

Stella peered through the window. She never tired of the view from the Televator. The horizon curved sharply at this height. A summer dusk poured indigo across the heavens. Far below, the Himalayas looked like scratches in the ground.

A child yawned in a nearby seat. In another couple of days, that little girl would wake up on a new world. Stella thought of all colonists she'd ferried to the spaceport. Thousands over the years. Just like this batch, another hundred or so bound for—where was it this time?

"Oh yes, Denebola Five." she murmured.

None of them ever came back. Sometimes that struck Stella as curious. But she was too busy with her work to worry about strangers. Over time, the faces all faded away. She rarely remembered an individual passenger, only the unspeakably rude ones.

There was that famous archaeologist. What was his name? The one that vanished on Mars.

"Professor Tiberius Magma. Right bossy boots."

And then there was that naughty boy. The time the Televator broke down. What was his name? Ugly looking kid with blue hair. Weird. Stella didn't like weirdoes.

Somebody screamed.

Stella rolled her eyes. Another anxiety attack?

A pale-faced woman was pointing at her window. Stella glanced out again. She screamed.

It was tiny. Very tiny. But hurtling nearer. A pencil-shaped object with a red tip. A flame blasted from the end. A vapour plume trailed away into snowy mountains.

Stella's mind raced. What did they call those things? She'd only seen them in the history iBooks. Outmoded technology from long ago, before magnodrives were invented. Torpedoes? Rockets? No, not quite. Oh, yes…missiles!

They were under attack. Terrorists! That crazy Martian State Brigade.

Images poured through Stella's mind at the speed of light. Mister Flopsy, her beloved tabby, waiting at home. Dear old Mummy, also waiting for her. The long-ago boyfriend who broke her heart.

Stella drew a deep breath. Panic was not an option. She had a job to do.

Red lights started flashing. The captain was activating emergency protocols. Stella switched her magnopad to loudspeaker.

"Attention! Sit down, fasten safety belts and assume crash position."

People obeyed her command, even as they cried and whimpered and prayed. Couples held hands. Parents hugged their children. Stella envied them.

She looked out again.

"Yes!" she cried, punching the air. The missile had peaked. It was beginning to drop, on a trajectory sure to miss the cabin. They were saved.

Her skin crawled. They were not saved. The missile was still on a collision course with the eighty-mile high tower, somewhere below.

Stella squealed and made a dash for her landing seat. She buckled herself in as fast as possible. The Televator was made of carbon nano-tubes, the strongest substance in the world. But was it strong enough to withstand a crash?

A faraway boom popped like a cork.

The cabin was tilting. Cups rolled away. Bags fell out of overhead lockers. There was only one explanation. The missile's impact was causing the tower to bend. But for every action, there is an equal and opposite reaction. Newton's third law. Like a pendulum, the tower was swinging to the left. Would it swing back again?

"It's okay," she shouted. "The Televator will right itself."

Thank heavens! The cabin was moving back to the centre. It was righting itself. Stella saw hope flicker across the sea of faces.

A noise of metal buckling and twisting echoed up the shaft. Stella pictured it, perhaps kilometres beneath, the tower snapping in two. For one ice-cold second nothing happened. And then they fell.

Part One

Chapter One

A Disturbingly High Ledge, Ophir Chasma, Mars

Zeke pushed down hard on his brakes. The bike skidded to a full stop, scattering dust into the valley below. He was a kilometre high, overlooking a stupendous view of the canyon.

The vast basin of Ophir Chasma gleamed red in the noonday sun. A petrified world, where everything was rock. Zeke's school, the Chasm, nestled among the northern cliffs like a concrete sea coral.

He took a deep breath of the cold Martian air. This far up, it reeked of a chalky sweetness. He glanced over the edge, to the sheer drop. His head swam. Any tumble would be fatal, low gravity or not.

"Albie."

A hologramatic dashboard flickered to life over the handlebars. Albie's name formed on its virtual screen. Albie was a unique travel app, left behind by Zeke's missing father. It could be downloaded into any vehicle to improve performance. It also gave Zeke total control of the vehicle. So far, Albie had been a bicycle, a gyrocopter, a grav-scooter and a Bronto.

"Please calculate how dangerous this route is for cycling," Zeke instructed. "Desired speed, Master Zeke?" Albie asked in a metallic voice.

Zeke scratched his chin for a moment.

"Recklessly fast," he replied.

The bicycle chassis pulsed with lights as Albie computed the factors. "Risk assessment complete, Master Zeke. Bicycle travel not recommended. Seventy percent chance of landslide."

Zeke felt temptation flutter in his ribs.

"Thanks, Albie, that's just the advice I need."

He shoved off with his right leg, immediately plunging down a steep incline.

"Wheeeeeeeee!" he cried as the bike hurtled downwards. The path was bumpy. Air whistled past his ears.

"Switch off rider assistance," he shouted.

"That is an unwise option—"

"Do it!"

The bicycle clicked.

A dip in the ledge appeared out of nowhere. The tyres lost contact with the ground. Zeke landed on the far side and kept peddling. Thanks to the low gravity, his calf muscles could push the bicycle much faster than on Earth. Adrenaline surged through his brain.

That's what you wanted, isn't it? The thrill? asked his inner voice.

A stone appeared on the path up ahead. He steered around it. The bicycle wobbled. His breath froze. Was he going to topple? He gripped the handlebars, his biceps straining. Yes! The bicycle stabilised.

He dared to glimpse down at the sand dunes, at the plains, at the lumpy rock formations. The planet he called home.

The path was getting bumpier. Zeke eased off on the pedal and freewheeled. Still the bicycle gained speed, as the ledge plunged ever more sharply.

"Oh, no!" A spur jutted out from the rock face. The path vanished. *Up!*

The word echoed through his synapses. His eyes burned bright. The bicycle lifted into the air, flew over the spur and landed on the other side, where the path resumed. Was it cheating to use psychic powers? Whatever.

On and on. He was lower now, about as high as a skyscraper. The way ahead smoothed out and cycling became easier. For about a hundred metres.

"Oops!" A bend was coming up. He hit the brakes. Dust spewed everywhere. Zeke took the bend full on, leaning inwards till the rock face was almost scraping his cheek. He regained balance.

The path curved back again. Zeke was pedalling furiously now. As if he wanted a crash. Faster and faster. Faster and faster. His left elbow bumped against a protuberance. *Grshda!* he cursed in the language of the long-dead Martians.

On and on. Now the way twisted like a snake. In and out, in and out. Zeke somehow kept the bicycle upright. The sound of his panting lungs filled his ears.

The finish line was in sight. Where the path melted into the valley floor. Just another twenty metres to go…no!

It was if Mars itself gave way. The wall beneath his wheels crumbled. Two billion years of erosion had left it as fragile as eggshells. A wave of ochre collapsed into the valley. Zeke and his bicycle were falling. Again, his eyes filled with light. He emerged from the dust cloud, pedalling thin air, twenty metres high and heading for a crash landing.

Slower, slower…

His powers decelerated the fall, but he was still coming in fast. The ground was racing up. Zeke closed his eyes. He felt the bang, the tumble and the slide, as sand scattered in all directions. Then a standstill.

He sat up, coughed out a spit ball of dirt and opened his eyes. Dust was settling all around him. The bike was nearby, miraculously in one piece.

He laughed. No doubt there'd be bruises tomorrow, but no broken bones.

Why do you keep taking these risks? asked his inner voice. The answer was easy. Zeke had survived the Infinity Trap. He'd escaped Gravity's Eye. He'd defeated the Particle Beast. Everyday Martian life was becoming dull. And that wasn't the only reason. The thrills kept his mind off the deaths. And the terrible future that might be waiting for everyone.

Zeke sat and listened to one of the very few noises of the Martian landscape. The hiss of dust devils. These were little whirlwinds, created by warm air rising out of the ground. They were forever gusting across the surface of Mars, just as they did on Earth, in the deserts.

A chill ran down his spine. This particular hissing was loud. Too loud. He took a deep gulp and slowly turned.

A dust devil gyrated a few meters away. Its vortex blew inwards, making the figure of a man. Head, torso, legs. And a face. Yes, a face that once was shapeless now had features. Spinning sand formed thick lips, a prominent nose, and eyes. Blank sand eyes.

Goosebumps raced around Zeke's body. The likeness was exact. Jimmy Swallow, one of the missing school students. As though a sculptor had moulded a sand statue.

Zeke gulped and said, *"Kshmlnwa."* Hesperian for hello.

The dust devil tilted its head to one side.

"Hello," it replied in English. And then, "you've changed colour."

Zeke frowned for a second. "Oh, my tunic. I'm a second year now. Blue's the colour for second years."

Silence.

"How...How are you?" Zeke asked.

"How am I what?"

"How are you feeling?"

Zeke could see the confusion on its shifting face. Arms emerged from the body, and it raised its hands.

"I feel with these."

Cultural misunderstanding, Zeke thought. He steadied his nerves. As fearsome as the Devil was, this was a rare opportunity to find out more.

"Why are you here?"

"You speak the old words. Only you and I. And—"

"And?" Zeke asked, scarcely daring to breath.

"You were Jimmy's friend."

"Didn't he hate me?"

"Yes. After you betrayed him."

Zeke opened his mouth to protest, then hesitated. From Jimmy's perspective, maybe there was a grain of truth in that sentiment. Zeke certainly regretted not taking Jimmy's illness seriously. The illness that was actually an ancient alien code turning Jimmy's body to sand.

"Is Jimmy alive?"

"No," the Devil replied. "His atomic signature mingles with mine. I see his memories."

The idea was fantastic. A two-billion-year old alien robot was crazy enough, but one spliced with a human boy…Rather, with the ghost of a boy. Unbelievable.

"What memories?"

Now the Devil lifted its head, as if staring into the distance.

"Hot buttered toast. A polished basketball court. Christmas trees. Girls."

Zeke bit his knuckle. Such everyday words, on the windblown lips of a monster.

It stepped forward, gliding a dozen metres till they were face to face. Zeke cringed. The stink of damp basalt was overwhelming.

"What about your memories? The Makers? Old Mars?" Zeke asked.

A spasm passed through its twisting body.

"Nothing."

"Nothing? But surely—"

"I have replicated many times. When I wear out, my atomic structure rebuilds itself. Every new devil is both the original and a copy. A million incarnations. A billion. My memory cells are not big enough to store that much information."

"A copy of a copy, times a million," Zeke muttered to himself.

"And now and again, an atom reforms in the wrong place. That mutation is passed on forever. Slowly getting worse."

It was inevitable that the Devil would get corroded, damaged, forgetful. Zeke's head swam with questions. "And the Infinity Trap? It is sealed, isn't it?" The Devil's purpose was to guard the Trap.

The Devil scratched its ear. Zeke shuddered. It was one of Jimmy's mannerisms.

"Yes," it answered.

"So, the Spiral can't get out?"

"We didn't only seal the Infinity Trap here. We sealed it across time and space. The entity you call the Spiral cannot escape. Yet, the Trap is a dimension in its own right, as big or small as it needs to be. Sometimes walls wear thin."

"Right, that's how I was able to see him in the pocket universe. But those walls won't break though, will they?"

The Devil shook its head. "Impossible. The Makers made sure."

"You said once you could still open the Trap."

The Devil nodded.

"But why would you? And surely you'd need five psychic brains."

An expression spread across the sand face. Zeke wasn't positive, but it seemed like a smirk.

"I could do it with one of your human psychic brains."

"B-but," Zeke stammered.

The smirk grew into a cruel smile.

"Five brains to open without my consent. One if I agree. Your professor did not understand that."

"But why? Why would you do that?"

"The day will dawn when you'll want me to unseal the Trap."

"Not in a month of Martian Sundays," Zeke said firmly.

"Things change."

The Devil swivelled a hundred and eighty degrees and took one step. A step that took it ten metres.

"Hey!" Zeke cried. "Why are you going?"

The Devil said nothing.

"Wait for me," he cried, breaking into a trot. "Please, there's so much I want to ask you." The Devil soared another ten metres.

Oh, no you don't, Zeke thought and translocated. He reappeared beside the Devil.

"Why can't you stay? You can help me."

The Devil whooshed further away. Again, Zeke translocated and caught up.

"When will I see you again?"

The Devil gazed blindly at him. The face creased into a new expression. Sadness.

"You won't" it said. "You will die."

Chapter Two

The Congregation Hall, Ophir Chasma, Mars

Zeke hesitated before the great, steel door. Overhead, the digital sign proclaimed: *Welcome to our freshers*. Once upon a time that was him. Not any more. But would his second year be any easier?

The Hall was packed with students and teachers. The walls were festooned with streamers and balloons. Macs scuttled around, serving snacks. A hologram of Country and Martian band *The Radiation Brothers* played in the corner.

The freshers were easy to spot in their silver uniforms. They all looked shell-shocked. Zeke smiled. They'd lived through their first translocation to Mars, the petrifying landing, and the principal's introductory lecture. No wonder they were shattered.

"Bro!"

It was Scuff, beside a punch bowl. Zeke decided to say nothing about his encounter with the Dust Devil. Not till he'd thought it over.

"A bit dead," Zeke remarked as he joined his friend.

Scuff nodded. The party was a quiet affair. Everyone was standing around, awkwardly trying to think of something to say.

"We need an icebreaker," Scuff said, and guzzled a glass of red punch.

Zeke glanced around the crowd.

"Looking for you-know-who?"

Zeke threw his friend a filthy look. No, he wasn't looking for her. Just checking who was there. Mariner Knimble, the translocation teacher, was chatting to Doctor Chandrasar. They both looked uncomfortable. Mariner Chinook, the psychokinesis teacher, towered above the teenagers, silent and brooding. Trixie Cutter, the official school bully, was working her way around the crowd, handing out business cards. Mariner Kepler, the telepathy teacher, was performing mind-reading tricks.

"Same old, same old," Scuff said.

Zeke nodded. "I like it."

"Yep, that's the thing about home," Scuff went on. "No matter how boring it gets, you never want it to change."

Zeke gazed at all the faces. Eating, drinking, chatting. Were they free of danger? Did he stop the Spiral for good, or was there a chance…?

A shadow passed over him.

"Hailey."

It was Mariner Ariyabata, the astral projection teacher. He was a tall, gangly man with a stoop and long black hair.

"Sir?"

"I hear you've enrolled for my class."

Astral projection was an optional subject that began in Year Two.

"Yes, Sir."

Ariyabata eyed Zeke from head to toe, his wide, dark eyes glistening.

"I hear you're a difficult student," he said, after a long pause.

Zeke's feelings boiled to the surface.

"Who told you that?"

The Indian gave a slight shrug and looked at the ceiling.

"Maybe nobody. Maybe I observed it myself. On my wanderings."

Zeke was too flustered to reply. Ariyabata placed his long, bony hand on Zeke's shoulder.

"Consider yourself warned. Any bad behaviour and you'll be in for a month of detentions."

With those words, the Mariner strolled off.

"Totally nuts, that one," Scuff said when the man was out of earshot.

Zeke was about to reply when someone tugged on his shirt. A

small boy with dirty cheeks, freckles and tousled brown curls stood before them. He was clutching his glass nervously.

"You Zeke Hailey?"

"Yes, how did you —"

"I looked you up, on Salford's Virtual Library. You being the last English boy before me to come 'ere like. Your 'air really is blue."

"Yes, it really is,"

"I thought we could be besties, both being English and all."

The boy stared at Zeke, a stare that was anxious and bold at the same time. They shook hands.

"Are you a Yank?" the boy asked Scuff.

"No," Scuff replied frostily. "Canadian."

"Alright, they're all dead polite up there, and eat maple leaves."

Without a word, Scuff filled his glass with punch and walked into the crowd. Zeke searched for something to say.

"So, what's your name?"

"Gary. Gary Aspeck."

"And how are you settling in?"

"My room is minging. A proper cave," Gary replied with a frown.

"Ah, the catacombs. I'm there too. It's where all poor students go."

Gary pulled a face.

"And…What did you make of the principal's lecture?"

"She's a right old boot," Gary said. "But it made sense. Earth's dying, so everyone's gotta move to the stars. And that's our job, or will be when we graduate."

"Yes, every Mariner translocates a colony ship out to deep space. Did you ever wonder why they don't come back?"

Gary looked confused. Zeke went on.

"We translocate ships around the solar system all the time. But every far-ship that's gone further, into deep space, never returns."

"Aw, you daft apeth. Why would they bother coming back 'ere?"

Zeke bit his lip. He knew there was something the Mariners' Institute was covering up. And that it was connected to his father's disappearance in deep space all those years before. But how to explain that to an innocent fresher?

"Gary, actually there's more to it—"

"Stop!"

The voice boomed across the Hall. Zeke turned to see the school principal materialising on the stage. He whistled. Projecting her voice in mid-translocation was quite a feat.

Principal Lutz glared at Zeke.

They don't keep me here because I'm beautiful.

Zeke blinked. Was she thinking in his head? Surely not!

Principal Lutz stood at her lectern, back straight, head high. Due to her rank, she wore cream-coloured robes instead of the white uniforms of the teachers. Her broad African face had a serious expression. Teachers and students alike fell quiet.

"This party is cancelled."

A chorus of disappointed sighs filled the air. Lutz's frown deepened.

"I have news. Terrible news. In all my years of running the school, this is the worst."

Zeke traded looks with Scuff. What was she going on about?

She cleared her throat.

"At 7.20 am, local Earth time, terrorists attacked the Televator. It was destroyed in a missile attack. The so-called Martian State Brigade claimed responsibility."

This time it was a chorus of gasps.

"Thankfully, the Televator cabin employed its parachutes. It landed intact with only a few casualties. But the consequences are immense."

Mariner Knimble raised his hand.

"The Televator is the only route from Earth into Space. Without it, all space travel will be brought to a halt. The colonists, supplies to Mars, everything."

The principal nodded.

"UNAAC is taking emergency action. They may even dig those antiquated rockets out of mothballs. But all that will take weeks, even months."

"Then Mars is cut off?" The panic in Mariner Kepler's voice was unmistakable.

"That's the least of our worries," Lutz said.

Zeke clenched his fists. What was she saying?

"Mars is at war."

For one sticky moment, nobody spoke.

"With those bandits, the Unpro?" Knimble asked.

"Yes," Lutz replied. "The Governor of Mars declared war on the Unpro in a pre-emptive strike. Yes, the Unpro deny any links to the terrorists called the Martian State. But both have the same goals. Independence for Mars. The Governor wants to get them before they get us."

Zeke's head was swimming with confusion. He thought of Ptolemy Cusp, the leader of the Unpro, and Isla the Incisor, his second-in-command, and their secret love. They were the enemy now?

"What do we do?" Mariner Chinook asked.

Lutz shrugged. "We do nothing. The Mariners' Institute is like my home country, neutral."

Knimble raised his hand again. "But surely—"

Lutz raised her hand to silence him.

"My words are being broadcast throughout the school. Listen carefully. Life will continue as normal. We do not involve ourselves with politics. The Mariners are on a more important mission. We are saving humanity.

"However, take note! Absolutely no student is allowed out of school until this crisis passes. You are all under curfew for your own protection."

Lutz threw Zeke a beady glare. He gulped.

"No one will communicate with the outside world either. We will look inward. We will continue our studies."

She glanced around the room.

"As this is no time for merriment, I suggest you all return to your rooms and focus on your coursework."

Students filed from the hall without a word. Gary tugged at Zeke's sleeve.

"What do we do now?"

Zeke struggled for a reply.

"A double chocolate moonshake, if you ask me," Scuff piped up.

They merged with the stream flowing out of the Congregation Hall. The great metal door clanged behind them.

"This isn't some kind of test, is it?" Gary asked. His eyes were wide with fear.

Before Zeke could answer, a bloodcurdling scream rang out. It came from behind the door and echoed through the cavernous corridor.

The principal!

Zeke wheeled around. A brief blur and he was inside the hall again. He'd translocated without even trying.

Lutz was on the floor, kicking wildly. The teachers surrounded her, too shocked to move. Her eyes glowed like magnesium flares.

A psychic fit!

"No, no, no," she shrieked, foaming at the mouth. "You have to stop it."

Knimble spotted Zeke.

"Get out!" he shouted.

"But, Sir—"

"Out!"

Zeke obligingly vanished.

Chapter Three
The Cranny Cafeteria

Gary sipped his moonshake.

"Mi 'ead 'urts."

The three boys were sitting at the panoramic window, looking out onto towering canyons. Sunlight streaked the cliffs in rust and shadow.

"War breaking out on your first day is pretty daunting," Zeke agreed.

Scuff slurped from his glass. His bulging eyes reminded Zeke of a frog on a lily pad.

"Mars is totally insane," Scuff remarked.

"Anything we can set straight?" Zeke asked.

Gary scratched his messy curls.

"Well, what is it with all these chasmas and valleys?"

Scuff gestured to the vast expanse of rock outside.

"Behold Mariners Valley. Largest canyon in the solar system. As wide as the USA and five miles deeper than the Martian surface."

"Nearly all the colonies and settlements are here," Zeke explained. "Our ancestors started terraforming Mars two centuries ago. As air levels rose, Mariners Valley became the first habitable region."

Gary's eyes lit up. "Because air pressure is strongest the deeper you go?"

"Simple gravity," Scuff said. "The air up on the surface is still very thin. Like being on the peak of Everest."

A new frown gathered on Gary's forehead.

"But aren't we in Ophir Chasma? And what is a chasma?"

Scuff smirked at the fresher's ignorance.

"Mariners Valley is a network of smaller canyons. I say small, but they're huge by Earth's standards. Chasma is Latin for canyon. The school is situated in Ophir Chasma, the northernmost. That's why the school is nicknamed the Chasm."

"Okay, I get that. But who or what are the Unpro?" Gary asked.

"That's easy," Zeke began. "Every colony is a protectorate of the nation that set it up. Obama Town belongs to the Americans, Hokusai Station the Japanese. Tithonium Central, our only city, is under UNAAC control. Even the School belongs to the Mariners' Institute. But some colonists want to be independent of Earth. Yuri-Gagarin Freetown, for example, it rebelled against the Russians and became self-governing. A few others did too. So those colonies are unprotected. They banded together and call themselves the Unpro."

"And the Unpro blew up the Televator?" Gary asked.

Zeke stared at the bubbles in his moonshake.

"Maybe. But they say they know nothing about the Martian State Brigade. That the Brigade are a bunch of extremists acting alone. And as not one of the Brigade has ever been caught, who knows?"

"Dead miserable of them, spoiling Freshers' Day," Gary remarked.

Scuff clicked his fingers at the nearest drinksomac. The robot wheeled over on squeaky castors.

"Three more moonshakes," Scuff said.

The robot bleeped and rumbled. A door in its chest popped open to reveal glasses brimming with froth.

"Here you are, Sir," said the robot's mechanical voice as it served the drinks.

Gary suddenly nudged Zeke.

"You got a girlfriend or what? She's mint."

Zeke stared blankly at his new friend. Gary nodded to the glass doorway and a Chinese girl with long, straight hair. Her face was round and pretty.

"Oh, her," Zeke replied and turned back to his drink.

"She definitely looked at you, our kid," Gary went on.

"We used to be friends, her name's Pin-Mei Liang."

"Ouch!" Gary cried as Scuff kicked him under the table.

Pin-mei crossed the cafeteria to the jukebox and pressed a button. Then she joined a couple of girls at a corner table. A Country and Martian band materialised out of nowhere. A hologram of the *Radiation Brothers*. They launched into the opening bars of *Moonstone Cowboy*.

Scuff tapped the table.

"We're forgetting the important thing. You saw Lutz in the grip of a psychic fit."

"That's when a pre-cog gets overloaded with a vision of the future?" Gary asked, still keeping an eye on the Chinese girl.

"Sure is, and Lutzie is a pre-cog," Scuff replied. "Zeke, did you get any clue what she was seeing?"

Zeke remembered her words. *No, no, no. You have to stop it.* A chill tickled his spine.

"No. I'm just worried…" his words trailed off.

"You're thinking the Spiral, aren't you?" Scuff said.

Zeke said nothing.

"What spiral?" Gary asked.

"The interdimensional demon who did for the ancient Martians," Scuff replied.

Gary's mouth dropped.

Scuff laughed. "You don't want to believe everything you read in textbooks. Two billion years ago, this planet was crawling with aliens."

"You are kiddin' me!"

Scuff shook his head. "No siree. And they were all wiped out by the Spiral."

"That's enough." Zeke sounded angry. "He doesn't need to know that."

"Hey, don't get in a strop," Gary snapped.

"Some things are better not knowing," Zeke added.

Gary jumped to his feet. "I'm no kid." His freckled cheeks were red. "You're well snide. I'm off."

He stormed off, banging into several chairs on the way.

"Where did that come from?" Zeke asked in a dazed tone.

"Space travel, culture shock, chocolate. It's a tough combo," Scuff suggested.

"He did look exhausted."

"Never mind him, tell me all about it."

"Nothing more to say," Zeke replied.

"Wasn't Lutz on the floor, thrashing about?"

"Yep."

"So, did you see her panties?"

"Scuff!" Zeke flicked drops of moonshake at his best friend with the straw.

Scuff picked at his nose.

"Not every day you see a psychic fit."

"Exactly," Zeke said. "The only one I've seen was Pin-mei's. First time I ever heard the Spiral's name."

Scuff lost his grin.

"That was a year ago. No reason why Lutz's premonition was Spiral-related. More likely it was some vision about this war. Some battle or massacre, maybe?"

Zeke gazed out at the vista of peaks. The sun was setting. A tide of darkness crept across the Valley.

"That doesn't make me feel any better," he remarked, after a long pause.

The buzzer buzzed. Zeke peered through the door's spyhole. It was Gary, looking very uncomfortable. The auto-door swished open.

"I've come to say sorry."

His hair was dirtier, the circles around his eyes darker and his silver tunic scruffier.

Zeke beckoned him in.

"Fancy a cuppa?"

"I'm gaggin' for a drink."

Zeke focussed on the fusion kettle and it clicked on.

"Whoa, magic!" Gary said, mouth gaping.

Zeke smiled.

"Psychokinesis. You can have the chair."

Zeke sat back on his bed and said, "Forget about today."

"Dunno what came over me. Just felt you were takin' the Mickey."

Zeke raised a hand to silence him.

"I get it. The transition to Mars is tough."

Gary beamed.

The kettle pinged. Two tea-cubes levitated out of their box and into each cup. The kettle lifted itself up and poured in boiling water.

"Milk and sugar?" Zeke asked.

Gary nodded vigorously.

"Five sugars please."

The milk jug and the sugar bowl added their contents. A spoon stirred the steamy contents. Finally, both cups glided through the air, one to Gary and one to Zeke.

"Don't burn yourself," Zeke said.

"Your eyes weren't glowing." Gary said.

"No," Zeke replied. "As time goes on, your mental muscles get stronger. That was easy for me."

"They told me every Mariner has a best skill. Is that yours?"

Zeke thought for a moment.

"No. I guess translocation is mine."

A suspicious look formed on Gary's face.

"Mariner Knimble told me nobody is allowed to try that till the fourth year. It's the most dangerous ability."

Zeke nodded.

"Yes, I chopped a man's foot off once. Get it wrong and you can materialise inside a wall or with your head in the ceiling."

"Then why do it, our kid?"

Zeke glanced away. It was all such a long story.

"Because I had to, if I wanted to survive. I don't want to go into it right now."

Gary pushed his bottom lip out.

"Tell me about your family," Zeke added hastily.

Gary stared at the floor.

"Got none. Grew up in the Salford Home for Unattached Children."

"Oh!" was all that Zeke could say.

"Mi' parents were washed away in the Great Mancunian Flood."

"That's awful. Global warming has a lot to answer for."

Gary sipped at his drink.

"I used to daydream about going back in a time machine. Fixing all those people who destroyed the environment. Hurting them the way they hurt me."

Zeke wrung his hands.

"You have to remember the twenty-first century was very primitive."

Gary scowled.

"Even cavemen had common sense. The world can only take so much poison."

Zeke decided to change the subject.

"We've got that in common. My dad is missing."

Gary raised his eyebrows. "Thought 'e were dead too?"

"He's just missing," Zeke remarked coldly.

"Sorry, our kid. Your file in the Salford Virtual Library said he was a Mariner and got killed on a mission."

Zeke took a few deep breaths.

"He was on a mission for them, yes. It was called the Flying Dutchman Project. The idea was to investigate why nobody ever returns from deep space. He translocated a team to the star Alpha Cephei as an experiment. And they, too, didn't return."

Gary laughed. "The ship probably blew a nuclear gasket. Or maybe they discovered a planet full of beautiful girls and—"

Zeke's frosty stare killed the words on his lips.

"Anyway, one day I'll go and find him. Bring him home," Zeke said. "When I graduate as a Mariner. Unless something comes along first."

"Good luck with that. Not like you find empty far-ships lying about the back garden."

Zeke's scalp tingled. "I might surprise you yet."

"Then I'll come with you. We're besties now."

"Besties?"

Gary's wide grin cracked again.

"You's a proper Londoner. Best mates." He blushed.

"Hey, why don't I teach you a trick?" Zeke said.

His magnopad rose from the bed and fluttered through the air. It dropped into Gary's lap. Gary whistled.

"Now, you send it back to me."

"I can't, our kid."

"Easy. Close your eyes. Relax. Picture the 'pad floating back to me. Don't think about how or why. Just visualise and accept it."

Gary shut his eyes tight and screwed up his face. His shoulders tensed and his fists balled. Sure enough, the magnopad jerked into the air. Briefly. Then it clanged onto the floor.

"Oh, I broke it."

Zeke reached out his hand and the 'pad flew to his grip.

"It's fine. Not bad for a beginner."

"Really?" Gary was even redder than before.

"Absolutely."

"I feel like mi' brain's waking up."

Zeke drained his tea.

"That'll be the lack of magnetism."

"Yup, I know that. Magnetism blanks out psychic powers. It wasn't till humanity moved into outer space, outside Earth's magnetosphere, that people discovered they were psychic."

"The one-in-a-million lucky enough to be gifted."

"Yup," Gary said. "But Mars has no magnetic field. So, they built the school here as the best training ground."

Zeke reached over and placed his cup on the bedside cabinet.

A scream pierced the air. Gary! He was kicking and struggling and falling. Falling upwards. Something was sucking him into the sky.

"Are you alright, our kid?"

Zeke blinked. Gary was sitting on the chair, as right as rain.

"Sorry, got distracted."

"You's gone an 'orrible white."

"I am feeling unwell. Better turn in."

Gary jumped up and shook Zeke's hand.

"Thanks for being my bestie. The Chasm's gonna be the best thing that ever 'appened to me."

Chapter Four
Astral projection 101

I t was a very unusual classroom.

"Come in, don't dally," said Mariner Ariyabata.

He was sitting with his long legs draped across the desk, casually reading an old-fashioned paper book. Doleful eyes gazed out through an untidy fringe.

There were no student desks or seats. Instead, the room was full of mats and pillows. Posters decorated the walls with pentacles, crescents, and stars. A bronze Buddha sat beneath the plasma board, with incense sticks smouldering away. The air reeked of sandalwood.

"Is this yoga class or what?" Dedy, the Indonesian student, joked. Ariyabata glared at him. Dedy mouthed a *sorry* and crept to the back.

Zeke glanced around, hoping Scuff had changed his mind and opted for this class rather than Remote Viewing 101. Obviously not. That was a pity. Scuff's company kept Zeke going. Most students regarded Zeke with suspicion, after his various misadventures with the Dust Devil, Fitch Crawley, and the collapse of the Melas Mine. The more he protested his innocence, the less they believed him. So, a sympathetic face would be nice. Sadly, it was not to be. Zeke joined Dedy in the back row.

Ariyabata leapt on top of the desk.

"This way," he said, sitting cross-legged on the desktop. "Welcome, my little psychonauts, to Astral Projection 101."

A few of the students were groaning as they forced their limbs into the required position.

"So, what brave soul will give us a definition of the subject?"

His dark, watery eyes gazed around the class. Zeke gulped.

"Out-of-body stuff?"

Ariyabata glared at him.

"Is that the best you can do? Okay, a quick textbook definition. When your consciousness goes on a journey while leaving your body behind. You travel as a disembodied spirit."

"Like a ghost?" asked a pimply girl in the front.

Ariyabata gave a condescending chuckle. "Hardly. Ghosts aren't real. We are."

"How is that different to translocation?" Zeke asked with a puzzled frown.

Ariyabata looked at him as if he were a dunce.

"Translocation? The ability to step outside space-time and to re-enter at another point. All to do with String Theory and the space inside atoms. How tedious!"

Twenty pairs of eyebrows shot up. Principal Lutz never stopped saying how crucial translocation was. Those graduates who mastered the skill would become heroes and pilot far-ships to the heart of the galaxy.

"My skill is quite different. Your body goes nowhere. The consciousness exits the brain, travels far from the body and returns. Unlike translocation, you don't leave the space-time continuum."

Zeke put up his hand.

"Sir, supposing the spirit didn't come back to the body?"

"Then you'd be dead."

A collective gasp echoed through the classroom. Ariyabata waved his long, scrawny hands.

"Fear not! We'll study for yonks before actually attempting it. Not till you're ready and then in strict supervision."

The students settled.

"For this term alone," Ariyabata began, "we will simply be practicing meditation techniques. The methods needed to reach the mental state of projection."

"Couldn't we accidentally slip out of our heads?" asked a blonde American girl.

Again, the condescending chuckle.

"Indian mystics took centuries to achieve astral travel. Nobody ever *slips out*, as you colourfully put it. Projecting is extremely hard. Many of you will never actually accomplish it. Those who do can expect to practice for months."

"What's it like?" Zeke asked, his curiosity piqued.

Those mournful eyes gleamed.

"Like a dream. You are the breeze. As light as a feather and quite unseen. Intangible. Able to swim through clouds or walk through a wall…"

Ariyabata's voice trailed off, lost in his own dream. "Oh, yes," he said after a few seconds. "And now a taster of lessons to come, my children. Today we will familiarise ourselves with the art of relaxation, the first step to setting the mind free."

The students exchanged uneasy looks.

"Tish, tish. Lay down and get comfortable," Ariyabata said. He clicked on his magnopad. The murmur of gentle waves filled the room.

"Close your eyes and feel a soft glow oozing up from your toes, soothing your muscles."

Zeke stretched out and put the pillow behind his head.

Hope I don't fall asleep, he thought.

Ariyabata continued talking. His tone was comforting, the words soothing. Zeke's feet and calves relaxed, next his thighs and then up into his stomach. He was surprised at how quickly his body responded to the teacher's suggestions. Even that surprise melted away.

Ariyabata's voice dropped to a whisper.

"Let the glow flow into your head. And all that tension and worry ebb away, through your skull, away."

Yes, it was working. Zeke's scalp tingled. Every muscle went limp. As though he were floating. Drifting.

Ariyabata fell silent. The only sound was the lapping of the sea. Soft, repetitive, reassuring.

Zeke focussed on the waves. Such a beautiful noise. As he listened, he sank deeper into this happy trance. On the verge of sleep. Not tired, but superbly relaxed. Deeper. Happier. Floating. Rising. Rising. Rising.

Zeke lazily opened his eyes. The concrete ceiling was a few inches above him. Below, he could see himself on the mat, taking long, slow breaths. Ariyabata was still on the desk, and the rest of the students lay around the classroom. A couple were snoring.

I did it! Zeke thought with a thrill. And yet he was not anxious. Even though he seemed to be nothing but pure thought, he felt safe.

Why stop here? he thought, and went higher. The ceiling came nearer and nearer. And then, without a hint of a bump, he merged into its concrete greyness.

Chapter Five
Above the Chasm

Zeke emerged through slates and kept rising. It was rather like being a balloon. He drifted a little to the left and a little to right. But always up, into the blue of the sky.

The school sprawled beneath him. There was the Grand Hall clinging to the canyon, an intricate coral of arches and parapets and buttresses, a hundred years old and still growing. A row of turrets had recently been added on Lutz's command. They poked out of the ancient structure like stubby fingers.

Towers dominated the school grounds. They were clumsy and mud-coloured. A city of termite mounds, as Zeke often described them. All fenced in by the school wall, with its stone gate. Engraved above the gate were the first sentence of the Mariners' mantra: *Gravity, magnetism and thought are the forces that bind the universe together.*

"And of these three, thought is the most powerful," Zeke recited.

He looked further. Beyond the school walls lay Ophir Chasma, a gigantic arena of sand and rocks, all enclosed within the eight-kilometre-high cliffs. A wilderness of stone untouched for two billion years. Around the school, the cliffs soared to dazzling heights. Nearer the horizon they appeared to shrink sharply. For such a small planet, Mars had a grand scale. The tallest volcanoes and the largest canyons.

The most striking feature, Zeke thought, was not what he could see but what he could hear. Rather, what he could not hear. Mars was so hushed. No tinkle of streams. No breeze in the treetops. No bird song. Not even the beep-beep of traffic.

Then a thought struck him. If his body, with his eyeballs, were back in the classroom and he were a disembodied spirit, how did he see? Maybe it was really just a dream.

Lutz's tower caught Zeke's attention. He focussed on the lofty minaret and found himself rushing towards it. He passed through the wall. Now he was outside Lutz's office. Marjorie Barnside, the school secretary, sat at her desk typing away. For all the world, she looked like a stout, grey-haired woman, bossy but human enough. Zeke was one of the few who knew her secret. Her skin was synthetic and electricity flowed through her plastic veins. The school secretary was an android!

Zeke had found out one fateful night when she tried to save him from the Dust Devil. But androids were illegal throughout the solar system. It was too easy to mistake them for real humans, and that opened up a lot of criminal opportunities. So why was Principal Lutz allowed one? Zeke's guess was that the principal needed an assistant who could last a long time. A very long time. Someone who could keep up with her extended lifespan. That was the other secret. Every time Lutz died she was cloned. A brain chip was passed on from clone to clone. This meant every new Lutz had all the previous clones' memories. It was a kind of immortality.

The intercom buzzed.

"Yes?" Marjorie asked in her thick Belfast accent.

"Come and take notes," a voice said. A voice that was not the principal's.

Zeke frowned, or imagined himself frowning. It was hard to be sure in his out-of-body state. He'd never known anyone but Lutz to use that intercom. Barnside walked into the next room with Zeke floating behind her.

His unease deepened. Mariner Knimble was occupying Lutz's chair. What would prompt him to do something so impudent as to take her seat? Lutz would kill him if she found out.

Mariner Bobby Chinook and Doctor Chandrasar sat across from Knimble. They all looked very grave. Barnside took the chair against the wall, grabbed her magnopad and nodded. Zeke hovered in mid-air.

"Doctor Chandrasar, your report for the record," Knimble said, scratching his bare head.

Zeke felt a hot sensation as Chandrasar stirred, her dark-as-the-night hair, catlike eyes and saffron skin. A flush? But how was that possible when he was made of pure thought?

"Lutz suffered an extreme psychic fit. It happens occasionally. Normally they pull out after a few minutes, but the principal sustained a severe mental shock. This has left her in a state of great anxiety, almost delirious. I can't pacify her. She's sedated for the present and resting in her apartment."

"Prognosis?" Knimble asked. He gazed upwards. His fathomless blue eyes peered right through Zeke, as though he were watching something very far away. Zeke gave an imaginary gulp. The teacher couldn't see him, surely? Or was Knimble able to sense Zeke on some other level? Telepathic, maybe?

"Oh, she'll make a full recovery. She needs a few days," Chandrasar said.

"So, it's not time to order Lutz Six, then?" Chinook asked in his booming baritone.

The adults laughed. Except Barnside, who scowled at them.

"No," the doctor replied. "But until she's okay, who's steering the ship?"

She and Chinook waited for Knimble to respond.

"I am the most senior staff member," he acknowledged. "Doesn't seem bonzer though, stepping into her shoes."

Chinook leaned forward.

"The most important school in the solar system cannot be leaderless. Least of all in the heat of war."

"You're right," Knimble said reluctantly. "And that burden falls to me."

"What will we tell the students?" Chandrasar asked.

Knimble scratched his chin.

"Nothing, let them believe Lutz is at the helm. Business as usual.

I'll brief the Institute later."

"That's agreed then," Chinook said.

Knimble nodded. "Deffo, mate. The outside world need never know. But for the next few days I'll mind the shop. Take the decisions, sign the orders, make the calls."

"Talking of decisions," Chinook began. "What about the Governor's request?"

Knimble's eyebrows raised.

"About Hailey, you mean?"

Zeke's absent heart skipped a beat.

Knimble considered for a moment.

"The Governor of Mars can bog off. The school is neutral."

The Governor? Request? What request? Zeke trembled. He had to know more.

"Hailey!"

His name echoed out of thin air. Nobody else in the room heard it.

"Hailey!" The voice had the lilting cadence of a cello.

Zeke's eyes opened with a start. He was back in the classroom, on his mat. The other students were gone and Ariyabata loomed over him.

"How dare you doze off in my lesson!"

"Sir, no! I was astral travelling!"

"Of course, you were," the teacher scoffed.

"Truly, Sir."

"Liar!"

"But, Sir—"

"It would take a genius to leave their body on the first day."

"Sir, I did leave my body"

Ariyabata shook his fist.

"You, boy, fell asleep and had a dream. As a punishment I will set you an extra homework. You scoundrel."

Zeke rolled his eyes. In the doghouse again.

Chapter Six

The South Cloister

"Bro, you were totally dreaming."

They were sitting in the shadow of the pillars. Overgrown cacti filled the courtyard, genetically modified for the cooler Martian climate. Zeke stared at them and pictured spiky green worms bursting from their pots.

Scuff clicked his fingers and a drinksomac trundled over. A basic fridge on wheels, the 'mac asked, "Anything to drink, Sir?"

"A Craterade, please."

The drinksomac beeped and popped open its chest door. A mechanical claw gave Scuff his can.

"Scuff, it was real, I'm sure of it."

The Canadian looked at his friend.

"But Lutz is still in command."

Zeke chewed on his knuckle.

"Is she? How would we know, if they don't tell us?"

"And why would the Governor of Mars be interested in you?"

Zeke's face fell.

"You know why."

"That Martian stuff is behind you now. Professor Magma is dead. So is Doctor Enki. That nutter Crawley is safely locked up. You got to move on."

Zeke stared down at the flagstones.

"And the Spiral is still lurking on the other side of the dimensional wall. And the Dust Devil is still out in the Valley, so is the Craton.

And who knows what other Hesperian devices are buried in the sand, waiting to be dug up?"

"Look on the bright side, why don't you?" Scuff said, pinging the tab of his can.

Zeke motioned a passing cafemac to stop. It resembled a huge coffee steamer.

"British instant, please. Milk, no sugar."

The 'mac hissed and bubbled till steam erupted from a vent on its head. A belly flap dropped down. Zeke fished out a mug of boiling coffee.

Scuff screwed up his face.

"Yuk, you Brits and your caffeine tendencies."

"I just don't like filter. Sorry, this is the way Mum made it."

An image of his mother, alone on Earth, flitted through his mind. He pushed it aside. Minutes ticked by while the two boys silently sipped their refreshments. Scuff spoke first.

"You think the Governor wants your help with something. You speaking Martian?"

"Hesperian. And yes," Zeke replied.

"So, go and ask Mariner Knimble, bro."

A gang of students drifted past, on their way to the next class. Zeke waited till they were out of earshot.

"And admit I was spying on them? No way."

Scuff narrowed his eyes.

"You've got a plan. I know that look."

Zeke grinned.

"It couldn't do any harm to call on the principal. Wish her a get-well-soon."

Scuff blew a raspberry.

"You'd never get into her room."

Before Zeke could answer, a string of first-years shuffled past. They all looked rather lost. Gary was among them. He glared at Zeke, then went and sat on the far side of the cloister.

"I thought you two were 'besties'," Scuff remarked, making air quotes with his fingers. He sounded jealous.

Zeke frowned. He walked around the courtyard and sat beside Gary. The boy was munching an enormous cheese sandwich.

"Go away, you," he snarled, spitting out grated cheese.

"What did I do?" Zeke protested, and flushed.

"You're a weirdo. You're in cahoots with them Martians."

"The Hesperians vanished two billion years ago. What are you on about?"

Gary swallowed a mouthful and said, "Trixie Cutter. She told me you got spooky alien powers and you killed three teenagers."

"What!"

Gary nodded vigorously.

"Trixie's the one who's dangerous," Zeke replied hotly. "She puts her psychokinesis to bad use. Not just bullying but all kinds of criminal activity. She runs a black-market operation—"

Zeke faltered as he recalled Trixie's side line in smuggling weapons to the Unpro. Now Mars was at war, her profits were probably on the up and up. His stomach churned. One day he'd put a stop to her shenanigans for good.

"Are you saying it's not true, then?" Gary asked in a loud voice.

Zeke took a deep breath.

"Okay, I am a little different. One year ago, I made the journey to Mars. The same as you. But I came across a Hesperian orb and it downloaded their language into my brain."

"Hang on a mo', our kid. What's a Hesperian?"

Zeke smiled. "You'd call them Martians. The creatures that lived on Mars during what scientists called the Hesperian period."

Gary thought it over.

"I think I know that. Mars has three geological periods, right? The Hesperian was when water flowed and the air was breathable?"

Zeke nodded.

"For millions of years. Then there was some kind of cataclysm. Mars died. For one point eight billion years it was a barren vacuum. We call that the Amazonian Period. Now we're at the beginning of the forth era of Mars. The Terran Period. Man is terra-forming the planet into another Earth."

"What happened to these, um, Hesperians?"

Zeke bit his lip. Should he say they were destroyed by a demon from beyond time and space? And the Spiral was still out there, in another dimension, seeking a way in. No, that was too scary. Instead, he said, "Nobody's really sure."

Gary cocked his head to one side as the information sank in.

"So, what about these students who died?"

"Well, a mad archaeologist called Magma opened the Infinity Trap. That was a Hesperian machine that could take you to any time or place. Not just in this universe but any universe."

Gary whistled.

"I closed it again. But Jasper Snod, one of my classmates, got lost. We don't know what happened to him."

A tinge of guilt nibbled at Zeke's heart. Actually, the Spiral ate Jasper along with the adults who were there. That terrible incident replayed itself in his mind. Zeke shuddered. But he couldn't confess that to innocent little Gary.

"There was another student there. Jimmy Swallow. And he got contaminated by the Dust Devil. It looked like the ordinary dust devils you see blowing across the desert, those little whirlwinds. But this one was a kind of an ancient robot. Anyway, it exploded but later on, Jimmy morphed into a new one. He's out there now. All wind and sand, haunting the canyons."

"Ooer," Gary said.

"Fate worse than death," Zeke remarked. "And there's nothing we can do for him."

"But he's not dead."

"I'm not too sure on that," Zeke said. A weight crushed upon his heart. "But Bartie Cain is dead. He was the son of Josiah Cain, leader of the Marmish, a religious colony that refuses to use technology. Bartie came along with us when another madman, Doctor Enki, forced us into a bubble universe. We found a deserted Hesperian citadel. We also found a monster, the Particle Beast, that killed poor Bartie."

"Flipping awful, our kid."

"Yes," Zeke said sadly. "That's why my best friend, Pin, fell out with me. She blames me, but I had nothing to do with it."

Gary wolfed down the last chunk of bread.

"This bubble universe, is it still there?"

"No, it got—"

"Destroyed. How did I guess?"

Gary leapt to his feet.

"Don't you see? Trixie's right. Everyone and everything around you comes to a sticky end."

"No, no," Zeke cried.

"Yes, they do. You're a danger. And anyway, aliens, madmen, monsters. It's all too much."

"You've got me wrong," Zeke said.

"Just keep away from me, you weirdo."

Gary was yelling now. He twisted on his heels and stormed off.

Across the cloister, Scuff raised a finger. "Does that make me number one bestie again?"

Chapter Seven

Teachers' Towers

Zeke stood before the reinforced door. In one hand he held a posy of flowers, in the other a *Get Well* electrocard. He pressed the buzzer with his nose.

A football-sized dome above the door opened to reveal a large electronic eye. It scanned Zeke with a red laser.

"Zeke Hailey," said a simulated feminine voice. "Access level zero. You are not authorised to enter these apartments." The dome closed.

"Yes, but I want to visit the principal. It's a…um…humanitarian mission."

Nothing.

Zeke considered pressing the buzzer again and arguing with the computer. Then he had a better idea. He peered through the frosted glass at the lobby beyond.

"This door is just atoms. Specks full of space. I pass through that space and—"

He was inside the building.

"That was easy." Indeed, translocation was fast becoming second nature for him. And other students weren't allowed to start until their fourth year. It was hard not to feel a tad cocky.

The lobby was small, with fake marble flooring. A portrait of Principal Lutz hung on the wall. Buttons outside the elevator had everyone's room number. Principal Lutz lived in Room 7, apparently the only apartment on that floor. Zeke could see the elevator needed a security pass, so reluctantly took the stairs.

Seventy exhausting steps later he reached seventh floor, a long gloomy corridor with a single door at the end. He wondered what she might be doing at that moment. Was he interrupting anything? It was hard to believe Lutz had any kind of life outside the school. He tried to picture her sewing or listening to classical music or watching a Holowood movie. He couldn't. Maybe she passed her off-duty hours in a cryogenic freezer. That was easier to imagine.

He knocked on the door. Footsteps approached. The door creaked open.

Zeke's jaw dropped.

It wasn't Principal Lutz, or Marjorie Barnside or even Mariner Knimble. It was somebody he never expected.

Pin-mei Liang.

"What are you doing here?" she asked.

"I—I came to—"

He waved the flowers in her face.

"Go away, Zeke. She's not well enough—"

Pin-mei's face blanked over. Her irises glowed.

"Okay, she says you can come in."

"You're talking telepathically to her now?"

Since when were his ex-best friend and his worst enemy on such good terms?

"Why not? She's not the battle-axe you make her out to be."

Zeke was too stunned to answer. Pin-mei led him to an armchair and she sat opposite on a sofa. The apartment was bare. Little furniture, no ornaments or pictures, and just a modest kitchenette in the corner. The kitchenette looked like it had never been used. The window was wide, with a dizzying view of Ophir Chasma. Canyon walls tumbled into the distance.

"How have you been?" he asked.

He marvelled at how Pin had changed. She was so gifted that she came to the Chasm four years early. Zeke had taken her under his wing and she called him her Martian big brother. But those days seemed as long ago as the dinosaurs. A tragic death had driven a wedge between them.

Pin-mei twisted a strand of hair.

"Good. Better."

"You look so grown up now."

"I am nearly thirteen."

In the last few months she had shot up, grown her hair long, experimented with makeup. He hardly recognised her. The shyness and innocence were replaced with quiet confidence. And some kick-ass Marjitzu moves. She spent her weekends at Yuri-Gagarin Freetown, studying with the commando Isla the Incisor.

Silence. Zeke shuffled on the cushion.

"So, what are you doing here?"

Pin-mei picked up an electrobook from the coffee table. On the cover a white whale erupted from the ocean in a shower of spray. It seized an old-fashioned sailor in its jaws and dived into the briny depths. The animation played over and over.

"Reading this to her. Helps the recovery."

"Cool," Zeke replied, avoiding eye contact.

He whistled aimlessly. But bottled-up feelings were stirring. Like that whale, bursting from the depths of Zeke's heart.

"Look, Pin—"

"Don't, Zeke."

"We ought to talk it out."

"Nothing to say."

"But it wasn't my fault."

"Wasn't it?"

"How can you say that?"

She jumped to her feet.

"You made him stay."

"And you took him along. You plucked him from Edenville."

"He was my friend. He was helping me."

"Unlike me, you mean?" Zeke was shouting.

"If the cap fits—"

"*Silencio!*"

Principal Lutz was standing in the doorway to her bedroom. Zeke blinked. Was this the same woman? Her hair was ash white. She was walking with a stick. Perhaps most unsettling of all was her dressing gown. Pink and fluffy.

She staggered to the sofa and sat down beside Pin-mei. Zeke waved the flowers in her face. The principal eyed them suspiciously.

"Really?" she remarked.

Zeke gulped and pressed a switch at the base of the bouquet. The blooms crackled and vanished.

"If I want holograms, I'll ask for holograms," she snapped.

"I've come to see how you're doing, Ma'am," Zeke began.

"You can't fool me with your lies. I've had a century of scheming boys."

Zeke's uniform was suddenly damp. He fiddled with his collar.

"Alright. The truth is I want to know about your premonition."

"What's it to do with you?" Lutz asked sullenly.

"Nothing, I hope."

Lutz pursed her lips. After a moment's contemplation she said, "Go back to your studies, and keep your nose out of people's business. *Capisci?*"

Zeke clenched his fists.

"The other Lutz had a death bed premonition. I want to see if they're the same."

Lutz leaned forward.

"My predecessor? That sour old goat?"

The current clone was the fifth incarnation of the original principal. Due to a mix-up, she'd arrived early, while Lutz Four was still alive. Lutz Five had seized office and banished Lutz Four to Yuri-Gagarin Freetown. The two women hated each other.

Zeke nodded. Lutz stroked her chin, "Tell me more of her prediction."

"She saw an apocalypse."

Lutz's face clouded over. She stared into mid-air and said, "The sky cracked. Something slithered out. People were screaming." Tiny glistening tears gathered on her eyelashes.

"Was I in it? Did you see me there?" Zeke said, raising his voice.

She gazed at him for a second as though they were strangers.

"No, you were dead."

Zeke's blood ran cold.

Lutz gripped Pin-mei by the wrist.

"Fetch me some water, there's a *bonne fille*."

"I need to know more," Zeke said, frowning.

Lutz rolled her eyes and turned away.

Zeke was about to speak when he heard a sound. Chopping noises. He crossed to the window.

It was midday and Ophir Chasma shone with sunlight. But there were three black specks in the sky. Three flies buzzing nearer. Autogyros.

"Zeke!" Pin-mei cried.

He twisted around. Lutz's eyes were alight, like magnesium flares. "They're coming," she said. "And it's you they want."

Chapter Eight
Ten-Thousand Metres High

The cabin shook on a wave of turbulence. Zeke grabbed the overhead handgrip. He felt like a sock in a tumble dryer.

"You're fine, kid," said a soldier through the onboard radio. The blades were so deafening, everyone used earphones and microphones to communicate.

Zeke was in the belly of a large autogyro, a big clunky vehicle called a Monarch. The cabin reeked of plastic and sweat. Four young soldiers sat opposite, three men and a woman. Mariner Bobby Chinook was beside him, tall impassive, silent.

Thank god he's here, Zeke thought. Chinook's presence gave him strength. The Mariner had the heart of an eagle.

The soldiers were all square jawed and bursting with muscle. Even the female. They chewed gum and stared at Zeke as if he were a zoo animal.

"So, you're a Mariner" one asked, his voice deep as a bass drum.

"Not yet." Zeke sounded squeaky in comparison.

"You're not psychic?" asked the woman. Her voice was almost as deep as her colleague's.

"Yes, I'm psychic. But I don't become a Mariner till I graduate."

"I getcha," she replied. "You're a baby Mariner."

The soldiers guffawed.

The Monarch rocked violently, wiping the smile of their faces. Zeke was numb. It all seemed crazy. He closed his eyes and replayed the last few hours in his mind.

The soldiers bursting into Telepathy 201 and escorting him out at gunpoint. Meeting the captain out in the courtyard, a horrible man who shouted a lot. Mariner Knimble, with a face like thunder, saying something about war diktats outranking his authority. Chinook volunteering to escort Zeke to Tithonium Central. Climbing onboard the Monarch and taking off. Watching through a porthole as the school dwindled down into a smudge in the Martian dirt.

Stay calm

Zeke tensed up. Chinook was talking to him in his head.

Permission to share thoughts?

Zeke mulled it over. He didn't like adults prying on his brain. But he could see advantages in their present situation. He gave a slight nod.

Any idea why these grunts have taken you? Chinook asked.

Do I! Same reason they always want me.

Chinook gestured for Zeke to continue.

Somebody wants some Hesperian translating.

I see.

Now that Doctor Enki's dead, I'm the only one alive who speaks it.

Chinook stroked his broad chin.

Then it's simple. Help them out and we'll soon be home.

Zeke balled his fists.

Never! There'll be some Hesperian technology they need help with. There always is. And every time I translate it, somebody dies.

Chinook raised his eyebrows.

You can't know that.

I can. I'd rather die than make another mistake.

"Hey kid, look outta the window," shouted one soldier, a Latino with a trace of a moustache.

Zeke twisted around. Through the smeared glass he could see the usual red wilderness. Riverbeds that dried out two billion years ago. Ancient craters and ash dunes. Blue bedrock bursting through ochre sand.

And then Zeke saw it! He caught his breath. In the distance, a circle of green. Grass! On Mars!

They were approaching fast. The green was peppered with white rectangles. Buildings. A few rose out of the greenery, two, three storeys high. A city. The first and only city on Mars. Tithonium Central.

It's nicknamed the Green Zone, Chinook thought.

Zeke's attention was drawn to a small hill overlooking the city. Not much more than a bump but topped with an odd-shaped building. Like an egg sliced down the middle and laid on its side.

That's the Ellipse, Chinook went on. *The official residence of the Governor of Mars.*

NANANANANANA!

The alarm siren. Red lights were flashing.

"We're—we're under attack!" came the pilot's astonished voice.

One soldier scanned his magnopad.

"Missile at seven o clock!" he cried.

"The Martian State Brigade. It has to be," said the female soldier.

A chorus of swear words rang in Zeke's ears.

"A thousand metres and gaining," said the first soldier.

The Monarch veered sharply to the left, throwing Zeke forward. His safety belt prevented a fall.

"Still closing. Eight hundred metres."

"We're going to die!" wailed the Latino soldier.

The Monarch rocketed upwards. Then down, then to the right. Zeke's stomach heaved.

"Must be heat-seeking, we'll never shake it," shouted the tallest soldier.

Zeke seized both handgrips so tightly his knuckles hurt.

"Six hundred metres and closing."

Sir, we've got to translocate out of here!

Chinook glanced at him.

And leave these grunts to die?

Zeke looked at them. Four soldiers in the cabin, plus the pilot and that awful captain in the cockpit. No way they could ferry them all out. Who would he save?

That's not the way of my ancestors, Chinook thought. His brow was furrowed and his jaw set.

"Four hundred metres and closing."

"I need to see it. Did you say seven o'clock?" Chinook said aloud. The soldier with the magnopad gave a terrified nod.

Chinook shifted around and peered out of the nearest porthole. With the Monarch shaking violently, this wasn't easy. Zeke copied his teacher's actions.

A white, red-tipped missile was zooming towards them. The vapour trail streaked across the empty Martian sky.

Chinook recited the Mariners' mantra.

"Gravity, magnetism and thought are the forces that bind the universe together. Of these three, thought is the strongest."

His eyes became dazzling sockets of light.

The missile began to dip.

"Two, no, a hundred-and-fifty metres."

It was losing altitude. Lower and lower as it neared the Monarch. Nearer, but lower, nearer but lower. Chinook was changing its trajectory by psychokinesis.

"Ninety metres and closing. Eighty, seventy."

The air stuck in Zeke's windpipe.

"Fifty, forty, thirty."

Chinook was still reciting. His eyes shone like lanterns. Zeke covered his face with his hands. Should he escape? He'd never trans-located from a moving vehicle before. Didn't they say it could be fatal? And if Chinook could be courageous, shouldn't he be, too?

"Twenty, ten."

The Latino muttered a prayer. The woman soldier uttered a few obscenities.

"Zero."

Nothing. Zeke dropped his hands. The four soldiers looked like babies now. Frightened, bewildered, even tearful.

The one with the magnopad spoke.

"Missed us by inches. Flew right under our feet. It's thirty metres away. Forty—"

An explosion roared. The blast caught the Monarch and hurled it through the air. It rotated a complete three-hundred-and-sixty-degrees. For a split-second, Zeke was upside down, blood coursing into his skull. Mercifully, the safety belts did their job.

The Monarch righted itself as the shockwave faded.

"Status A-okay," said the pilot over the radio. "ETA is fifteen minutes."

A volley of whoops and cheers erupted. The tall soldier kissed the female. She slapped him and laughed.

"Game over, man," said the Latino and high-fived the tall soldier.

A stink of vomit tinged the air, although nobody appeared to be sick. Zeke stole a sideways look at Chinook. Yes, there was that impassive gaze, but also, the tiniest trace of a smile. Zeke broke into a grin himself.

Quite the welcoming committee, Chinook thought.

It was, indeed. Soon they would land. What would be waiting for him at the capital city? Zeke's short-lived grin died on his lips.

Chapter Nine
The Ellipse Office

A bear-sized security man ushered Zeke and Chinook into the office. The room was shaped like a stretched circle and reeked of percolated coffee. A huge mahogany desk dominated the scene, where the governor signed laws and treaties. Two flags hung on the wall. The flag of UNAAC, a world map surrounded by olive branches, and the Earth flag, six interlocking circles. Leather sofas, potted plants and a water cooler filled the space. Dark paintings hung on the walls, scenes from long ago. In one, a crowd gathered around a torchlight to watch a dying man. In another, a horse and coach galloped out of the night.

Gloomy, Zeke thought.

A tiny man sat at the desk. His hair was grey and his face pinched, like a sharp-beaked bird. Despite the formal setting, he wore golfing slacks and a cardigan.

"Your Honour," Chinook said, and bowed low.

Zeke blinked. This seemed out of character for the proud Arctic hunter.

The man jumped up to greet them.

"Thank heavens, you're okay. My people briefed me all about the missile attack."

He shook their hands with great enthusiasm.

"Welcome," he said to Zeke. "Welcome to the Ellipse. You're the young man who's going to solve our little problem."

"And you are?"

The man, Chinook and the three security officers laughed aloud, as if Zeke was saying something stupid.

"Why, boy," he said in a drawl. "You've gone to the very top. I'm Duane Esterhazy. Governor of Mars."

He beamed, as though expecting Zeke to gasp in awe. Zeke scowled. The governor did not notice. He beckoned for them to sit down. A maid came in and served tea from a silver teapot. Next came cookies, sugary snaps with a tinge of lemon. Zeke hadn't eaten since breakfast, and wolfed down a whole packet.

"Now, boy, I must apologise for dragging your carcass outta class and half way across Mariners Valley."

Zeke grunted. He wasn't sure what to say.

"As you must rightly know, the good people of Mars are at war with the Unpro and the Martian State Brigade. I need your help with a matter of vital importance."

Zeke's body ran cold. Esterhazy went on.

"Let me cut to the chase. We found ourselves a genuine Martian artefact. A kind of metal statue and covered in engravings. We want to translate them."

"Why?" Zeke asked. He stared into the governor's eyes. They were grey with darker flecks, the colour of storm clouds.

The governor was taken aback.

"*Why*, boy? To stop this conflict before it goes any further. Those damned terrorists nearly killed you this afternoon."

"But how will this artefact do that?"

The governor's smile dropped.

"It's a brain surveillance device. It can scan every life form on the planet instantly and tell you what they're thinking. We'll use it to list the whereabouts of every rebel on Mars. We'll be able to find them immediately, arrest them and halt the war dead in its tracks."

Zeke chewed on his thumb.

"Isn't it easy to find them? All the Unpro colonies."

The governor looked uncomfortable.

"Yes, but the rebels have scattered out across Mariners Valley and beyond. They're hiding out there, watching us. This way we can pick them off, before they alert each other."

Chinook leaned forward.

"This is excellent. The war can be brought to an end without any bloodshed."

The Governor nodded enthusiastically.

"That's the beauty of it."

He put his hand on Zeke's shoulder.

"I bet you're itching to help, after that close call you had with the Martian State Brigade. Put an end to this conflict now, without firing a single bullet."

Zeke didn't feel so sure.

"Where did this artefact come from? And how do you know what it does?"

Governor Esterhazy guzzled down his tea.

"We found it near Noctis Labyrinthus. That's in the far west of Mariners Valley."

"I know. I've been there," Zeke replied coldly.

"Our best linguist worked for months on the runes. But he only got so far before he was stumped. That Martian writing sure is a tricky business. So, he recommended you. You should be proud of your reputation."

Goosebumps tickled Zeke's skin.

"What linguist?"

The governor was sweating. He aimed a remote at a side door and it swished open. A man stepped into the room. A small, portly man with a bald head, a goatee beard and olive skin. Doctor Enki.

"You!" Zeke screamed.

Enki gave a stupid grin and waved. Zeke leapt up and tore towards the newcomer.

"I'll kill you!"

He was almost upon Enki, waving his fists, when a million volts seared through his body. His brain imploded.

Pain thundered through Zeke's head like a stampede of elephants. The room re-formed. He was lying on the sofa. Chinook sat across from him, with Governor Esterhazy at his desk with dark-suited security men in the background. Esterhazy was chewing gum.

Zeke tried to sit up. The pain ricocheted around the inside of his skull. He collapsed back.

"Lay still, they gave you a shot for pain relief," Chinook said, his expression as hard as ever to read.

"You used a neural disruptor on me," Zeke protested weakly.

"Why, boy," the governor piped up, "you meant to do bodily harm. We will not tolerate such actions in Tithonium. Isn't peace the very thing we're fighting for?"

"He killed Bartie," Zeke cried out, his voice hoarse with rage.

The governor spat his gum in the bin.

"As I understand it, the Particle Beast killed that unfortunate boy."

"And Enki forced him to go into the citadel."

The governor tapped a pencil against his chin.

"No, the boy volunteered."

"He didn't" Zeke cried.

"Were you there when they entered?"

"B-but," Zeke clamoured. "I was there when Enki held them prisoner."

"For their own protection, from this beast," the governor replied.

"Enki killed Bartie," Zeke repeated, this time in hushed voice.

"Do you have any witnesses to this alleged abduction?" the governor asked.

Zeke sighed. The only witness was Pin-mei and she wasn't talking to him. Surely there was something he could do. Or not do? He gritted his teeth.

"Let's go," he said to Chinook. "We're finished here."

A look of alarm flashed across the governor's face.

"Don't be hasty, boy. I'll start an investigation."

Zeke sat up. The headache was fading.

"Investigation?"

The Governor nodded.

"Once the war is over, I'll have my best men look into your allegations. If Enki did anything wrong he'll get some Martian justice. I promise you."

"Well, okay," Zeke said. It seemed a step in the right direction.

"First, I need your help with the brain surveillance device. Help me win this war and, so help me, if Enki's guilty, he'll do serious prison time. But in the meantime, we have to concentrate all our resources on stopping the Unpro."

Zeke scratched his ear. So much had happened in one day. Whisked off by the military, a missile attack, Enki back from the dead, not to mention Zeke's brain cells getting scrambled.

"In any case, boy, why don't you sleep on it for the night?"

Zeke gazed into those stormy eyes. The governor seemed kindly enough. Could he be trusted? And what was this device anyway? Maybe it might shed some light on the mystery of the Hesperians.

"I guess I can do that," he said.

Chapter Ten

The West Patio

Zeke stumbled out into the soft morning light, yawning his head off. Mango trees and frangipani surrounded a white-tiled patio. Shiny tropical birds fluttered around the branches, cooing and clucking. Crickets chirruped invisibly.

The governor was sitting at a white iron table.

"Come, join me," he beamed amiably.

A breakfast banquet covered the table top. Zeke drooled. There were sausages, bacon, fried eggs, toast, stewed tomatoes, hash browns, cheeses, croissants, pastries, yoghurt, fruit, fruit juice, tea and coffee. Zeke's belly rumbled like an earthquake. He dived in.

For a few minutes neither spoke. Zeke shovelled down the food with the frenzy of a starving man. The eggs were so creamy, the bacon so tangy, the fruit so sweet. It was the best food he'd eaten since leaving Earth.

A bird swooped down from a treetop, over their heads. It froze in mid-air, wings blurred.

"Damn glitch in the software," the governor grumbled.

"Oh," Zeke said through a mouthful of toast. "The birds are holograms."

"You bet your bottom dollar" the governor chuckled.

He aimed a remote at a small console in the trees. The birds vanished, and the crickets fell silent.

"The trees?" Zeke asked.

"They're real enough, boy. Genetically modified, naturally, for the cooler, drier climate. Cool palms."

Zeke nodded and stuffed a Danish pastry in his mouth.

"Where's Enki?"

"I'm keeping him out of sight until you two boys learn to play nice."

Zeke nearly smiled at this quip, but forced it back.

"I want to see him, now."

The governor raised his eyebrows but said nothing. He typed a command into his magnopad. Three croissants later, Enki appeared from the dark interior, flanked by two beefy guards. He sat down at the breakfast table without a word.

"Tuck in, Doctor," the governor said.

Enki glanced at the spread with distaste.

"Quite full, thank you, Duane." And he giggled.

"I swear, for a man packing your extra pounds, you sure don't eat much. I've never seen you eat," said the governor.

Enki giggled some more.

Zeke stared hard at his adversary. At the beady eyes, the puffy cheeks, the sweaty bald head. A chill slithered down Zeke's spine. There was something wrong, but he couldn't put his finger on it. Something different in the way Enki walked, talked, breathed. As if the man before them was a waxwork imitation.

"How did you escape?" Zeke asked at last.

Enki snickered. His falsetto laugh was annoying.

"I can't say, Zeke. I was lost. In a dark place. Floating. There were terrible convulsions, tremors, quakes. Then, all of a sudden, the bubble universe spat me out. Like this."

Enki spat into the fruit bowl.

"Spare us the demonstration," the governor remarked, reddening slightly.

Enki leaned across the table and grabbed Zeke's hand. Zeke snatched it away.

"Zeke, forget about the past. We need to work together now. To save lives."

"What about the Spiral?" Zeke asked, glaring.

Enki giggled. His eyes rolled from side to side. Zeke wondered if he'd gone crazy.

"I haven't a clue what you're on about."

"Yes, you do. The Great Spiral. The demon from a hell dimension."

Enki pursed his lips and rocked his head from side to side.

"A demon, you say? I'm not acquainted. All I remember is darkness."

Zeke shifted on the iron chair. He dredged up the unpleasant memories of the citadel's last hours. He had left Enki unconscious, in a trance. Maybe the man was telling the truth.

The governor sensed his uncertainty.

"So, you'll finish off the translations? Help me put an end to this war before anyone dies?"

Zeke looked the governor straight in the eye. The most powerful man on the planet. Zeke mulled it over for a nanosecond and then replied.

"No."

The governor's grip on the cutlery tightened.

"Hi."

It was Mariner Chinook, jogging up the garden path in borrowed running gear. His smooth, muscular limbs rippled with each stride.

The governor drew a deep breath and called back.

"Mariner Chinook, can you help us with a little translocation?"

They were high up. Three miles. The air was cold and hard to breath. But the view was staggering.

Zeke and the governor stood on the brink of a ledge as large as a tennis court. It jutted out from the canyon wall and sloped down to the valley below. An ocean of red ash flooded the valley. Layers of bedrock writhed through the swell like sea serpents. In the distance, the white jewel of the city gleamed brightly. A stench of sulphates tickled Zeke's nostrils.

What catastrophic events created this vista long ago, while Earth was a primordial soup? Earthquakes, volcanoes, a stray asteroid? And what of the Hesperians? What was their part in all this prehistory? Nobody would ever know, Zeke thought glumly.

"Magnificent, isn't it?" the governor said, resting his hand on Zeke's shoulder.

"Yes, Sir," Zeke mumbled, awestruck.

"Think how vast this canyon is," the governor continued, "then add on all the others—Ophir, Candor, Ius, Noctis, Oudemans—and what do we get?"

"Mariners Valley?"

The governor smiled as if Zeke were a dim-witted child. "Think bigger. The cradle of civilization!"

"Oh, sure. That's what I meant."

"The dawn of a new humanity. We'll build a society that lasts forever. Doesn't that stir your soul, boy?"

Zeke nodded. Perhaps he spent too much time thinking of the long-ago past. The governor was right. Mars had a future too. Millions of years yet to come.

"And I'm offering you a stake in that future."

Zeke blinked.

"Sir?"

The governor gestured to the lands below.

"A share in all these things I will give you, if you come down and work for me."

Zeke pushed his hands in his pockets. The cold was numbing him.

"I don't understand. Mars belongs to Earth, not you. Isn't that what you want?"

"Ah, that's where the rebels lie about me. I believe in independence for Mars. We're the Martians now. New Martians. But I want it done properly."

Zeke was still baffled.

"I mean, we need a withdrawal achieved through diplomacy. Not by a bloodbath."

"So, you actually back Mars cutting ties with Earth."

"For sure, boy. We call it MESS."

Zeke eyes widened.

"A mess?"

The governor laughed.

"The acronym needs some work. M, E, S, S. The Martian Exit Strategic Solution."

"And who will be in charge, after we quit the Earth Union?"

The governor gave a little shrug and smirked.

"Little ol' me, at least to kick it off."

Zeke turned back to the vista of ashes, deep in thought. After a moment he called out to Chinook, patiently waiting a few yards away.

"Can we go now, Sir? I'm missing some important lessons."

The governor puffed out his chest.

"Now don't go off all hasty like. At least have a look at the runes. That's the least you can do."

Zeke glanced at Chinook.

Where's the harm in looking? And antagonising this man won't do the school any favours, the Alaskan thought back.

Zeke stared at his feet.

"Okay, that I'll do."

Chapter Eleven
The Tithonium Mental Health Facility

"Sixty-Four F, Sixty-Five F…ah, here we are," the doctor said as he led Zeke down the sterile corridor. "Sixty-Six F, patient Fitch Crawley. Are you sure about this?"

Zeke took a deep breath and nodded.

"Yes, I've got time to kill before a meeting."

"Well, any trouble and shout, these two will be outside." The doctor gestured to the two beefy orderlies behind them. "As long as you don't annoy him, you'll be fine." The look on his face said otherwise.

"How's he coming along?" Zeke asked.

"Oh, the boy's quite a challenge, I can say that."

Zeke grabbed the man's arm. "But what's your opinion, as a doctor?"

The doctor considered for a moment.

"A nutcase, he's a complete and utter nutcase."

He unlocked the fortified door. "And steer clear of the teeth."

The room had changed since Zeke's last visit. Then it was a white cube, now it was dark with graffiti. Cartoons, scribbles, words. Not very nice words. Zeke studied the walls. Frenzied drawings of beaks and tentacles, of people ripped in half, of crumbling cities. The same images as his dreams. As his visions.

"You took your time," came a voice.

Fitch sat behind a table in the corner of the bare room, surrounded by drawing paper and eCrayons. Ice-blue eyes gleamed through bedraggled hair. They burned with a cold hatred.

"Excuse me?"

Fitch shifted on his seat.

"What is it? Nine months? And you never visited."

Words failed Zeke. Why would he come and see the boy who almost killed him? The boy working for the Spiral, quite happy to unleash an apocalypse?

"How are they treating you?" Zeke said as last.

Fitch snorted.

"Peachy."

He flicked a stub of eCrayon at Zeke. It missed.

"Play nice," Zeke said, echoing the Governor's phrase.

"That's all I can do, now."

Fitch scratched his scalp. Zeke was rather glad the dirty curls obscured the scars. Principal Lutz gave the order for Fitch to be lobotomised. The psychic parts of his brain were cut out. Zeke understood perfectly why she did so. Fitch was a genius at mind control. He was ruthless and enjoyed killing. Yet Zeke also felt Fitch's loss. The revulsion at becoming normal.

Zeke changed the subject.

"How long will they keep you here?"

"That idiot doctor says until I'm cured."

"Cured?"

"No longer a madman bent on world domination," Fitch laughed like a gurgling drain. "In other words, never."

"Maybe you should go along with the treatment. Be that good person."

Fitch looked down at his paper and began scribbling.

"Once a tiger, always a tiger, Zeke. And they know when I'm lying."

"Maybe with time—"

"Time? There isn't much of that left, you know."

Zeke said nothing.

"The Spiral will break me out of here. Then, there'll be murder to pay. I'll start with that doctor and his goons." Fitch glanced up. "Then I'm coming for you."

"You despise me that much?"

Fitch looked down again.

"It's not too late. The Spiral likes you. Says you're special. Work with us and he'll spare you. Reward you."

Zeke stuffed his hands in his pockets.

"Like you said, never."

Silence filled the room like cold air. Fitch busied himself with his scribbling.

"Thought you enjoyed our little adventures."

Zeke didn't speak.

"Remember when we broke into Lutz's office? And defeated that homicidal boulder? What about when we escaped from Yuri-Gagarin Freetown?"

Zeke sighed. "I remember you leaving Trixie and me for dead. And nearly incinerating my friends. And your plans to open a portal for the Spiral."

Fitch guffawed. "Good times."

Zeke took a closer look at the graffiti. Scratchy drawings of a huge gaping mouth, with tentacles seizing stick people. Some of the stick people seemed to be flying upwards, towards the mouth. Zeke's skin crawled.

"Quite the artist," he remarked.

Fitch spat on the floor.

"Something has to occupy the long days. Here all alone with the loonies."

"It can't be that bad."

"Can't it?" Fitch bellowed in a sudden fury. "You've no idea how lonely it gets. And you never visit."

"It's too far!" Zeke cried.

"You could translocate! Two seconds from the Chasm to here."

"But—" Zeke couldn't think of an excuse.

"I thought we were friends," Fitch said, tears in his eyes.

He is totally mad, Zeke thought. *One minute he wants to kill me, the next I'm his best mate.*

"Friends don't brainwash friends," Zeke remarked.

Fitch blushed slightly. "What harm is there in a little manipulation? No different to little Miss Pinny. She controls your heart. I tinker with your brain cells."

"I can't believe you're saying that."

"Everybody wants to influence their friends, one way or the other. Don't blame me because I'm good at it."

Zeke opened his mouth, then closed it again. What was the point in arguing with a lunatic?

"How is the delightful Miss Liang? And that American buffoon?"

"Canadian, and, well, I mean, they're fine."

Fitch stared at him through narrowed eyes. Even with his lobotomy, he still seemed able to read Zeke's mind.

"You look uncomfortable. Oh, they don't like you anymore?"

"Yes, they do, it's just Pin-mei—" Zeke cursed himself. "It's none of your business."

"Zeke, maybe I'm your true friend, after all. Think about it."

Zeke's blood boiled. Fitch was playing mind games with him. Maybe he should change the subject again.

"Did you know Mars is at war with Earth?"

Fitch stroked his chin.

"Don't care. There's a bigger war coming."

"The Spiral versus humanity?"

"Got it in one, Zekey babe."

"That isn't going to happen. The laws of physics prevent it."

"The Spiral will find a way into our universe."

"No, he won't. We destroyed Gravity's Eye. Remember?"

Fitch chewed on an eCrayon. "There's wishful thinking, Zeke, even in hell." A minute or two ticked away while both boys were lost in thought.

"So, you didn't come to the city to see me?" Fitch asked.

"Hardly," Zeke replied. He wasn't sure if he was angry or afraid.

"Then why did you come?" Fitch flashed him a crafty look.

"Oh, business," Zeke answered. He was sworn to secrecy. The Governor saw to that.

Fitch smirked. "It has to be something to do with your skills in speaking Hesperian."

"Not necessarily."

"Why else would anyone want you? I'm not stupid, Zeke."

Zeke cursed under his breath. Fitch was running rings around him.

"Oh!" Fitch cried, dropping an eCrayon. "They've found it!" His face paled.

"Found what?" Zeke asked.

"Electron's Blade."

"Electron's what?"

Fitch hesitated. "Nah, I'm just messing with you."

"Do you know something?" Zeke said, trying to sound forceful. Fitch appeared ill at ease.

"Well, this has all been very sweet, but I'd like you to go now."

"Tell me, what do you know?"

Fitch bared his teeth and growled. Those glacial eyes glared malevolently. Zeke gulped. Maybe it was time to go.

"Guards! I mean, orderlies!"

Zeke translocated straight back to the Ellipse, materialising in the governor's office.

The governor himself was at his desk, scowling.

"You're late."

Enki and Chinook sat on the sofa. Enki wore that insane grin on his bloated face. Chinook looked stiff and uncomfortable. All three held dainty cups and an aroma of coffee beans laced the air.

"You said I was free till you came out of your meeting."

"Yes, the war cabinet ended an hour ago."

Zeke glanced at his watch. "Sorry, I must have lost track of time."

"Where were you?"

Zeke scuffed the oriental carpet with the toecap on his boot. The governor didn't need to know about the villainous Fitch Crawley.

"Oh, out exploring. You've built a wonderful city."

The grimace dropped from the governor's face and he beamed.

"I've sweated blood and tears on the Green Zone. I raised this city from dust. And I'm real proud of it."

"Didn't Earth help with that?" Zeke asked.

The governor nodded.

"With the subsidies, yes. But where did those greenbacks come from? Martian taxation. Every cent Earth gave me they clawed back from my people."

My people? Something about those words jarred in Zeke's head. As if Esterhazy was a king, not an elected official.

"Then why are you fighting the Unpro? Don't you want the same thing? Independence?"

"I told you up on the canyon, boy. Their way is anarchy and chaos. Mine is the path of peace and stability."

Zeke shrugged. Politics was confusing.

The governor adopted a silkier tone. "Help out with our brain surveillance device and you'll save thousands of lives. Be a hero for Mars."

Zeke sat down between Enki and Chinook. Maybe the governor had a point.

"If I can."

Enki thrust his magnopad into Zeke's hands. The governor leaned forward, eyes gleaming. "Let's see that gift in action—"

Zeke faltered. How could he explain it to them? He was the only human alive to be altered by the orb. It had downloaded an entire language into his subconscious. And more. Visions of an apocalypse. But they wouldn't understand. He lowered his head and focussed on the transcripts.

"Hey, this is just a list of words," he cried with a sinking heart.

Enki tittered.

"So?" asked the governor sternly.

Zeke's mind raced. He was expecting to see text copied from this brain surveillance device. Instead the magnopad showed a handful of words in the geometrical script of the Hesperians. But words without meaning, or at least none known to Zeke. Were they keeping something back? He skimmed through the list, *sacca, wunna, lee, va.* Gibberish.

"I need to see the whole thing. Where is this machine? Show it to me."

The governor jumped up and started pacing.

"That's on a need-to-know basis. Don't forget there's a war on. That means wartime security. For your own protection."

"Then, I'm not doing it," Zeke snapped, dropping the 'pad into Enki's lap.

The Governor exploded. He thumped his fist down on the desk, and bellowed,

"Do as you're told, boy. This is for the good of my career!"

Silence. Everyone stared at him.

"Your career?" Zeke asked in a tiny voice.

The governor stood up straight and adjusted his cardigan.

"I mean the good of the citizens."

"You said *career*," Zeke added.

"I'm tired. Running a war is no picnic, you know."

Chinook coughed.

"Zeke has made his decision. It's time we returned to the school."

The Governor was all smiles again.

"Friends, friends, don't be running off. Let's talk this through."

Chinook stood up. His bulk seemed to fill the room. The three security men stirred uneasily.

"Nonetheless, we should go."

The governor threw out his arms.

"Mariner Chinook, please appreciate the importance of this. We must do everything we can."

"The Ophir Chasma School for Psychic Endeavour is neutral. A wise bear avoids thin ice."

"Spare me your folksy garbage," the governor snarled. "I'm fighting terrorists. Either you're with me or against me."

Chinook squared up his shoulders. The security men slipped their hands inside their jackets.

"Come Zeke, I'll translocate us back."

"Boys, boys!" the governor cried. His smile was back. "Please enjoy my hospitality a touch longer. Sleep on it. Let me know your decision tomorrow, Zeke. I promise to respect it."

It's your call, Chinook thought.

Zeke chewed his knuckle. Stopping the war was the right thing to do. Who could argue with that? Yet surely nothing good could come from a Hesperian machine? Look at the Infinity Trap and Gravity's Eye, both with the power to destroy humanity.

"I don't know what to do," he burst out.

The governor grinned like some kindly uncle.

"You're exhausted, boy. Go grab some zees. Let's start again in the morning, when you're all refreshed."

The governor's words made sense. Zeke nodded.

"Okay, one more night."

Chapter Twelve
Stephen Hawking Boulevard

Zeke had no intention of going to bed. His mind was too full of worries. He slipped out of the building, smiled sweetly at the security 'mac and passed through the barrier.

He found himself on a wide boulevard. Every block was filled with prefabs, white cube-shaped buildings shipped from Earth. Cool palms lined the pavements. Photon lamps glowed like pearls. Bright, but not too bright to blank out the stars. The Milky Way filled the sky like a swarm of cosmic fireflies.

Zeke began walking, without direction. The cold air cleared his head. And his old friends, the stars above, raised his spirits. It was good to get away.

Where is everyone? he wondered.

The streets were deserted. Tithonium Central had to be the quietest city in the solar system. Very different to Zeke's home town of London. He missed its busy streets.

Guitar chords drifted over rooftops. The slow harmonies of Country and Martian. When he first came to Mars, he'd found the music rather odd. Now, he loved it.

Zeke tracked the sound through the maze of blocks. He turned a corner and came face to face with a blue building. Neon lettering proclaimed the name: *The Lonesome Crater*.

"Oh, it's real," Zeke said to himself. The name was famous from the hit song, *I'm All Washed Up in The Lonesome Crater*. So the bar was not a made-up place at all.

He could hear chatter and the clink of glasses. The windows were blacked out, but the auto-door was open. His curiosity was piqued.

The interior was dark. People slumped around tables in small groups, drinking and snacking. A jukebox projected a hologram of the famous trio, *The Harmony Robots*, strumming banjos, onto a tiny stage.

Zeke squeezed past chairs and servomacs, till he reached the bar. He grabbed the one spare barstool and beckoned to a flask-shaped 'mac behind the counter. It waddled over on four short legs.

"Good evening, Sir," the machine began. "I'm a Mixomac 3000. What may I get for you tonight?" A digital display on the wall flashed a menu of cocktails.

"Hmm, I'm not sure," Zeke replied. This was a first for him. He scrutinised the menu. A *Manhattan Project*, a *Tequila Starburst*, an *Amber Moon*, a *Bucks Phys*, they all sounded very exotic.

"Try a *Sirius Sling*," drawled an American voice.

Zeke spun round on his stool. A lanky, scruffy older boy with tombstone teeth sat beside him.

"Justice!"

"Zekey boy, what the heck brings you to the city?"

Justice ruffled Zeke's blue hair.

"Um, business," Zeke said uncomfortably.

"If I know you, it's funny business, am I right?"

Zeke shrugged. Justice wasn't wrong.

"I can ask you the same question," he said. "Shouldn't you be up at the observatory, the Perspicillum?"

"Try that drink and we'll have a good ol' catch up."

Zeke hesitated. "Mum wouldn't like me drinking alcohol."

Justice slapped Zeke on the back and laughed.

"Then you've come to the right place. Mars has run dry."

"Excuse me?"

Justice grew sombre.

"The Televator's down. Supplies are running low. Booze was the first thing to go. On account of it being so needful up here on Mars."

Zeke gulped. Now that Justice mentioned it, how would the New

Martians fare with the Earth to Mars trade route closed?

"Barkeep," Justice said. "A *Sirius Sling* for my buddy and I'll have a *Marstini*."

The mixomac poured three different bottles into a vent on its head. Next, it vibrated like a washing machine on rinse cycle. Finally, a tall glass popped out of its chest. Foamy, strawberry-red liquid bubbled in the glass while a pineapple slice balanced on the rim.

Zeke gingerly put the straw in his mouth.

"Ooh." The cocktail was too sugary. Revolting. He sipped some more. Actually, it wasn't so bad. He sipped again. In fact, it was rather delicious.

"I'm here for a little R and R," Justice said. "It gets mighty dullsville up there above the airline."

Zeke coughed on an ice cube.

"But how's Professor Van Hiss? And Bobbi?"

"The ol' professor is full of bats. No change there. And Bobbi is just Bobbi. You'd think, him being a robotoid and all, he'd have more conversation."

"Guess so," Zeke mumbled.

Justice took his drink from the 'mac. It was clear, with a speared olive.

"It's been tough up at the Perspicillum," he said, his voice suddenly morose. "The professor works so hard, looking for his precious genesis particle, scouring the galaxy through that oversized magnifying glass."

"Yes," Zeke said. "He told us about that. I never really understood what all the fuss was about."

"I ain't no scientist," Justice replied, "but I think it's big. He talks to himself, you know. When he thinks I'm out of the way."

Zeke leaned forward.

"This much I know," Justice went on. "It's mighty important to the government. Earth, I mean, UNAAC and all them fellas."

Zeke burped. A light-headedness seeped into his skull.

"Do you ever think Earth is in trouble? I mean, the way they're sending colonists into space at breakneck speed?" he asked.

Justice narrowed his eyes.

"We've all heard the rumours. Earth is doomed. Something bad happened a few hundred years ago. But nobody in power ever comes out and says anything. But the professor, he's dropped some mighty big hints. Putting two and two together, I think his hunt for the genesis particle is connected in some way."

"Why don't you ask him."

Justice took a slurp from his Marstini.

"I plain well did. And he never said nothing."

A light fired up in his eyes.

"Hey, why don't you ask him? You made an impression on him."

"Send him an email on the Mars-Wide-Web?"

"No siree, pay us a visit, why don't you?"

"Kind of busy with schoolwork. And there's a war on."

Justice clicked his tongue.

"War! War on the Big Pumpkin. Downright crazy if you ask me. Those dratted terrorists stirring up a hornets' nest."

"You ever met any?" Zeke asked, waving his empty glass at the mixomac.

"Can't say I have," Justice answered. "But the radio is always on about them. Tune into Raymond Gamma the Third. He's got the low-down. They're just crooks, plain and simple."

They fell silent while the mixomac shuddered and juddered and produced another *Sirius Sling* from its mechanical innards.

"Now truly, young Ezekiel, ol' Hiss gets real blue some days. Pop over for a weekend and cheer him up. Heck, cheer us both up. Do your translocating thing and you'll be there lickety split."

Zeke gazed at his friend's face. Justice was always so perky and devil-may-care. But now he seemed sad.

"I'll see what I can do," Zeke said. "Just coming here has lost me two days at the Chasm."

"Yeah, why are you in the big, bad city, anyways?"

Zeke drew a deep breath and launched into his story. Justice's face grew paler and paler.

"Zekey boy, you've gotta do something."

"About what?"

Justice thumped the counter with his fist.

"If you can stop this war, you gotta!"

Zeke finished off his second drink.

"You think I should do what the Governor says?"

"Is there any doubt?" Justice raised his voice. "Those Martian State fellas are lower than a snake's belly."

"Come again?" Zeke asked and hiccupped.

"They're varmints. First class."

"Oh, right," Zeke said. The room was swaying.

"And what are you up to?" boomed a voice.

Both boys jumped. Mariner Chinook loomed over them.

"Where the heck did you come from?" Justice exclaimed.

"I translocated here," the Mariner said.

"But…but how did you find me, Sir?"

"I followed the trail of stray thoughts. Mental breadcrumbs. There's a lot on your mind, young man."

"Well, not any more, my friend here has talked some sense into me," Zeke said, blinking. Chinook was rather blurry. He picked up Zeke's glass and sniffed the sludge in the bottom.

"These drinks might be free of hooch, but they're laced with synthetic chemicals."

"You're darn tootin'," Justice said, his words slurred. He downed his third *Marstini*. "Life on the Big Pumpkin ain't easy, Mister Mariner, Sir. We gotta loosen the collar once in a red moon."

Chinook's expression was stern but Zeke fancied there was a ghost of a smile on his lips.

"Bedtime for you, young man," he said to Zeke.

Zeke frowned as he tried to think of a good reason to stay. He wiggled his forefinger at his teacher. "I don't think so." Another hiccup.

At that precise moment the bomb went off. The roar pounded Zeke's eardrums. Windows shattered. Photon lamps flickered. A shockwave threw him into the air. For a split second that lasted forever, he flew through a blizzard of glass. His head crashed against a foot rail. There was a terrible silence and then wailing.

Chapter Thirteen
The Ellipse Guest Bedroom

Zeke lay in darkness, unable to sleep. The nanoplaster on his forehead itched as it released nanomacs, microscopic robots designed to heal. He pictured them sinking into the sea of his flesh, fixing damaged tissue.

The explosion left him with a nasty bruise. But nothing worse, and for that he was grateful. Luckily, nobody got seriously hurt. *Think what it was like before the invention of scratchproof glass*, Chinook had said. The Mariner also sustained a couple of bumps but showed no sign of distress. Justice came out of it without a single injury. Not a physical one, anyway. After the blast, Justice couldn't stop being jolly, singing at the top of his voice and shaking the hand of everyone in the bar. *Shock*, Chinook remarked.

The Tithonium militia arrived surprisingly quickly, checked the victims for injuries before sending everyone home. The female soldier from the Monarch was among them. She saw Zeke and winked like they were old pals. She told him the bomb had gone off on the street.

And now Zeke was in bed, anger surged through his veins. Anger at the Martian State Brigade. What cowards. Hiding in the shadows and striking down innocent citizens. Zeke couldn't wait for sunrise and to start translating the text. He'd show the terrorists. He'd make them pay.

His eyes were heavy.

Where were the terrorists now? Out in the wilderness, holed up in some cave? Plotting their next attack? The *phsstrargs*, he thought, slipping into Hesperian. He'd show them.

His eyes shut and a warmth flowed over him. The edge of sleep. The divide between waking and dreaming. A sensation of floating.

Zeke opened his eyes and gazed down at the blue-haired boy in the bed. He seemed familiar. Oh, it was *him*! And Chinook asleep in the adjacent bed. It was another of those dreams, the same as in Ariyabata's class. He might as well enjoy it.

Zeke drifted through the wall, out into the gloomy corridor. For a while, he bobbed aimlessly through the warren of identical corridors. Then he caught a glimpse of the governor, up ahead, hurrying somewhere.

"Hey, wait for me," he called out, then remembered nobody could hear him in this out-of-body state. And in any case, he was dreaming. He glided after the politician. The governor strode through a hologram sign saying *No Entry*. Zeke followed. Zeke had never seen this part of the building before. The Governor stamped a code into a security panel and disappeared through an auto-door. Zeke simply passed through the wall as if it were just another hologram.

"Oh."

The tiny room was dwarfed by a strange object. Zeke guessed at once what it was. A thick blade of metal, six feet tall and the shape of a sword, embedded in a circular stone base.

Enki sat beside the object, muttering softly to himself.

"It still takes my breath away," the governor remarked softly.

Enki twittered away, like a bird driven mad.

"Don't you think it's real pretty?" the governor asked, stroking the blade. The metal shimmered. The governor stroked it again and this time it made a chiming noise. The sound a finger makes on a wine glass. The sound atoms made in the void between realities. Zeke shivered. If a spirit could shiver.

"The rupture, the rupture, the rupture," Enki mumbled. Zeke hovered in front of his old adversary. The man's face was passive and waxen. Zeke thought of a doll, or a ventriloquist's dummy.

"What's that, Doctor?" the governor asked.

Enki giggled. "Your secret will bring about the rupture."

The governor laughed.

"The Rapture? You sound like my old pastor back in Texas. Didn't know you were a man of faith, Doctor."

"No, the rupture, the rupture,"

"I don't think so. This little beauty is going to bring on the New Martian era."

"The rupture."

"Whatever, little man. I suggest you get some sleep."

"Enki no longer sleeps," Enki said, staring into mid-air.

"Eggheads, they're all cuckoo," the governor muttered.

"Okay, maybe Enki rest." the doctor said, standing up. "Good night," he said to the object.

The Governor smiled. "Yes, good night, you wonderful machine. Good night, Electron's Blade."

Zeke woke up with a start. He was in bed. Daylight streamed through the ventilation grill. Chinook was whistling in the shower.

Was it all a dream? Zeke wondered.

Chinook walked out, with a towel round his waist, drying his hair with another. His body looked carved from oak. Zeke felt puny in comparison.

"Ah, you're awake. The governor's invited us for breakfast. Look sharp."

Thirty minutes later and they were back on the West Garden patio. Another feast of breakfast goodies. The scent of coffee mixed with the earthy reek of cool palms. The governor was alone, bar two security men and they didn't seem to count as people.

Chinook tucked into the feast. Zeke had lost his appetite. He nibbled a bacon sandwich and left it at that.

The governor licked his lips. "Let's cut to the chase, why don't we?" he said with a glint in his eye. Zeke pushed out his bottom lip, as if to say 'go on'.

The governor leaned closer. His grey hair was immaculately combed. Pungent aftershave clawed at Zeke's nostrils. The man's face was charming, but Zeke still saw storms in those narrow eyes.

"Zeke, my son—and I feel like a father to you—how soon can you start work? Today?"

Chinook coughed politely. "He has schoolwork, Sir."

The Governor threw him a withering glare. "And I'm confident Lutz will give the boy leave of absence, this being war. The old bat owes me more favours than I care to remember."

Chinook stiffened.

Zeke raised his hand.

"Sir, let me get right to the point. I'm not translating anything."

The governor's jaw dropped.

"But boy, you saw for yourself how dangerous the Martian State Brigade are. You can't be serious."

"I am," Zeke said, looking down at his bacon sandwich.

"You'd do that? You'd walk away from the good people of Mars?" The governor was turning purple.

"My mind's made up."

"Boy, you haven't thought this through. Spend another day and—"

"No," Zeke said in a louder voice. Their eyes met. The governor's face twisted with rage. He banged the table with his fist.

"I hereby order you to—"

Chinook stood up. His shadow fell across both Zeke and the governor.

"Mariners do not take orders from you, Sir."

The governor jumped to his feet, knocking his coffee cup to the floor.

"In a time of war, I outrank everyone, even you, Eskimo."

Zeke saw a ripple pass through Chinook's imposing frame. But his face remained as inscrutable as ever.

"Up to a point, Governor. But you cannot keep us prisoner."

The governor's cheeks were the colour of aubergines.

"Actually, I can. Men!"

The two security men whipped out guns from their jackets and stepped closer. Chinook glanced at them. His eyes flickered with light. The guns leapt from each man's grip and hurtled away. They rattled to a stop somewhere beyond the cool palms.

"We're leaving," Chinook snapped. He placed his hand on Zeke's shoulder.

"B-b-but—" the Governor cried.

The West Patio blurred. Dimmed. Zeke and Chinook were in the darkness. Atoms sang their metallic song. The universe reshaped. They were standing on the steps of the Grand Hall. They were home.

Part Two

Chapter Fourteen
Telepathy 201

A large brain hovered at the front of the classroom. Or, rather, half a brain. A dissected brain as large as a sofa. Zeke hesitated in the doorway.

"You're late," Mariner Zoë Kepler snapped from her desk. She flicked back her long, raven hair and glared at him with beady eyes.

"Oh, be fair, Miss. I was abducted by soldiers."

"It's always excuses, excuses with you, Hailey. Find a seat."

He scanned the sea of faces. Pin-mei was at the front. Their eyes met, then she looked away.

"Ahem," Scuff said, in the back row. There was an empty seat beside him.

"Now, class," Kepler began. "Using your magnopads, label these areas of the brain."

She aimed her 'pad at the hologrammatic brain. Lines appeared, linking parts of the cerebral cross-section to numbers.

Without looking up from his magnopad, Scuff thought, *So you're back then?*

Yes.

Guess you had plenty of adventures?

Bad ones.

Scuff gazed down at his 'pad, pretending to work on the assignment.

Yup, ain't all adventures bad at the time? It's only later they seem exciting.

Zeke shrugged.

So, like, it's all happening here too, Scuff thought. They exchanged looks.

For starters, three students have gone down with future fever.

What? Zeke thought back.

Future fever, same as Lutz, Scuff explained. *Starts off with a psychic fit, but the patient gets hysterical, distressed, raving on about an apocalypse.*

A shiver ran up Zeke's spine.

And Knimble has had us all out in the quad doing safety drills. In case of attack. My feet are killing me.

My sympathies to your feet, Zeke thought, and grinned his lopsided grin.

And there's one more thing, Scuff thought in an ominous tone.

Which is?

"Are you two thinking in class!" Kepler bellowed from the front.

"No, Miss," Zeke and Scuff cried together.

"You better not be," she bellowed some more. "I will not have students thinking in class!"

At break, I'll show you. My room, Scuff thought quietly, then focused on the assignment.

The bell rang at two-thirty and the students streamed out of the teaching block, into the anaemic sunlight. As they crossed the gravel to the students' dorms, Zeke filled Scuff in on the trip to Tithonium.

Scuff whistled. "You sure land in hot water. Do you think the governor's going to drop it there?"

Zeke chewed his thumb.

"He wouldn't dare cross the Mariners."

"You don't sound too sure."

"I'm not."

Scuff scratched the folds of his double chin.

"Are you doing the right thing, bro?"

"Meaning?" Zeke asked sharply.

"You had a chance to stop the war. Save lives."

Zeke stopped dead in his tracks.

"Scuff! Nobody's seen as much Hesperian technology as you and me. And how often has it done any good?"

Scuff paused, deep in thought.

"Okay, gotcha. We were nearly killed on three occasions."

"Some people did get killed," Zeke said in a low voice. "Even if my dream was just a dream, I don't trust him. And I definitely don't trust Enki. They're hiding something."

"Okey-dokey, it's your call."

They trudged up the steps to Scuff's room on the fifth floor. Scuff waved his 'pad at the auto-door and it swished open. The interior was a toxic dump. As if a storm had hit. Dirty socks and jocks were strewn on the floor. Old pizza boxes littered the bed. A half-finished mini-robot stood on the desk, with wires spewing from its chest.

"No change here, then," Zeke remarked, stepping over a pile of books and comics.

Scuff pointed to a corner near the wardrobe.

"Scuff!" Zeke cried.

There, next to an overflowing bin, lay a sphere as big as a medicine ball. The Black Orb.

"Why did you go into my room?" Zeke said in a raised voice.

Scuff pushed out his bottom lip. "I didn't, bro."

Zeke went to answer, but stopped.

"I woke up this morning and there it was," Scuff continued.

Zeke scratched his head. "It found its own way here?"

Scuff nodded.

"Hmm. S'pose it's not the first time," Zeke agreed.

"I think we better recap. It might shed some light," Scuff said.

Zeke pushed aside the pizza boxes and sat on the bed. There was a stink of stale anchovies.

"Okay," he began.

Scuff sank into his chair, winced and jumped up again.

"That's where I left the screwdriver."

He tossed it onto the carpet and took his seat.

"So, what do we know about the Black Orb?" he asked.

Zeke bit his lip.

"Not much."

Scuff gave Zeke his best '*Are-you-nuts?*' stare.

"Think, Zekey boy. Where did you come across it?"

"At Yuri-Gagarin Freetown. You know that. Ptolemy Cusp had it, along with the Orb of Words and the Orb of Can Do."

"And he got them from Trixie Cutter?"

Zeke frowned.

"No, she swiped the first two from Magma's camp and sold them to Cusp. He hoped all three would give him some advantage if war ever broke out."

"Which it has," Scuff said. "So, we've no idea where this one came from?"

Zeke shook his head.

"Go on," Scuff prompted.

"Well, he wanted me to touch it. Only psychics have enough brain power to activate the orbs. He was hoping I'd trigger some power, but it's dead. I got zero response."

"But when you woke up in the Medical Facility, a few days later, it mysteriously appeared beneath your bed."

"Right. I took it back to my room for safekeeping and forgot all about it."

"Until it makes its way to my room."

"Did someone sneak it in? For a joke?"

"Doubt it, bro. My auto-door has double authentication. And why?"

"Then what?" Zeke asked.

"It was looking for you. Obviously."

Zeke crouched down and gingerly poked it. Nothing. He heaved it up and dumped it on the floor between them.

"Weighs a ton," he remarked.

"I've got an idea." Scuff said, rubbing his squat nose. "And what about the dodecahedron?"

"Never go anywhere without it," Zeke replied, and fished the multi-pointed rock star from his pocket. "Why?"

"Just, it's another lump of Martian technology. Also, a mystery."

"Don't think so," Zeke said, tossing it in the air. "This does absolutely nothing. Except for making a great paperweight and all-round good luck charm. I think it was an ornament."

"Dullsville. An alien artefact rescued from a dying universe and no super powers?"

Zeke pushed it back in his pocket. "So, your idea?"

Scuff sniffed.

"First we speak to Trixie. She might know something. Second, we pay a visit to Mariner Cortez."

"The psychometry teacher? These objects have two billion years of history. It might blow her mind."

"Look on the bright side, why don't you?"

"Why does it matter so much to you, anyway?" Zeke asked.

"Because of this." Scuff leaned forward and touched the Orb. Rings of light rippled out from his finger and around the orb.

"It's definitely not dead for me," he said.

They found Trixie Cutter in the school library, of all places. She was sitting in a quiet corner, hidden behind a forest of lofty bookcases. Photon lamps dangled from the high ceiling, painting the scene in a dull, brownish light. Silence reigned, with every head buried in an electrobook or a holoreader.

"You could hear an atom split," Scuff whispered.

They approached Trixie warily, as one would a wild beast.

"Ah, my least favourite earthworms," she said, looking up from a pile of books.

"Gee, its mutual," Scuff said, flushing. "Why are you even pretending to study? Cheating's more your style."

An electrobook levitated off the table, and smacked Scuff on the top of his head.

"Yeouch!"

It flapped over to Zeke. The book smacked him on the skull too. "Hey, what did I do?" he protested.

"Inch of prevention's worth a pound of cure," Trixie replied, with a cruel smile, seizing the book from mid-air. She straightened her perfect, blonde ponytail. Zeke glanced at her flawless skin, the cherry red lipstick, the hint of eyeliner. Trixie was stunning, he thought, like a shark in make-up.

"I can see from your grubby faces, you're after something. Spill the beans, what can Auntie Trixie do for you?"

"Information" Scuff replied.

"It'll cost you."

Scuff waved his magnopad. "You take M dollars?"

Don't Scuff, it's not that important, Zeke thought.

No point having a millionaire dad if I can't flash the cash, Scuff thought back.

You'll both get another whack if you don't stop with the telepathy, Trixie's voice boomed in their brains.

"We'll cut to the chase," Scuff said. "We want to know about the Black Orb. Did you sell it to Ptolemy Cusp?"

Trixie lost her smile.

"Why are you asking about that?"

"Doesn't matter. Just tell us where it came from?"

"No idea,' Trixie replied. "Wait. Tolly told me some freetowner found it out in the wilderness. Brought it to Tolly, who of course guessed it was an alien relic and took ownership. Then it vanished, right after our jolly little visit with that creep Crawley. Tolly was hopping mad. Blamed me."

"But what does it do?" Zeke asked.

"Never did anything. Dead as a dodo."

Trixie's eyes narrowed. "Have you worms found it?"

She didn't know they had it!

"N—n—no, just some research I'm doing," Zeke stuttered.

"Whatever, fifty Ms, please."

"Fifty!" Scuff squeaked. Without a word Trixie began inspecting her pretty, rose pink nails. The menace was unmistakable. Scuff gulped and tapped his magnopad.

"Fifty M dollars emailed to your account."

The boys turned to go. Zeke hesitated

"Why are you here?" he asked.

"You think I'd cheat on my final exam? No way old Lutzie would fall for that."

"But you said when you graduated you would stay in the solar system and build up your black-market empire."

The powdered tint of red deepened on Trixie's cheeks.

"It would break Daddy's heart if I didn't get an A Plus."

"The one person you care about," Zeke said without thinking.

"That's none of your business, earthworm," Trixie screeched. An electrobook whizzed through the air and clunked him on the forehead.

Chapter Fifteen
A Dream

The disc was as big as a football field. Smooth and shiny as if made from bronze. Zeke was standing in the centre like the pivot of a clock. The galaxy streamed around him, a swarm of stars and supernova. He could reach out and touch them. White dwarfs were mere pinpoints, sparks in the night. Yellow stars were the size of marbles. Then came the giants, the supergiants, the rare hypergiant, dazzling oranges, reds and blues. They floated past, most no bigger than a tennis ball. The colours of the cosmos against the inky universe.

A nebula drifted by, a cloud of illuminated gases, fiery greens and pinks. Zeke pursed his lips and blew. The nebula coiled away, like smoke.

I'm dreaming, he thought.

A large white star approached. Zeke, with his knowledge of astronomy, recognised it at once. Alpha Cephei or Alderamin. The destination of his father's secret mission, over fifteen years before.

The star grew bigger. Zeke stepped back, alarmed. But there was no heat. A tiny planet swung into view.

"In real life you'd be as big as Jupiter," he told it.

The planet continued to swell.

"Oh." There was a moon, a little nugget spinning around the gas giant. Zeke leaned in for a better view. The moon was streaked with purples and blues. The blues had to be water, a world of rivers rather than oceans. As for the purple, Zeke couldn't tell.

"Are you there, Dad?"

The word 'dad' stuck to his tongue. He'd never known his father. Could you call a man you'd never met 'dad' or was that impolite? What was the protocol with a father? If they ever met, how should he greet him. A hug? A manly handshake?

The stars fizzled out. About twenty metres away, pillars materialised out of nothing. Three great columns of stone, pocked with age. In their shadow was a bed. Zeke rushed towards it. But he stopped short. A body lay on the bed, under a sheet. Was somebody dead? The sheet fell a couple of inches short, exposing a mop of hair. Blue hair.

A man was kneeling at the foot of the bed. His face was buried in his hands and he was weeping. His hair was a faded blue, streaked with white. His beard was all white.

Beep, beep, beep, beep, beep.

Zeke shot up in his bed. His bicycle headlamp flashed in the darkness of his room.

"Alarm off," he muttered, rubbing his eyes.

"Good morning, Master Zeke," the bike said.

Zeke grunted.

"I beg your pardon, Master Zeke?"

"Good morning, Albie," Zeke snapped. Sometimes, the app's relentless cheerfulness could be annoying.

"Lights," Zeke said aloud and photons bathed the little cave with radiance.

"No!"

Zeke saw it at once, or rather he didn't. The night before he had brought back the Black Orb for safe keeping. He'd dumped it on the floor in the middle of the room. Now it was nowhere to be seen.

Scuff! he thought, then remembered Scuff's room was too far away for brainwaves. He snatched his magnopad from the bedside cabinet and thumbed in Scuff's number.

After an eternity of buzzing, Scuff answered.

"Bro, wazzup?"

"The Orb. It's gone."

"Not exactly, it's here."

"It really does like you," Zeke replied, and staggered to the shower.

Mariner Cortez kept a classroom at the top of the teaching block. Psychometry was a specialist subject only open to final year students. As such, she had a lighter timetable than most teachers. When Zeke and Scuff knocked on her door, she was sat at a window and gazing out through a pair of diginoculars. She was a stout, older woman with a bouffant of butterscotch-coloured hair. The smell of lemons filled the room and her magnopad was tuned to Mars Valley Radio, and the harmonies of Country and Martian.

Cortez suspiciously eyed the Black Orb in Scuff's arms.

"Come in *chicos*, come in."

They walked over, Scuff struggling under the weight of the orb.

She resumed observing the landscape with the diginoculars.

"Mars, it's never the same, don't you think, *chicos*?"

The boys exchanged looks.

"Hasn't changed in two billion years," Zeke replied.

"Ah, that's where you're wrong. It's always shifting, moving. Take those dust devils. Always blowing the sand this way and that."

Zeke stiffened at the mention of devils.

"Sometimes I think they are *fantasmas*!" Cortez said.

"Why would you say a thing like that?" Zeke asked, feeling a chill in the air.

Cortez lowered the diginoculars and laughed. "An old woman's fancies."

She picked up her cup and sipped lemon tea.

"Let me guess. You think you've found some ancient Martian artefact and want me to read it."

"Whoa, how'd you know, Miss?" Scuff exclaimed.

Mariner Cortez smiled.

"Every term some *niño* trips over a lump of rock out there and brings it to me. I say to them and I say to you, you've more chance of winning the *lotteria*, than finding alien relics."

"But supposing you did?" Zeke prompted her.

"*Mi chico, los Marcianos* lived millions of years ago."

"Billions," Zeke said gently.

"*Si, billónes*, any energy field would be long gone."

"Energy field?" Scuff asked.

"*Si*, living creatures leave energy fields on objects they touch. If they touch an object over a long period, the energy field becomes strong enough to read. If you are *el vidente*, the psychic. But the field lasts only a few years. A hundred at best, but *billónes*, that is the *imposibilitad*."

"So, there'd be no harm in trying?" Zeke ventured.

Cortez raised an eyebrow.

"In Lima, young people are not so pushy."

She gestured for Scuff to step nearer. He placed the orb on the floor and she leaned down and placed a hand on its dull surface.

"*Mi dios!* You have some dirty habits," she remarked at Scuff. He blushed.

"But before Scuff, anything?" Zeke cried.

Cortez stroked the Orb a few times.

"*Nada*."

Once again, she lifted the diginoculars to the view.

"There they are again!"

"What, Miss?" Zeke asked.

"The tiny people, running and hiding. Like little black ants."

She pointed out, beyond the school wall. The boys looked too. The morning sun caught Ophir Chasma in a blaze of purple. To the west, canyon walls soared out of sight. Ash dunes flowed away to the east. Towers of basalt rose from the dunes, craggy and gnarled. Zeke imagined some vast subterranean monster, waking from eternity and breaking through the planet's crust.

"*Aqui, aqui*," Cortez said, thrusting the diginoculars on Zeke. They were set for twenty miles. Zeke peered through the lens. Faraway blurs became crystal clear. Rock formations invisible at that distance, could now be seen in detail. He was looking at a crop of slabs, jutting at an angle. A shadow flashed between them.

"Oh!" He gripped the diginoculars. Seconds ticked away. There was no more movement. "Um, I thought, I mean, well, I can't see anything now."

"Are you certain?" Cortez asked. Zeke shrugged and was about to hand back the diginoculars, when Scuff said, "Show her the dodecahedron."

Zeke gave the diginoculars to Scuff instead and fished in his pocket. He passed the blue and pink rock star to Cortez.

"Ooh?" she remarked, feeling its weight. "This is an *objeto interesante*." She pressed each of the dodecahedron's points into her palm. Then, she rubbed her finger along the edges, muttering in Spanish.

Hey ho, we've got a live one, Scuff thought.

She kept stroking the star, mumbling to herself. Embers smouldered in the irises of her eyes. Simmered. Erupted. Her eyes blazed with light.

"*Madre de Dios*, someone's inside!" she screamed, and hurled the star across the room.

"Stop!" Zeke shouted. The alien paperweight froze a few inches from the floor. It flew back and he caught it in his hand.

"What did you mean? Inside?" he asked.

Cortez slouched over in her chair, panting heavily. Scuff handed her the cup of lemon tea and she took a deep swallow. The glare in her eyes ebbed away.

"Not what, *qui*, who," she said between puffs.

"I don't understand," Zeke said in an impatient tone.

Steady on, Scuff thought in Zeke's head. *She's had a goddamm shock.*

Cortez patted her chest, still gasping for air.

"*No entiendo*. I cannot say. A soul, I sensed inside. Trapped."

"An alien?" Zeke cried, excitement bubbling up in his chest.

Mariner Cortez stared at Scuff, as pale as a Martian polar cap.

"It felt human enough to me, *chico*."

Zeke held the star in the palm of his hand. Who knew what feats of technology the Hesperians could achieve. He'd already see a portal to everywhere, and a pocket universe. But a human consciousness, trapped inside a relic brought from a parallel dimension where no person ever stepped? That was the *imposibilitad*.

"Maybe they had a way of tapping into atomic structure. Like a quantum computer?" Scuff suggested.

"No, no," Cortez interrupted, the colour returning to her cheeks. "I am mistaken. It's just a lump of rock, nothing more."

Zeke frowned. "But you said—"

"I know what I said. I was wrong. Too much staring at the desert. *Vamos!*" Cortez raised her voice. The boys were about to leave when Scuff grabbed Zeke's arm.

"Listen."

The music on the radio had stopped.

"This is Ray Gamma the Third with breaking news," said a smooth voice. "Reports are coming in of an attack on a convey travelling to Hokusai Station. The convey was under the protection of the Governor's Office and protected by the military. A gang of cowardly Unpro thugs, aided by the so-called Martian State Brigade, opened fire on our brave boys. Luckily our boys repelled the attackers, but not before they stole several crates of food. We go now to the Ellipse to get the governor's reaction…"

Cortez switched off her magnopad. She turned her face away from them.

"With the Televator down, this is only the start," she muttered, more to herself.

Neither Zeke nor Scuff knew how to reply, and silently slipped from the classroom.

Chapter Sixteen

Ophir Chasma

Zeke cleared a gully and freewheeled out into the open vastness. The ground ahead was embedded with large stones, as flat as floor tiles. His bike bounced across them, jarring his spine.

For a small planet, Mars always seems so big, he thought.

The canyon stretched for miles in every direction. Slabs of basalt dotted the distant plains. Closer to hand, a pile of boulders resembled a clumsy fort, with smaller stones at the top like battlements.

Zeke pedalled faster. He loved cycling on Mars. The weak gravity made it easy. The crisp air, reeking of chlorine, lifted his spirits. A dust devil whirled across his path and fizzled out beside the fort.

"What the—"

Someone was watching him, up in the battlements. Zeke skidded to a halt and stared up at the fort. Nothing. Perhaps it was a trick of the light. He dismounted and aimed the handlebars.

"Albie, scan for life."

The head lamp shone a green beam across the rocky pile. Yet another of Albie's useful features.

"No life detected, Master Zeke," Albie said.

"Are you sure?"

"To a percentage of ninety-nine point nine, nine, nine, nine, nine—"

"Okay, I get the picture."

Zeke propped the bike against an ash-coloured boulder. He studied the boulder for a second. Everything else was ochre, thanks to the high levels of iron oxide. So why was this one different? Then, he dismissed it. There was too much on his mind to waste time on geology. He took two steps away, bursting with worries. Was Cortez crazy? She kept saying she saw phantoms. And what about that whole 'there's someone inside' thing? Could there be a life form stored inside the dodecahedron? If so, could it get out, and was it dangerous?

Then there was the Black Orb, suddenly acting so strangely. Zeke felt a twinge of jealousy. Why was it working for Scuff and not him? He was the special one. The Orb of Words chose him for the gift of Hesperian. Could Scuff and the Black Orb be a mistake?

These worries paled in comparison to the war. Zeke thought of Isla the Incisor, fighting alongside Ptolemy Cusp and his army of commandoes. Zeke's dislike for Ptolemy grew with every meeting. But Isla claimed to be Zeke's friend. Did that still apply in the heat of battle?

Isla's last words to him flitted through his memory. "Zeke, when the war starts, make sure you pick the right side."

But which side? The rebels started the war, and had done terrible things. But he couldn't think of Isla as a criminal. The governor represented the rule of Earth. And yet something about him scared Zeke to the bone.

Zeke's head hurt.

"Master Zeke, an email has arrived," Albie's metallic voice chimed.

"From?"

"The Office of the Governor of Mars."

"Delete it."

"Yes, Master."

That was the great thing about robots. They never argued.

Zeke pondered his three days in Tithonium Central. Suppose he'd done the wrong thing. Maybe he ought to work with the Governor and this Electron's Blade, if it saved lives. After all, how long before the planet began running out of supplies? The colonists had worked for decades to achieve self-sufficiency, but they weren't there, not yet.

The bomb attack surfaced in Zeke's memory. The deafening explosion, the storm of debris, the shock. He realised he'd forgotten Justice's invitation to visit Professor Van Hiss and find out what was really going on. Why the genesis particle was so important. Was it connected to the mystery of the never-returning colonists? And his never-returning father?

A sudden sound broke this spell of doubts. A pebble falling, tumbling down through the crannies in the boulder fort.

"Who's there?" he shouted.

Nobody answered. The fort was deserted. Zeke stood alone in the great valley of emptiness. A blanket of silence smothered the scene. He was quite alone.

It was at that moment the sooty-grey boulder wobbled and the bicycle fell over. Zeke jumped in surprise. Before he could react, the boulder unfurled. Limbs appeared. It stood up! A human-shaped creature made of rock. Crystal shards pierced its lips, arms and torso. Empty, black eyes regarded him. The Craton!

Translocate!

Too late. The Craton's jaw dropped and spewed a jet of sticky, pungent vomit. Blinded and breathless, Zeke tumbled backwards. A chemical reek, like ant acid flooded his nostrils...

When Zeke awoke he was lying in the cold dirt, wrapped in dried vomit like a fly in a spider's web. At least the Craton hadn't taken him anywhere, yet. He struggled against the sticky bonds but it was useless. His arms were tied to his sides. His legs were bound together. Only his face was clear, although his nose was bunged up with the stuff. The smell was revolting.

The Craton was nearby, hopping from stony foot to stony foot. Zeke took it for a victory dance.

"*Kshnmlnwa,*" he said weakly.

The creature froze, for all the world like an unfinished statue, then scrambled over. It got down on all fours and poked its face into Zeke's.

"Kshnmlnwa, child from the third planet," it replied in Hesperian.

"Are you still angry with me?" Zeke continued.

It smiled, its cheeks cracking with hairline fractures.

"Craton knows you did not help the hoomans. The man who wanted Craton for its secrets."

Scaly fingers caressed Zeke's hair.

"Craton likes you. You speak the words of the long-ago makers. You and Craton are same. Touched by their magic. Their strange science."

Touched in the head, more like, Zeke thought. *"Then why did you attack me?"*

Craton sat back onto its haunches.

"I am saving you, child. Evil is coming. Great evil. But we will hide in the ground, sleep the long sleep. We will out-sleep the danger."

Zeke knew it was pointless reasoning with the Craton. In any case, he was an apprentice Mariner. He would escape soon using his translocation. The important thing was to find out more.

"Maybe I will come with you. But you must help me first."

"Hoomans, always making deals," it snorted.

"When we met before, you said if I give you your name, you'll give me the others. The missing humans from all those years ago."

The Craton spat a dollop of hissing bile onto the ground.

The bonds were loosening a little. Zeke propped himself up on his elbows.

"You were once human. Don't you remember any of it?"

The Craton scowled. Zeke took that as a *no*.

"Where are they. Please. You can tell me."

"They are stored."

"Under the ground, in your lair?"

"No," the creature replied. *"In the yellow orb."*

Finally, a clue! *"And where is that?"*

"Child from the third planet asking too many questions. The orb is hidden. Where no hooman can ever find it."

Zeke hesitated, he didn't want to push it into a hasty reaction.

"Forgive me. Curiosity falls like rain in the deserts of ignorance."

It was a Hesperian idiom. Like all their prehistoric words, it bubbled up from Zeke's subconscious. The Craton clicked its ossified tongue. It seemed appeased.

"The orb took them. Those hoomans. Into its atomic structure. Orbs do wondrous things."

They certainly do, Zeke thought.

"Now we will go, my tunnels are waiting." It leaned over him, placing its jagged hands on either side of his torso. Zeke trembled. The Craton's lair was beneath the abandoned Beagle Research Station, where the bedrock was laced with iron. The deposits generated a magnetic field, weak but powerful enough to dampen his psychic powers.

"Are you Tom Ganister? Wheeler? Maddie or Veronica?" he shouted in desperation, summoning the only names he recalled off the top of his head. The Craton said nothing, but its dark eyes began to glow. It was building up for a translocation. Zeke knew that if he materialized under the research station, he'd be trapped and at the creature's mercy.

Zeke screwed up his face and thought hard. Mars vanished. So too did most of the Craton's dried bonds, left behind in the valley. Zeke was afloat in the never-where between atoms, a dimension simultaneously everywhere and nowhere. Devoid of light, airless, yet with that endless ringing. Like an orchestra of chimes. No, a trillion orchestras.

But a hand grabbed him by the calf. Tiny blades of crystal sliced through his trousers and punctured his skin. The Craton was yanking him back.

Never! He thought.

Zeke kicked wildly. But in the void thought was stronger than muscles. Zeke pictured his room. It was a little ball of reality, up ahead, out of reach.

You will stay. I will save you! The alien words boomed through Zeke's head. The hand was pulling him back, to the valley.

Not today, Zeke thought back. He concentrated on the image in his mind's eye. The room was becoming bigger, nearer, solid. Still it was distorted, as though seen through a fish-eye lens. But he could almost touch it now.

The Craton's grip hardened. Zeke yelped as the crystals cut deeper. The Craton's ugly, petrified face leered out of the darkness. Zeke could take no more. He booted it on the jaw. A silent scream erupted from its sliver of a mouth. Zeke felt it let go. The face fell away.

Zeke was outside his room, as if it were a blown-up photograph. *In! In!*

And, as his teachers never tired of saying, thought is the most powerful force in the universe.

He flopped onto the floor of his room, back in atomic reality. Safe.

Chapter Seventeen
Zeke's Room

Zeke stepped out of the shower and dried himself. He felt better. Soap and shampoo instead of dried alien vomit. He jumped into his spare uniform. The tunic and trousers were ice-cold, where he'd left them on the floor of his cave.

"Albie, book the laundromac to pick up my dirty clothes."

Albie pinged and said, "Done, Master Zeke."

Zeke pulled a can of Craterade from his fridge, plonked down in his easy chair and picked a leather journal from the floor. The words *Beagle UK Research Station Logbook. Year 2089* were embossed on the cover.

Zeke and Scuff had stumbled across the deserted Beagle Research station in a sandstorm. Early British astronauts had built it a hundred and seventy years earlier. This was during the first human landings on Mars, long before terra-forming kicked in. In those days Mars was a death trap, with no breathable oxygen and deadly radiation levels.

The journal was kept by the astronauts working there, all of whom vanished. Well, bar one, the Craton. As soon as Zeke heard the Craton speak English, he realized it was an ex-human, mutated by Hesperian science. Scuff even came up with a theory to explain it. Supposing the yellow orb was rewriting the human's DNA to make him (or her) Hesperian. But maybe the Hesperians were a silicon life form, not carbon-based. Then the transformation would go horribly wrong, as carbon reacts differently to silicon.

As mad as the Craton seemed, there was a consistency to its ramblings. First, it no longer remembered its human identity. Second, that the astronauts were not dead, despite the passage of time. They were preserved in some way, using the powers of the yellow orb. Which meant they might yet be saved. But the Craton would only reveal their whereabouts if Zeke helped him (or her) remember who it once was.

This was where the journal came in. It was Zeke's only chance of finding answers. Indeed, he made it his mission. Yet as the Martian months crawled by, the journal gathered dust on his floor. He had some mental block that he could not put into words. Maybe he was afraid of learning the truth. The events at the Beagle Research Station might prove too horrific.

"Block, no longer," he muttered and took a sip. The metallic taste of Craterade tingled on his tongue and energy flooded through him. He opened the frontispiece and refreshed his memory on the crew.

Mission Leader: Doctor Tom Ganister. Geologist
Medical Officer: Doctor Jed Wiley. Physician, Psychologist
Harry Silverman: Lab Technician, IT support (and a helluva cook!!!)
Doctor Veronica Skye: Meteorologist, volcanologist
Clyde Wheeler: Transportation Engineer
Doctor Claire Welt: Terraform Researcher
Prof. Madeline Willow: Agriculturalist, hydroponics

The journal was kept by the team leader, Tom Ganister, although a few others also contributed. The first few weeks were all recordings of data, experiment results and scientific findings. Which, of course, was the purpose of the journal. But then it grew darker, and sporadic. Pages were torn out. The last few had bloodstains.

Zeke had read Tom's growing alarm as some dark force took over the station. They'd found the yellow orb, only for it to disappear. Zeke's guess was that one of the crew was psychic. But the twenty-first century was a dark age, before humanity's psychic abilities were understood. The yellow orb had called to that crew member, just as the Orb of Words had called to him. But this person, not grasping his or her powers, had been driven mad, slowly mutating into the Craton.

The pages unfolded a story of how one crew member, Clyde Wheeler, seemingly vanished outside in the vacuum. Of course, he would have instantly died, but there was no corpse and someone was tapping on the walls at night. Then the two buggy engines were stolen, leaving the crew trapped. And someone smashed the radio, their only lifeline to base camp.

Zeke glanced around his room. He had an uncanny feeling he was being watched. Goosebumps tickled his arms.

"It's just a book," he said aloud. "Books never harmed anyone."

He came to a well-thumbed page and dived in where he had left off.

Aug 12th

I'm desperate. We all are. And mad. Wiley walking round the station like a zombie and muttering about ghosts. Martian ghosts. Maddie keeps weeping. Says we're all going to die. If only I could find the yellow orb. I'm convinced that's the cause of the trouble.

Fact: the orb is an alien artefact. There's nothing else it could be.

Inference: everything we know about Mars is wrong.

Conjecture: Whatever purpose the orb served, it is now messing with our minds. Even if we found it, we don't have the equipment or skills to figure out how it works.

Conclusion: The orb is killing us.

Solutions:

1. Find and destroy it.

2. Find the missing buggy engines and escape. With over a hundred and fifty kilometres to base camp, even that would be touch and go.

3. Murder the others. Human scum.

Doctor Tom Ganister
Aug 13th

Both Wiley and Maddie claim they heard Wheeler moving outside the Station last night. Obviously impossible.

New plan. Tomorrow we search the ground, looking for the orb and the engines. And Wheeler's body. Sounds cruel, but we really want to know he's dead right now.

Doctor Tom Ganister

Aug 13th midnight

Dreams so real. Too real. A gentle sea, a beach as white as sugar. But there was something behind me. Every time I turned to see it, nothing. Like a blind spot. A boy waded out of the sea. In a peculiar school uniform. He was crying. There was an axe in my hand and I decided to shut the little piggy up.

Doctor Tom Ganister

Aug 14th

First thing we saw outside were Wheeler's footprints, vanishing into the dunes. After an hour the metal detector found the engines. Half-buried. Both smashed beyond repair.

I'm never going to see my wife and kids again.

Doctor Tom Ganister

Aug 14th

Addendum: Something bugging me about those footprints.

Tom had helpfully tacked a photo below the entry. Zeke stared at it for a moment. There was nothing odd about them. Well, naked feet in a vacuum, that was pretty odd. But the feet themselves were human enough.

Aug 14th Midnight

Before I die I must find out which cockroach did this. And cut their heads off.

Doctor Tom Ganister

Aug 15th

Unbelievable! Veronica found the orb! Veronica and Claire share a bedroom and she found it in Claire's storage unit. Claire is now missing. Vanished. Nobody feels like going out to look for her.

At least we know the culprit now. My theory is that the Orb is controlling her mind. Maybe Wheeler is in on it. Or he is dead. Who cares about him, the third-planet mutant. We will live now. I will live.

Doctor Tom Ganister

Aug 16th

Working together we tried to drill into the orb. Nothing could scratch it. The spectrometer tells us it's simple basalt but atomically altered, in a way beyond our ability to scan.

Someone has to take it as far away as we can get. So, we are outside its influence. As our oxygen tanks have a maximum of two hours, that's one hour away and one back. Maddie was a power walker back on Earth (trust her, the sports fanatic, lol). She volunteered. Left forty minutes ago.

Doctor Tom Ganister

Aug 17th

Maddie never came back.

Doctor Tom Ganister

Aug 18th

Locked in my room. Barricaded the door. One of them is trying to kill me. Maybe more than one. Who?

Facts: Wheeler, Claire and Maddie vanished. So, they're dead. Or maybe that's what they want us to think.

Claire Welt was hiding the orb before she vanished.

Wiley acting like a man possessed. Very suspicious.

That leaves Veronica. First, she supported me but switched allegiances to the team. Highly suspicious, the third planet witch.

And Silverman. No evidence whatsoever to incriminate him. That seems incriminating in itself to me.

That's the entire team apart from me.

Conjecture: It's Claire. Maybe.

Fell asleep. Dreamt of spires on a rusty horizon. They were all gigantic shells. The ground rocked. The buildings crumbled. The sky broke in two. And something came through the crack.

Doctor Tom Ganister

Zeke turned to the last page.

Aug 19th

Fact: humans are traitorous killers.

Conjecture: If they are dead they can't hurt me.

Action Plan: Eradicate the station of human contagion. An axe should do the job.

Doctor Tom Ganister

Chapter Eighteen
The Cranny Cafeteria

"Wow! That's a little bedtime reading I can do without," Scuff remarked, and pushed the journal back across the table to Zeke.

They were sitting beside the panoramic window. It was half past three, Martian Standard Time, and Year Two were on a free period. The cafeteria was full with their classmates. Pin-mei Liang was in an alcove, head buried in an electrobook.

"What do you think it all means?" Zeke asked.

Scuff thoughtfully rammed his little finger up his left nostril and prised a bogie from deep inside. He inspected it carefully and then flicked it under the table.

"Tom Ganister is the Craton. He's clearly turning into a psycho."

"What about Wheeler, though? No one walks off into a vacuum and survives. Not unless they have some alien tech."

Scuff sighed. "Anyway, Claire Welt and the other woman—"

"Maddie Willow."

"Also vanished. So, it could be any of them. Supposing more than one of the crew were affected?"

Zeke shook his head. "You know the odds of being born with psychic powers. Isn't it three million to one?"

"Two million, nine hundred and eight-one thousand, two hundred and sixty-four."

"Yes, that. Therefore, it couldn't be more than one at the station."

Scuff pushed out his lip, then said, "Ganister was seeing things,

Hesperian cities. Isn't that precognition?"

"Postcognition I think, seeing something after it occurred. But the orb could download those images into his head. I think it was driving them all crazy, but only one would develop psychic powers like ours."

"Then I don't have a clue, bro."

"What about the footprints?" Zeke pushed the journal back. Scuff stared at the photo.

"They're a bit tiny," he said.

"Sorry?"

"These are a woman's footprints. Wheeler was a dude, right? So not his."

Zeke frowned. He only felt more confused now.

"Maybe Wheeler was a very small person?"

Scuff rolled his eyes. "Bro, look at the width, too narrow for a man, and see the curve of the side and the way the big toe doesn't stick out so much. A woman's feet, absolutely."

So, one of the women went outside, and therefore was the culprit. Or maybe…Zeke's head began to swim. Too many possibilities and not enough evidence.

"Another thing," Scuff said. "The second dream totally describes Martian architecture. We know that from the Citadel."

Zeke nodded. Scuff went on.

"So, the dreams must be Mars too, when it had seas. But what would a human boy be doing on ancient Mars? And he mentions a school uniform."

"So?"

Scuff gestured to their shiny blue tunics.

"Bro, only school on Mars."

"I think you're reading too much into a madman's ravings."

Scuff pushed his bottom lip out.

"Guess so, billions of years before humanity existed. It could never happen."

For a while they were both lost in thought. Then Scuff stirred and said, "Can't you bluff the Craton or something?"

"No, he or she is telepathic, they'd see through that."

Scuff leaned forward. "Even if you do work it out, then what?"

"Well, I'm not sure. But, if I could help it realise who it really was, it would lead me to the hidden orb. And maybe we can reverse the whole process. Free the astronauts, even the Craton's mutation."

"A lot of maybes," Scuff remarked. He whistled at a toastomac and it wheeled over.

"Care for a toastie, Sir?" the 'mac asked. It was a large aluminium box on wheels.

"Cheese and pepper," Scuff replied. The mac rattled. The smell of melted cheese tinged the air.

"I've got to try. Being the Craton must be a living hell," Zeke went on.

The toastomac beeped. A grilled sandwich popped out of its top and landed on the table. Scuff sank his teeth into the crusts, squirting yellow goo in Zeke's direction.

"And Jimmy. A living death for both of them," Zeke added. Scuff nodded.

"What are you keeping from me?" Scuff said in a suspicious tone.

"Pardon me?"

"You're keeping something back."

Zeke's neck grew hot.

"Are you reading my mind? That's illegal."

Scuff stuffed the last of his toastie into his huge mouth.

"Nope. It's impolite, not illegal. But we are best buds."

"You tell me, then," Zeke snapped.

"Bro, I'm not reading your actual thoughts. Just, being an A grade telepathist, I get the general drift. Something's upset you."

Zeke pushed back from the table. Scuff, the most insensitive of people, could be so sensitive when it came to mindreading.

"On the day of the Fresher's party, I saw the Dust Devil. It told me I was going to die."

Scuff choked on a mouthful of toastie.

"First Principal Lutz, now the Devil. Zeke, that's some seriously bad mojo."

Zeke said nothing.

"Aren't you scared, bro?"

"I haven't really thought about it," Zeke answered, not all together truthfully.

"Yup, trust you to go all Egyptian."

Zeke gave Scuff a baffled look.

"You're in de Nile, bro."

Another baffled look.

"Denial!" Scuff bellowed.

"Oh," Zeke said in a small voice.

Psychics weren't always right. He'd studied quantum decoherence in Precognition 101. How the universe adjusted to a different outcome but nobody noticed. Because the universe adjusted them, too. So, predictions that started off correct could become wrong. In any case, Lutz was clearly cracking up. As for the Dust Devil, a malfunctioning piece of alien equipment, who knows what it meant? Did it even have the right translation when it was speaking English?

Ping!

Something chipped the window. Both boys jumped. A spider's web of fractures splintered the glass.

"Bro?" Scuff said.

"Shush," Zeke cried. "Did you hear that, a pop?"

Scuff shook his head. Zeke peered out of the window straight down. The Cranny was three miles up, so it was hard to make out the school. But one thing he could see.

"Smoke!"

Chapter Nineteen
Still the Cranny Cafeteria

Scuff thrust a pair of diginoculars in Zeke's hands.
"Forgot to give them back to Mariner Cortez," he added apologetically.

Zeke put them to his eyes and pressed the focus button. The school gate came into view. Or rather, it didn't. All Zeke could see was billowing smoke. The ground was scorched and littered with rubble. There was only one explanation. Someone blew up the school gate.

"I told you remote viewing would come in handy," Scuff said. Zeke glanced over. The Canadian's eyes were filled with a pearly light.

Zeke returned to the diginoculars. A dark river flowed from the smoky ruins. Fighters! Men and women wrapped in black. Only their eyes were visible. They brandished bulky cylinder rifles.

"We're under attack!" Zeke cried.

"Ninjas!" Scuff shouted.

Furniture scuffed on floorboards as everyone leapt up and stampeded to the window. Twenty faces pressed against the glass.

Zeke watched the river break into smaller streams, as the commandoes or ninjas or whatever they were stormed the school buildings. Three fifth years came rushing over from the sport courts. A ninja aimed his rifle and fired. The boys flinched and shielded themselves. They looked bewildered as if nothing had happened. Only it had. As Zeke knew well, the ninjas were armed with ferromagnetic rifles. Weapons that neutralised psychic power by blasting out magnetic ions.

"You should see Mariner Chinook," Scuff said, his eyes as bright as lightbulbs.

"Is he letting them have it with his psychokinesis?" Juanita Almera asked, standing beside Zeke.

"Nope, they got him as soon as they burst through the door," Scuff replied. "But he's socking it to them. You go, Sir! Three of them but they can't beat him. Ouch!"

"What?" Zeke cried.

"He just felled one with a punch. Knockout. Wham! Down goes another and—"

"And?" half a dozen students cried.

"The third whacked him out with a baton. Chinook's out for the count."

Zeke's heart was racing.

"Maybe we should take out the hover-lift?" he suggested, hands trembling.

A chorus of *yup*s and *go-for-it*s passed through the crowd.

"Don't bother, bro," Scuff said. "Three of them with jet packs are at the foot of the cliff."

Heidi, the swiss student, squealed.

"And…they've blasted off," Scuff added.

Zeke pushed through his schoolmates and ran to the door.

"We've got to do something," he cried, then stopped dead in his tracks. But what?

"Slower than the hover-lift, but they'll be here soon," Scuff remarked.

"Fuse!" Zeke shouted, aiming his hand at a small aluminium panel beside the auto-door. It sizzled in a shower of sparks. "That'll keep them out."

"But for how long?" wailed Dedy, the Indonesian student.

"I can translocate us all out of here, in groups," Zeke said.

"Where to, though?" came a quiet, confident voice. Pin-mei.

Zeke's brain whizzed through the options. There was no way he was going back to Tithonium and the clutches of the governor. But Yuri-Gagarin Freetown were the very people currently storming the gates. The same went for Edenville, the Marmish community. They'd thrown their lot in with the Unpro after the tragedy at the Melas Mine.

"The deserts! We'll hide out in the deserts."

Pin-mei stared at him with a withering expression.

"That's your best plan? Starve to death in the wilderness?"

"The flyboys are a third of the way up," Scuff said.

Zeke glared back. Was she going to punish him forever?

"We'll have time to figure out a better plan. Fight back."

Pin-mei put her hands on her hips.

"Nobody lasts out there for long. No water, no food, no thermals. It's a mad idea."

"But we can't just stay here," piped up Farai, a tall gangly boy from South Africa.

"Right," Zeke said. "Who's with me?"

"Halfway," Scuff piped in.

Panic erupted. Students ran around the cafeteria, crying. Some wrung their hands, a few hid under the tables.

"Calm down, calm down," Zeke shouted. It was useless, they were deaf with fear.

"Sheesh, the flyboys are nearly at the top," Scuff said. His eyes flickered and dulled, leaving the eyelids puffy. "What do we do, Zekey boy?"

"I don't know, I don't know," he replied, biting on his knuckle.

Juanita screamed, pointing at the auto-door. Three black-garbed commandoes were on the other side of the glass.

"Let us in," boomed a voice.

"That's it! Who's coming with me?" Zeke cried.

Hands shot up everywhere.

"No!" Pin-mei said.

"But they're going to kill us," Heidi said, white with fear.

Pin-mei scrambled onto a table.

"If they wanted to kill us, they'd be carrying real guns. I know

Ptolemy Cusp, how his mind works. He wants our psychic talent. For the war."

"And what, you're going to give it to him? Betray Earth, our families?" Zeke asked angrily. Was his ex-best friend a traitor? Maybe she was a part of the Unpro plot.

Pin-mei sneered.

"Obviously not. We wait our chance. Fight back from the inside. Sooner or later our powers will come back and then—"

"Look!" Dedy cried. One of the commandoes was fixing a round, black device, the size of a smoke alarm, onto the door.

"If we run away, we're sure to die," Pin-mei went on, speaking faster. "Stay here and we live and have a real chance of beating them."

Zeke scanned the faces in the room. They were all gazing at Pin-mei with hope in their eyes. He'd lost his argument.

Crack!

The auto-door shattered into a shower of fragments. The commandoes burst into the cafeteria, ferromagnetic rifles blasting. Screams filled the air.

"Bro?" Scuff cried, seizing Zeke's arm.

A commando came running towards them, aiming his rifle. Zeke seized his friend and they toppled.

The two of them rolled through oblivion. Emptiness. The space between atoms. Next, they hit the ground, still rolling, tumbling downwards. An avalanche of shale engulfed them. All Zeke could see was sky and rock, swirling like a kaleidoscope. The cold burned his flesh. His lungs clawed for air.

They whacked into a small boulder, breaking the fall. Zeke looked around, gasping. He saw a great barren slope rising around them, cluttered with rocks. The caldera of the long extinct volcano, Ascraeus Mons. The second highest peak on Mars, eleven miles above the surface. But that meant they were above the airline. Scuff lay beside him, purple-cheeked and convulsing like an epileptic. Dizziness and nausea swept over Zeke. They were close to death. In seconds, he would pass out and asphyxiate.

Where was it? Zeke had overshot his target, but it couldn't be far.

There! Perched on the rim of the volcano, high above them. The Perspicillum, glittering gold in the sunset, the transparent dome splashed with reds and indigos.

Zeke's vision was blurring. Bells rang in his ears. He grabbed Scuff's tunic by the chest, focussed on the Perspicillum, and wished harder than he had ever wished before.

Chapter Twenty

Lutz's Office
or Possibly a Dream

A tall Japanese man was lounging in Principal's Lutz's chair. Worse, his feet were up on the desk, exam papers scrunched beneath his army boots. She'd have a fit if she ever knew. Ptolemy Cusp was handsome and broad-shouldered. He had cropped hair and he wore sand-coloured military fatigues. He was grinning.

The door swung open and three men marched in. The first was Mariner Knimble, flanked by two ninjas. His left eye was bruised. A tight metallic bracelet was fitted to his upper arm.

Magnetized, Zeke thought from his viewpoint in the corner, to cancel out Knimble's psychic strength.

"My dear Alistair, please," Cusp said genially, waving at the seat across the desk.

Knimble sullenly sat down.

"Alright, Alistair, let's cut to the chase."

"This is an outrage," Knimble snarled.

"Life at the school will go on as normal. I have no intention of stopping these young heroes from their mission."

"The Institute will stop you."

"I appreciate that for the moment, lessons will be all theory and no practical. Not until we can trust the students enough to remove the bracelets."

Oh, Zeke thought, *they've chained every psychic in the school! That's a lot of bracelets. How long has Cusp been planning this?*

"And I'm adding two new subjects to the curriculum. Revolutionary

Studies, opening up their young minds to the crimes of UNAAC, Earth and the Governor's Office."

"Propaganda!" Knimble spat the word out.

"And military skills. The students will warm to that. It's fun, target practice, manoeuvres, survival classes."

"You're turning them into child soldiers?" Kimble was incredulous.

"Tsk, tsk, Alistair. They're young adults, not children. And you should thank me for training them. We are at war, you know."

"Yes, I heard all about your failed attack on the convoy to Hokusai."

Cusp threw his head back and laughed out loud.

"What is it they say? The first casualty in a war is truth? We made off with the entire loot. You don't want to believe the fake news coming out of Tithonium."

"And I suppose the Martian State Brigade are totally bonzer?"

The smile dropped from Cusp's face.

"Listen, whoever those guys are, they're nothing to do with us."

"Like I'd believe that."

"Seriously," Cusp replied. "I've never met them. They're shadows in the dark. And they don't speak for Unpro. We use force only when necessary."

For an organization that drops a lot of bombs, how come nobody ever seems to have met them? Zeke wondered. It seemed odd.

"Can I go back to the cell with the other teachers now?" Knimble asked, with a sarcastic leer.

Cusp removed his feet from the desk.

"You're looking at this all wrong. I'm extending the hand of friendship. A treaty, if you will, between the Unpro and the school."

"The Mariners' Institute is neutral."

Cusp leaned nearer.

"Then break with them. Become the leader of a new faction of Mariners. With your students, we can win the war in days. Blood-free."

Knimble looked away.

Cusp went on. "Remote viewing, psychokinesis, telepathy, translocation! Your boys and girls can defeat the governor without ever stepping onto a battleground."

"It's obscene." Knimble retorted.

Cusp pushed back in his chair.

"Hypocrite! Every graduation, you send another generation to their doom. Lambs to the slaughter. And you call me obscene? I'm the one trying to save them. To free them from Earth's death regime."

Knimble was red with hatred.

"It's not like that."

"Oh, isn't it?"

"And we will never comply."

Cusp sighed. He pulled a clunky iPistol from the holster under his jacket.

"Listen. You're overlooking one fact. We're at war. And in a war, people do anything to survive. Bad things." Cusp aimed the weapon at the Mariner's head.

Zeke felt his heart, which was not actually there, skip a beat. He imagined the iPisitol leaping from Cusp's hand. Nothing. Apparently, his powers didn't work out-of-body.

Isla the Incisor stormed into the room. Zeke hadn't seen her for nearly a year. She appeared a little older. But her ginger hair was still cut to the skull, and her emerald eyes were as sparkling as ever. If anything, she was more stunning than Zeke remembered. Her fatigues fitted her curves like a glove. She also looked really, really miserable.

Cusp quickly put the iPistol away.

"No sign of him. Flown the coop."

"Typical of Hailey," Cusp said, rolling his eyes. "When the going gets tough, he does a runner."

Zeke bristled. Cusp turned to Knimble.

"Where is he?"

"Why do you want him so?"

Cusp shrugged.

"I want every student in the school. But Hailey is the cherry on the sundae. His ability to speak Martian could come in very handy."

Knimble gestured for Cusp to go on.

"You might as well know." Cusp said. "Could change your pig-headedness. The governor has a secret Martian weapon. Electron's Blade. Enki told him where to find it. To the west of Mariner's Valley, somewhere. My spies gleaned that much. What it does, we don't know. But Hailey could get in, figure that out, maybe even steal it for us."

Now it was Knimble's turn to laugh.

"Zeke would never do that, the boy's a born pacifist."

"Oh, I'd find a way to persuade him. Miss Liang is very important to him, is she not?"

Isla stiffened. She and Cusp traded looks. Neither were psychic but they had a telepathy all of their own. Zeke guessed the word for it was love. Cusp was suddenly crestfallen.

"Those two have fallen out," Knimble said.

Does everyone in the school know my business? Zeke thought.

"Whatever, we'll find a way. Now one more time. Where's the boy?"

Knimble stared his captor straight in the eye.

"He could be anywhere on Mars. That boy has a talent for translocation I've never seen before."

Zeke felt his absent cheeks flush.

"But where? Where's his bolthole?"

Knimble lowered his gaze. He looked very tired.

"I honestly don't know, Ptolemy."

Cusp clicked his fingers and the guards dragged Knimble from the room. Zeke felt an urge to slap Cusp, and damn hard. Too bad he was lacking his body.

Isla and Cusp were alone.

"Trixie wants to see you," Isla said. "Probably hoping to gain favour with the new leadership."

Cusp drummed his fingers on the desk.

"What do you think?"

Isla walked over and stroked the nape of his neck.

"I wouldn't give that sewer rat house room. She's poison."

Cusp had a smile like a cat getting the cream.

"Speaking as a woman?"

"Speaking as a soldier."

"Well, take her bracelet off. Tell her she's now head prefect. And the slightest hint of rebellion and I'll blow her head away."

Isla nodded approvingly. "That ought to work."

"But first we need to revise the plan."

"As the number one player is bunking off school?"

Zeke floated closer.

"Exactly."

"Tolly, you wouldn't really hurt Zeke or Pin, would you?"

Ptolemy took Isla's hand.

"I thought you, of all people, knew I am a peacemaker. It's all bluster. And to save lives, don't lose sight of that."

"I guess so," Isla replied. Her voice wavered.

"And so, the plan. I need you to—"

The strum of a guitar reverberated out of nowhere. Neither Cusp nor Isla heard it. They continued chatting, unaware of the plucking sounds. Yet the chords continued, loud but stumbling. Someone was attempting to play *I'm All Washed up in the Lonesome Crater*, and murdering the melody.

Zeke glanced around the room. Where was it coming from?

He was sitting up on a long seat, next to a window. Outside lay the fathomless dark of the Martian night. The room was circular. One half of the room was a kitchenette. The other had a pool table and comfy chairs. Justice was teaching Scuff to play his iGuitar. A smell of baking tortillas warmed the air.

"Welcome back, blue haired visitor," chimed a robotic voice from behind. Zeke whipped around to see two red bulbs staring back at him. A sleek, cylindrical 'mac hovered in mid-air, thanks to antigravity coils in its base. It was Bobbi, the only robotoid in existence.

Chapter Twenty-One
The Perspicillum

"**W**here's the professor?" Zeke asked. He was sitting with Scuff and Justice at the dining table. Bobbi floated beside the magno-oven, serving up dinner with his steel grabbers. They looked clumsy, but he dished out the tortillas and side dishes with a finesse many human cooks would envy.

"Up on the observation deck, as ever," Justice replied, unable to take his eyes of the tortillas. Scuff, too, was hypnotised by the smells of maize, beans and fried onions. Even Zeke was struggling to keep his mind off the food. He had a hole in his stomach the size of a small asteroid.

Justice turned towards the shaft for the gravity pedestal. "Professor, we're all about to eat the vittals!" he bellowed. "Dang me, if that man's head isn't full of stars. If I wasn't here, he'd plain starve to death."

"He gets lost in his work?" Zeke ventured. Justice nodded.

"Side effect of genius," Scuff piped in. "Happens to me a lot."

"Only thing you get lost in, is your comics," Zeke remarked, and laughed.

"Dinner is served," Bobbi said, gliding over with dinner plates.

For five minutes, the only sounds were the clinks of cutlery and the chomping of jaws. Zeke glanced at Justice and cleared his throat.

"How are you recovering from the bomb attack?"

"Weren't that a hoot," Justice replied. "I took me some nanomac therapy when I got back, for post traumatic thingummy-jig. Happy as a pig in mud, now."

"The governor's medics gave me some. I get flashbacks, though. That split second everything was flying through the air."

Justice pulled a face.

"You gotta learn not to think so deeply, Zekey boy. Look at me. Always moving forward, never looking back."

"Back to what?" Zeke asked out of idle curiosity.

The grin full of oversized teeth vanished. "Earth wasn't so kind to me, Zeke. My father wasn't a hero like yours. Plain fact is, he wasn't even particularly nice."

There was a hurt, angry expression on Justice's face. Zeke was about to ask what he meant when a foot stabbed his shin under the table.

Don't think he wants to talk about it! Scuff thought.

Typical you, Zeke thought back. *Not a hint of sensitivity.*

Scuff pouted and looked around for something to change the subject.

"So, Bobbi, how's the whole robotoid thing working out for you?" he asked.

"I cannot scan the syntax in your question," Bobbi said, hovering nearby like a waiter.

"My bad," Scuff replied. "You're super-advanced. More than the sum of your parts, able to exceed your programming. You can make emotional responses. No other machine has ever done that. Even androids. What I meant was, how is your life as a robotoid?"

Bobbi sighed. His grabbers interlocked, as if he were wringing his hands.

"It gets lonely up here, rotund visitor. Mister Justice and the professor are kind companions. However, I yearn for a friend who shares my parameters."

"There's the rub, Bobbi my ol' buddy," Justice cut in. "You're yoo-nique. No one like you in the whole dang solar system."

"The professor made you, right?" Zeke asked.

"Affirmative."

"Can't he make another one?"

Bobbi's head rotated a full circle.

"The professor decided against that possibility. Not until he has completed his study of robotoid psychology. I am his guinea pig."

"An experiment," Scuff said, reaching for another tortilla.

"That is my nature, rotund visitor. I am an unimportant unit of circuits."

"Aw shucks, Bobbi. The prof and I couldn't do it without you," Justice said.

"Thank you, Mister Justice. However, I hope one day to make my existence worthwhile. The small female visitor believes I can."

Zeke shifted uncomfortably in his seat. Bobbi was referring to Pin-mei. On their last visit, she'd made some vague prediction, a remark about Bobbi one day being very important.

"Where is the small female visitor?" Bobbi asked.

"Cosying up with the enemy," Zeke remarked bitterly.

The others said nothing, clearly stunned. Scuff coughed. "The prof's dinner is getting cold," he said, nodding to the meal on the worktop.

"Why don't you take it to him, Zeke?" Justice suggested. "After all, ain't that why you're here? To get ol' Jacob to spill the beans. Figurative beans, that is, not these refried variety."

"What do you mean?" Zeke asked.

Justice smirked. "Heck, it's not three hours since you two appeared out of thin air, flapping and flopping like fish out of water. And you haven't said yet why you chose the Perspicillum, out of the whole wide Martian planet."

"First place that popped into my head," Zeke replied. "Still, while, I'm here..." He grabbed the plate and headed for the gravity pedestal.

Stars. Thousands and thousands of stars. Zeke emerged through the floor and into the dazzle of the galaxy. The observation deck was cupped by a dome of super-polymer plastic, uncrackable and invisible. And the Perspicillum perched on top of an eleven-mile-high volcano, way above the airline. The view was spectacular. Red giants, supernovae, nebulas, faraway galaxies, all the mysteries of the universe slowly swirled above Zeke's head.

The dream surfaced in his mind's eye. The one on the space disc. Maybe his subconscious was playing with his memories of the Perspicillum.

A large telescope stood in the centre, all cogs and pulleys and dials. The barrel jutted out, through the dome, and into the sub-zero night. The telescope's magnification, combined with its location, gave it an exceptional glimpse into space.

Professor Jacob Van Hiss had his eye glued to one of the telescope's eyepieces. He was muttering to himself in Dutch.

"Sir," Zeke said gently, placing the meal on a counter.

The professor looked up. He was of Dutch-African descent, with grizzled coils of hair and enormous spectacles. His forehead was creased in a permanent frown.

"Ach, it's you," he said with a nervy smile. He gave Zeke a slight hug, looking rather uncomfortable. "Have you brought my dinner?"

Hiss ravenously seized the tortillas. While he devoured his food, Zeke peered out of the dome. One half of the Perspicillum looked down into the caldera of Ascraeus Mons. The other faced towards the south east, to a landscape of gullies and craters. But now it was night and everything was hidden. The Perspicillum rose above the ocean of darkness like a golden lighthouse.

"So, what were you doing, Sir?" Zeke asked as Hiss cleared the plate.

"Not so formal, my *jonge vriend*."

"Sorry —"

"Don't stand on ceremony, call me Professor."

"Oh? Well, Professor?"

"I was searching the Andromeda Galaxy. There." He pointed a long bony finger at a computer on his work station. The screen showed a live picture of a giant blue star. The great sphere bubbled and sizzled, as though made of burning ice.

"Why is your mouth dropping?" Hiss asked.

Zeke hastily closed it. "I've never seen a star in another galaxy, so close up and personal."

Hiss smiled. "Ach so, I've named her the Snow Queen. A character from ancient literature."

Zeke stared blankly.

"We used to name celestial bodies after mythological characters. Ancient Greek, Roman. When they got used up, we started on the others. Hindu, American Native, African. But there are so many objects in the Milky Way alone, we ran out of gods. For Andromeda I started with stories. Yesterday I discovered the Dracula Nebula, a bat-shaped cloud of gases, and Lilliput, a tiny moon."

Hiss clapped his hands, clearly pleased with himself.

"I don't have much time for reading," Zeke said. Then a thought struck him.

"Could you show me Alpha Cephei? Please?"

Hiss beamed and aimed his magnopad at the machinery. The dome rotated, shifting the telescope's angle. Hiss crossed to his work station and tapped in a few more adjustments on the control panel. A shining white sun appeared on the screen.

"Behold, the Fifth Star of the Celestial Hook."

"Pardon me, Sir?"

"Its Chinese name."

"Any planets?"

"Of course." Hiss fiddled with a knob. A gas giant appeared, with green and yellow bands. Zeke cooed. Exactly the same as his dream.

"Any moons, are there any moons?" he cried.

Hiss threw him a puzzled glance but fine-tuned the focus. Sure enough, a blue and purple moon came into view.

"I think that's where my dad went."

"Ach, now I am understanding." Hiss threw a few switches and the view magnified. A black crescent licked the moon's far side, that was the night. But most of the moon was bathed in the crystal light of its sun. Purple blotches, streaked with veins of blue, were clearly visible.

Hiss studied a line of gauges in the machinery.

"Oxygen, nitrogen, carbon dioxide, bio-organic compounds, surface water. You know, my *jonge vriend*, this moon could sustain life."

Zeke grabbed Hiss by the hand. A rush flowed through every cell in his body. For a second, he couldn't speak.

"My father. He's alive!"

Chapter Twenty-Two
The Observation Deck

Zeke glanced at the timer in the corner of the screen. "Oh." Twenty minutes had passed. Twenty minutes of staring at the blue and purple moon and fantasising about meeting his father.

"How do you do," he would say, shaking hands firmly. His father would be tall and muscular, maybe with a beard. After all, the batteries for his razor probably conked out years ago.

"I always knew you'd come," his dad would reply, tears creeping into those intense brown eyes.

And then they hugged. The search, the wait, the loss, it was all over now. A new life could begin.

Zeke shook himself. It was nearly midnight and he wasn't finished. Professor Van Hiss was on the other side of the machinery, tinkering with a control panel, all blinking lights and LED displays.

"Professor?"

The man jumped. "Ach, you are still here, *mijn kind.*"

"What are you doing?"

"Calibrating. The telescope works on many levels, light, radio, radiation, x-ray, quantum, etcetera. The computer fuses the data into one image, as you were seeing."

"It is stunning," Zeke agreed. "But I meant your research in general, what are you really doing?"

Van Hiss looked away. "This and that, all very boring for a *jonge man* like you."

Zeke stepped closer.

"I already know you're searching for the genesis particle. And you can't find it."

Van Hiss flashed him a look of shock. "How are you knowing this?"

"You told me, last time we were here."

"Me? I am being forgetful." He gave a little giggle. Then a fake yawn. "It is getting late, time for bed."

Zeke shot his arm out, barring the Professor's way. Hiss's eyes widened. "Please, I am not enjoying the confrontations."

"I'm not a child," Zeke said, his feelings rising. "I know Earth is in trouble. I want to know the truth. Tell me."

Professor Van Hiss glanced around his observatory, as though seeking escape. Then he stared into Zeke's face. "I think there is much iron in your blood." Zeke didn't answer. Van Hiss sighed. "Come," he beckoned.

They sat down in a couple of office chairs at the far side of the deck. Outside, the Milky Way poured through the heavens like a river of phosphor.

"Understanding our ancestors is not easy. They were reckless, destructive. Abusing the Earth quite intentionally. They overheated the planet. They wiped out the animals. Do you know there was once a forest covering South America?"

"Yes, we did history, Professor. How technology saved us from technology. What's that got to do with today?

"There was once a place called the Collider."

Zeke gave him a blank look.

"A giant particle accelerator, a ring of superconductors many miles wide. By shooting subatomic elements at great speeds, so they crashed together, many theories could be tested. A collider proved the existence of the Bosun Higgs, micro-holes in the space-time continuum, tachyons and five extra dimensions."

Zeke stroked his cheek. "Something went wrong?"

Van Hiss scratched his ash-grey curls.

"By the end of the twenty-first century, the largest mega-collider ever was up and running in Switzerland. And it was doing such good work. But one day, the good Swiss citizens woke up to find it missing."

"Missing?" Zeke said. Van Hiss nodded. "Vanished. Leaving a perfectly spherical crater in the ground. The collider, its buildings and soil, a bubble if you will, scooped out of existence."

"Where did it go?" Zeke asked, leaning forward.

Van Hiss shrugged. "Nobody knows. Another dimension. Another time. Maybe it didn't go anywhere, it just ceased."

"How awful. Were there people inside?"

"*Natuurlijk!* The night shift, the cleaning crew, a man walking his dog outside, and in the fields, many, many cows."

"Terrible," Zeke said, hands on cheeks.

"It is getting worse."

"Worse?"

"We may never know what happed that night, at the Mega Collider. But we do know from their online logs that scientists there created a handful of particles. The tiniest bits of subatomic matter. We call them apocalypse quarks. An incredibly rare particle. Theory states they only exist when universes end. They are a by-product of the breakup of the space-time continuum. Some experts say they are what cause that breakup."

A cold chill snaked down Zeke's back. Van Hiss drew a deep breath before continuing.

"And so, a handful of these particles began drifting to the Earth's core. They are incredibly heavy, you see. They are sinking through thousands of miles of rock, lava and molten metal. Apocalypse quarks are not stopped by matter, they are too small. They slip between atomic bonds. Thankfully, all that dense material slows them down. They've been sinking for two centuries, but..."

"But what?"

"When they arrive, they will settle together, that is certain. They exert a pull on each other, as magnets do. They will join up and this is triggering their power."

"Which is?" Zeke cried, on the edge of his seat.

"Start a cascade, a collapse of the planet. Earth will implode and shrink down into a few tons of rock." .

Zeke gasped and fell off his chair. Van Hiss helped him back onto it.

"When, Professor? When will this happen?"

Van Hiss gazed out at the star meadows, at the vast swathes of the galaxy.

"Nobody is knowing that answer. Scientists think it will be sometime in the next fifty years. Maybe tomorrow, maybe in the year 2310. And anytime in-between."

Zeke jumped to his feet.

"My Mum's on Earth!" he shouted.

"And my wife and daughter," Van Hiss replied. He sounded old and tired. "UNAAC is keeping them there, to motivate me in my search."

"What good will that do?" Zeke demanded, towering over the professor.

"I am seeking the genesis particles. Theory suggests they are the exact opposite of these catastrophic particles."

Zeke impatiently gestured for him to continue.

"The genesis particle is cross-dimensional, passing from one dimension to another. If it enters a non-dimension it acts as a catalyst. It kickstarts a universe."

"You mean it causes the Big Bang?"

"Absolutely, my *jonge vriend.*" Hiss gestured to the galaxy around them with a wave of the hand. "None of what you see through this glass could exist without genesis particles."

Zeke's head was spinning. Images of his mother falling into an abyss flooded his brain.

"B-but, that was billions of years ago."

"*Ja, ja.* And particles might still be passing through our universe, via a rift in the fabric of existence. I have to find them and analyse them with the tools at my disposal."

"You mean like a spectrometer or an atomic sequencer?"

Van Hiss grinned. "Very good, exactly. When we know their composition, perhaps they can be recreated on Earth. Genesis particles and apocalypse quarks instantly cancel each other out. Thanks to quantum entanglement, even if they are a few thousand miles apart, they react to each other. Earth would be saved."

Zeke sank back into his chair. "All this is theory, you say?"

Van Hiss nodded.

"And in all the years you've been looking, you haven't found any?"

"Ach, no. It is like looking for a molecule in a haystack. Theory dictates there will be tell-tale signs, trails. But I am finding *niets*, nothing." There were tears in the old man's eyes.

Zeke buried his face in his hands. "Then, my mother's as good as dead."

Chapter Twenty-Three

Another Dream

The great bronze disc slowly turned. This time the galaxy was no longer near enough to touch. The constellations twinkling around Zeke were light years away. Yet so bright they seemed closer.

Zeke was sitting in the dead centre of the disc.

My subconscious is remembering the observation deck, he thought, quite aware he was dreaming. But this dream had a purpose, he sensed it. He recalled the orb of words. How it changed his life forever. First it downloaded the Hesperian language into his brain. Then there were the hallucinations. Or were they visions? Zeke wasn't sure of the difference.

But there was more. As though a voice was forever whispering in his ear. Too soft to make out its words, but nonetheless there. Something, or someone, wanted to give him a message. A crucial message. But he couldn't hear it, he couldn't figure it out. Like a jigsaw with missing pieces.

"I am the message."

Zeke looked up. A huge tangle of tentacles with a beaked mouth rotated over his head. The Spiral.

"Get lost," Zeke replied. He was unafraid. Dreams were harmless.

"That voice you hear at the back of your head. It's me, Zeke. Trying to help."

Zeke stared at the metallic floor.

"I can save everyone. On Earth," the Spiral went on in its deep voice.

"Lies!" Zeke snapped. Yet despite himself, he glanced back up. He eyes locked on the Spiral and it began to turn a little faster.

"Not so, Zeke. I am limitless. There is room for every man, woman and child in my belly."

"Ha!" Zeke scoffed. "And just how is eating the human race saving them?"

A shudder passed through the tentacles.

"You know that already. No one dies inside me. Yes, I break down their bodies for food. But their consciousness lives on. As a part of me."

"That sounds like a living hell," Zeke said with a sneer.

The tentacles shook violently. They writhed and twisted. The beak opened and retched. A large ball of spit erupted and landed nearby. Zeke leapt to his feet. Now he was afraid.

The globule of green spit rose up, formed limbs, a torso and a head. The colour changed, as the blob transformed into trousers, a jacket, skin and hair.

Zeke felt his blood drain away. It was the late Professor Tiberius Magma.

"Greetings, young Sir," the man said. His pallor was deathly and his eyes blank. Zeke had no doubt what he was seeing. Death walking.

"You're the young man who defeated me," Magma said in a flat tone. "I can't quite recall your name."

"Zeke Hailey."

"Ah yes," the resurrected Magma said. "No hard feelings, old boy. More important matters to worry about now."

"Like what?" Zeke said, his attention flitting between Magma and the Spiral.

"Rescuing the peoples of Earth. Any day now the planet will crumble. If you could just help the Spiral come in, he'll save them all."

"And end up zombies, like you. I'd rather die."

"But you won't be the one dying, will you?"

Zeke snorted.

"Can you condemn billions of lives to a bloody end? Even your own mother?" boomed the Spiral.

"Shut up!" Zeke shouted, shaking a fist. "This is only a *lrxiichng* dream." The Hesperian verb meant something unmentionable, which perfectly expressed Zeke's anger.

"It's not a dream," the Spiral said. "You know I cannot physically enter your universe. Not yet. But I can send in my brainwaves. Too weak to be heard by the waking mind, but in sleep, that's different. Yes, I am real. I am speaking to you now from the Infinity Trap."

Zeke yelled with incoherent rage. It was trying to hypnotise him. He shut his eyes and covered his ears.

"Wake up, wake up, wake up!" he cried.

"As you wish, but I leave with a warning," the Spiral said, its voice growing faint. "Whatever happens, never use Electron's Blade."

After an ice-cold shower, Zeke ascended on the gravity pedestal to the living quarters. An early morning gloom lay across the kitchenette and recreation area. It was only seven and nobody was up yet. Or so it seemed.

"Oh."

Zeke spotted Scuff in an easy chair by a tall, thin window. The sun was pushing up over the horizon, catching Scuff with a finger of pale light. His eyes were red.

Zeke sat down next to him. They exchanged silent glances. And with that telepathy that really close friends sometimes share, Zeke guessed at once.

"You know?"

Scuff nodded. "I've been up all night."

"But how?"

Scuff coloured. A rush of annoyance swept over Zeke.

"Were you eavesdropping last night? Reading my thoughts while I was in with Van Hiss?"

Scuff shrugged. "Kinda. Just your surface thoughts."

Zeke took a deep breath. Irritating as it was to have someone spy on your inner self, they had bigger things to consider. Way bigger.

"Everything makes sense now," Zeke remarked. "The rushed emigrations to space. The secretiveness."

"My family are going to die, Zeke. Mom, my little sister, even Pops. Sure, he hates me, but I don't wanna see him cooking in a sea of lava."

Zeke sighed. "Yes, I get it. All I can think of is my mother. All alone in London, and about to die."

"What can we do?" Scuff asked, his eyes watering.

"I don't know," Zeke said. They lapsed into silence. Ideas and memories coursed through Zeke's mind. But nothing that could actually happen. Last night, on discovering his father's moon, he was elated. Now he was at the bottom of a very deep and very dark pit.

The sun was up. Its blueish radiance filled the room. How long had they been sitting there, each lost in his own thoughts? Zeke stirred and absentmindedly fished for his magnopad from his tunic pocket. He switched it on.

"Another email from the governor. The idiot."

"You should read it, Zeke."

"It can only be bad news."

Scuff attempted a half-smile.

"The school's fallen. Earth is doomed. What could be worse?"

Zeke pressed a tab and placed the pad on the coffee table between them. A hologram attachment beeped. The figure of the governor emerged from the screen, standing six inches high. Zeke decided the man really did look like a rat.

"Howdy, Mister Hailey. Boy, you sure do play hard to get. Where the heck are you on this miserable planet, anyway? Whatever, we've got some serious business to do. You have doubts. I get that. And ordinarily I'd not push it. But as governor of Mars I have to do everything in my power to avoid any more bloodshed."

"More bloodshed?" Scuff said.

As if the hologram could hear them, it said. "That's right. More. Yesterday my forces launched a bid to recapture Yuri-Gagarin Freetown. Needless to say, good prevailed. We liberated the citizens. Sad to say, most of them perished in the heat of battle."

Zeke's mouth ran dry. A picture of burning tents and bloodied corpses formed in his head.

"Anyways, Zeke, in the name of peace, I must leave no stone unturned. So, I'm offering you a first-class trip to Alpha Cephei."

Zeke's jaw dropped.

"You heard correctly, my little man. I used every trick in my toolbox to requisition a far-ship. It's in orbit now, waiting for you to take the helm. The Mariner who was going to use it will teach you everything you need to know. Just come on back to the Ellipse, translate the gizmo, catapult into space and rendezvous with the ship. In as few as two days you could be frying hotdogs with your pa. Anyways, you'll know where to find me. I'll be seeing you."

The hologrammatic governor crackled and faded.

Scuff leapt up, fired with a sudden enthusiasm. He danced on the spot.

"We're saved!" he cried over and over.

"Slow down," Zeke said.

"Don't you see, Zekey Boy. You've gone and done it. You can stop the war, save our families and take us all with you to meet your dad."

"Calm down."

"I always knew being your buddy would work out in the end."

"Scuff, stop it." Zeke said in a raised voice. Scuff pulled a face and sat down.

"It's probably some sort of trap," Zeke began. "And in any case, there are a few huge obstacles. I've never flown a far-ship."

"Like the gov' said, they'll teach you. You with the phenomenal talent."

"The Televator's been blown up, remember? How would our families get into space?"

Scuff sobered up. "That is a big one. Earth's magnetic field means translocation skills won't work. Even if they did, gravity would stop anyone from taking off."

"You see."

"But there's talk of space balloons, rockets, catapults."

"Talk!" Zeke snapped, combing his hair with his fingers. Scuff put a hand on his shoulder.

"Zeke, we've gotta think positive. Chances like this don't come along every day. And think of what's at stake."

"Meaning?"

"Throw it back on the governor. Tell him you accept, once he's figured out how to get our relatives into space, so they can dock with your far-ship."

Zeke scratched his chin. It was as good an idea as any.

"Alright, but help me with the reply. You're good at words."

"You ain't wrong," Scuff replied, grinning from ear to ear.

Together they composed Zeke's answer. Yes, Zeke would help. But only if their families were taken into Earth orbit to meet the far-ship. And the governor needed to confirm how.

"It's as polished as a pearl," Scuff said. "Send it now."

Zeke gritted his teeth and pressed the tab. The email disappeared. A few seconds later, his magnopad pinged.

"Wow, that was quick," Scuff remarked.

Zeke looked up, his eyes wide with alarm.

"No, it's from Pin-mei and marked 'save me'".

Chapter Twenty-Four

The Kitchenette

Everyone looked serious. Van Hiss, Justice, Scuff and Zeke were wedged around the dining table. Bobbi was loading the breakfast plates into the dishwasher. The air reeked of scrambled eggs and toast.

"I am not knowing what to suggest," Van Hiss said. "But your plan is the one with many risks."

"Tell me one more time," Justice said.

Zeke drew a deep breath.

"Pin-mei's counterattack against the Unpro failed. Cusp declared her an enemy of the Martian state and sentenced her to death by laser squad. The execution is tomorrow."

"Harsh," Justice remarked.

"So, Scuff and I are sneaking back into school to save her."

"But you are walking into the den of the lion. And you mere *kinderen*. Perhaps I should not allow it," Van Hiss said. He raised his eyes to Zeke's, to that dark, intense stare. Then he lowered them again.

"Ach, all success to you."

"Any chance it's a trap?" Justice asked.

Zeke shook his head.

"The biometric data confirms Pin sent it."

Justice paused for a moment.

"You did say there'd been a falling out."

Zeke glared at him.

"And this is our chance to make it up. And really, really, deep down, she never stopped being my friend. I see that now. Pin wouldn't sell me out."

"So why in tarnation ain't I coming on the joyride?"

"You?" Zeke replied, a little fazed by the idea.

"Ol' Pinny is my buddy too. And you never take me on them adventures."

"Bro, do you seriously want that?" Scuff piped in. "Remember Bartie."

Zeke pushed back his mop of blue hair.

"No. Stealth is the word. And, I'm sorry Justice, but you are a…"

"Normal? Heck, I can still handle myself in a tight corner."

"But not the way Scuff and I can, with our powers. I'm sorry but my mind is made up."

Justice looked away. "Whatever. You're calling the shots, Zekey Boy."

"Pin's in what Cusp is calling *detention*, but we don't know where. We're going to translocate into her room. It's the one place that will be empty. We can lie low there, while Scuff tracks down Pin's thoughts."

"And what is it you are doing afterwards?" Van Hiss asked.

Zeke paused.

"Guess we'll seek refuge at Tithonium. Find out if the Governor's offer is genuine."

"Heck, you got the whole damn shooting match figured out," Justice remarked and shook Zeke's hand vigorously.

"And we're going now, we can't lose a second," Zeke said, standing up.

"Slow down, cowboy," Scuff said. "I gotta request."

Zeke flashed him a puzzled look.

"Can I do the translocation?"

"What?" Zeke cried. "You know it's against school rules. Not till the fourth year."

Scuff clenched his fists.

"If you ask me, school's out. Indefinitely."

"Everyone knows how dangerous translocation can be," Zeke protested.

"You do it," Scuff said.

"That's different," Zeke replied. "I'm…I'm—"

"Gifted?" Scuff suggested, rolling his eyes.

"Lucky," Zeke answered, shifting uncomfortably. "And why? Why do you suddenly want to risk your life?"

A look passed across Scuff's face. An odd look Zeke couldn't read. "I gotta hunch. In my bones," Scuff began. "Sometime soon I'm going to need to get somewhere in a hurry. And like, it's a matter of life or death. Mine."

Zeke frowned. Hunches and gut feelings often turned out to be a form of precognition. An early warning from the subconscious mind. And anyway, if there was one person in the known universe he trusted, it was his best friend.

"Okay. Let's do it together."

Without another word the two boys walked to the middle of the room. They linked arms.

Justice gave a little wave. He looked like he was about to burst into tears. Hiss chewed on his nails and said, "Come back soon. I am showing you some comets heading our way. Amazing. Never seen before." Bobbi flashed his bulbs and spun his head.

"I'll be the back-up, if anything goes wrong." Zeke said. Scuff gave a nervous smile. He closed his eyes and concentrated. After a few seconds, he peeked through one eye.

"We're still here, aren't we?"

"Try a mental metaphor," Zeke said. "The Mariners always go on about them."

"Like what?"

"Well," Zeke replied, scratching his head. "When you hear Mariner Knimble describing translocation, how do you imagine it?"

Scuff thought for a moment. "Dunno if this is silly. I picture a hand pulling a black screen across. Wiping reality away."

"Go with it."

Scuff screwed his face up again. Zeke waved hopefully at Justice and Van Hiss. And then, for the briefest of seconds, the room flickered.

"Yes!" Zeke said. "Try harder!"

Scuff nodded, too overwhelmed to speak. Sparks danced around his eyelids. Day and night wrestled as the Perspicillum, and everything in it, wavered on the brink of nothingness.

He needs a push, Zeke thought, and focused.

They were floating in the abyss, arms linked, as cold as ice. Greyness formed into dust plains and distant cliffs. The icy morning air nipped at their cheeks.

"Oh," Scuff said, with a downcast expression. "I got us lost."

"For a first time, that was really good," Zeke said.

"I was aiming for Pin's room," Scuff protested.

"And you got us back to Mariners Valley. Definitely the right direction."

"You didn't interfere, did you?" Scuff asked with a frown.

"Not at all," Zeke replied, staring at faraway canyons.

"Only I felt as if someone chipped in."

"The first time always feels that way," Zeke said, now studying his feet.

"And you think I did good?" Scuff asked, flushing beetroot red.

Zeke nodded.

"Awesome, even?"

"Don't push it. How does it feel?" Zeke asked.

"Draining. Maybe you should take it from here?"

A ghost of a smile crept across Zeke's lips. "Sure." They locked arms and Zeke pictured Pin-mei's room. Mars evaporated. For a few seconds, they drifted in the endless void. Ground formed beneath their feet. They were there but it was still dark. The photon lamps were out.

Then the room blazed with light. Soldiers were everywhere, pointing rifles at them. "Shoot!" screamed a voice. The rifles fired.

Chapter Twenty-Five
The Office of Ex-Principal Lutz

A lot can happen in twenty-four hours, Zeke thought. Especially when there's a war on. The two soldiers shoved him through the principal's door. The first thing he saw was Trixie Cutter at the school secretary's desk. Her feet were resting on the desktop while she filed her nails.

"You're back, then," she remarked without looking up.

Zeke's mouth was too wide open to reply. Marjorie Barnside was propped against the wall, deactivated. Her head and shoulders slumped forward and her eyes were blank. Somebody had written a very, very rude word across her forehead.

"Yeah, the school secretary was an android all along. Who knew?" Trixie went on, still filing away.

"Me, actually," Zeke muttered. A fuse ignited somewhere deep inside him. Okay, there was never any love lost between him and the secretary. She was such a battle axe. But to treat her in that way. As though she wasn't...a person.

"What are you doing in her chair?" Zeke asked though gritted teeth.

Finally, Trixie lifted her face.

"Promotion. I'm in charge of the Unpro Information Office."

"The what?"

"Tolly's got me pounding out bulletins every five minutes. How we're winning the war. And in-between that I'm typing up the Thoughts of Ptolemy Cusp, the Great Martian Hope." Trixie made a gagging gesture.

"Your arm," Zeke said. There was no metallic armband around her upper arm. Zeke already had his locked on. Magnetized bio-metal. When the ferromagnetic ions from the rifles wore off, the armband would keep his powers neutralised.

"All you have to do is swear allegiance to the revolution and they take it off. There's already a dozen students freed and working on stuff."

Zeke didn't know what to say. Trixie leaned nearer.

"This war is a total bore," she whispered. "Ruining my nails. And terrible for business. Isn't it about time you brought it to an end?"

"Me?" Zeke cried.

"You're the one who speaks Martian. Get the governor's device thingy working."

"How do you know about that?" Zeke snapped.

Trixie fiddled with her perfect ponytail. "You should know not much escapes my attention. Anyway, don't tell Tolly I said that, will you?" and she gave a conspiratorial wink.

"Send him in," came a voice on the intercom.

"Maybe I should jack the whole thing in," Trixie said, more to herself. "Get a fresh start, out in the colonies."

Zeke's mouth dropped again. Trixie was ever the hard-hearted businesswoman, with fingers in all kinds of black-market operations. This just wasn't her.

Inside Lutz's inner sanctum, Ptolemy was seated at her desk, exactly as in Zeke's dream. Only it wasn't a dream, Zeke was sure now. He really had been astral projecting.

"Sit," Cusp barked. He had dark circles around his eyes. Zeke obeyed.

Cusp folded his arms.

"I apologize for my little ruse to get you back."

"Where's Pin?" Zeke snarled.

"She's fine. We faked the email. Biometric data is a lot easier to copy than you'd think. Pin was moved to another room. I wouldn't hurt a hair on her head. Isla would kill me."

Cusp broke into a cheesy grin. Zeke glared back. He'd never

realized it before, but he hated the man.

"Well, I think Principal Lutz will kill you first, sitting in her place," Zeke replied.

"If she ever recovers. This epidemic of future fever has left her an invalid."

"Oh!" Zeke's heart sank.

Cusp unfolded his arms.

"Look, Hailey. Cards on the table. I want you to join the Unpro and fight for our cause. A boy—I mean, a man—of your talents could make all the difference."

"Join a bunch of murderers?"

A look of annoyance flashed across Cusp's face.

"In a war, good people do bad things. To survive. Any bloodshed has been self-defence."

Zeke clicked his tongue. "What about the Martian State Brigade?"

"They're nothing to do with us. Nobody I know has even met them," Cusp replied.

"Oh really?" That was hard to believe. Two factions in the fight against Earth and there were no links between them?

Cusp shrugged. "Great men are not distracted by morals, Hailey. They focus on the important things. Now listen."

Zeke pushed out his bottom lip.

"I want you to go on a mission for us. In a nutshell, it's this. Return to Tithonium. Steal the governor's secret weapon and translocate it back to us."

Zeke eyebrows shot up. Was Cusp even crazier than he thought? The idea of lying his way back to the Ellipse Building and seizing the weapon. Hauling that big heavy rock through the void and… and…Zeke scratched his chin. Actually, it wasn't so impossible. The governor would welcome him back with open arms. And once he was in the same room as Electron's Blade, he could easily translocate out. After all, hadn't he lifted that huge boulder back in the bubble universe, purely by thought?

"How do you know you can trust me?"

"Easy," Cusp said. "Pin-mei, and all your other little playmates, will be in my protective custody."

"Suppose you want to put the device to similar use?" Zeke asked.

Cusp smiled. "We can track down our opponents in one fell swoop. Could avoid a lot of deaths."

The atomic clock on the wall ticked away as Zeke mulled over his options. He could betray Cusp and help the Governor bring the war to an end. Or throw his lot in with Cusp. There again, maybe he should just destroy the Blade.

Zeke slapped his forehead. He was forgetting about his once-in-a-lifetime chance to take a far-ship, rescue his mother and reach his father. That was the important thing. Wasn't it? Oh, his head was hurting. He didn't know what to do.

"Why the slap?" Cusp asked.

"I need time to think this through," Zeke said, still glaring.

"Think away. Go back to your classes. Spend time with your buddies. But don't take too long, every day more people die."

Cusp's words stabbed at Zeke's heart.

"I'll think it over, but I want you to do one thing for me first."

Cusp arched an imperial eyebrow.

"Clean Barnside up and switch her back on."

"Compromise," Cusp retorted. "My soldiers were a bit out of order. We'll wipe off the obscenity and store her somewhere safe and out of the way. I can't activate her. An android loyal to the school would be nothing but trouble."

"Okay," Zeke agreed. It was a start.

"It's nearly eleven AM. Which class do you study at this time?"

"Psychokinesis 201."

"Ah!"

"Ah?"

Cusp glanced away.

"I'm afraid that course is cancelled. Your teacher ran away, first chance he got."

"What?" Zeke cried.

"Your precious Mariner Chinook overpowered his guard and made a break for it. He's out there now, in the desert. I guess he was a just big coward."

"Bobby Chinook is no coward," Zeke said, clenching his fists.

"Whatever. Either way he's as good as dead. Nobody lasts long out there without supplies. Thanks to the armbands, he doesn't even have his powers."

Zeke was lost for words. He stared out of the window, at the crags and twisted pillars. Miles of cold, red sand stretched to the horizon. Zeke gulped. Chinook didn't stand a chance.

The bell rang. Mariner Ariyabata let out a long sigh, as if the noise displeased him even more than his students.

"Dismissed, dismissed."

Everyone jumped up from their mats and filed out between two rebel guards stationed at the door. Both men wore huge smirks across their stubbly faces. Clearly, they found the astral projection teacher hilarious.

Zeke hung back, till all of his classmates had left.

"Sir."

Ariyabata stared at him, as if he were some small, disgusting beetle.

"Sir, I did leave my body. Last week. I wasn't dreaming."

"Piffle," the teacher said. He turned around and began picking up his notes.

"And I've done it since. Twice."

Ariyabata ignored him.

"Sir!" Zeke said in a louder voice. Ariyabata wheeled around and stamped his foot.

"What took the ancient yogis a lifetime to master, you did in five minutes?"

"Well, they were living on Earth. The magnetosphere would have limited their powers. I'm on Mars."

"I did notice, boy. So, you have independent proof of these miracles?"

"Proof, Sir?"

"There must always be proof, otherwise it's only speculation."

Zeke stared at him blankly. The teacher went on.

"For example, seeing something that you didn't know was there and that someone else later confirmed to be correct."

Zeke's shoulders drooped.

"Not exactly, Sir."

"Impudent ragamuffin. Come back to me when you do. I anticipate a very long wait."

Ariyabata tried to leave, but Zeke stepped in his way.

"Sir, how far can someone astral project?"

"How far?" the teacher laughed sarcastically. "The fact you ask that question shows you've no idea."

"Sir?"

Ariyabata rolled his eyes. "Distance means nothing in the realm of the mind. It's irrelevant. If the soul can leave the body and travel a mile, it can travel a million miles. Or a million light years."

"Surely not," Zeke replied, eyes wide.

Ariyabata looked down his long nose at Zeke.

"A few of the ancient yogis travelled the stars. They returned with tales of encounters with alien civilisations."

"Gosh. And what proof did they have?"

The nostrils on that long nose flared.

"Proof? You don't ask the yogis and swamis for proof. How insolent!"

Zeke was about to say something when he thought better of it, instead he said "But how could a disembodied spirit travel across the galaxy?"

"We Mariners can cross the gulf of space in a twinkling, boy."

Zeke frowned. "You mean translocation. But that's science. Adjusted Quantum Theory explains it. But how could a spirit, without substance, travel vast distances? It's hard to believe. How would it move? How would it get back?"

Ariyabata's eyes gleamed. "Reality is your master. But reality is an illusion. Thought is the most powerful force, as the Mariners so teach. Once you grasp that the universe is non-existent, you become the master of reality."

Zeke blinked. His brain was spinning. Ariyabata went on, his voice rising. "There are levels beyond the mundane, where you can hold the universe in the palm of your hand. Once you've done that, no world is too far."

"Oi, are you going to chatter all day. Only we've gotta lock up," one of the rebels grumbled.

"Sir, could you help me study astral projection in greater depth?"

"You? Why ever would you wish that?"

Zeke thought for second. "I've got a feeling it might come in useful."

Ariyabata stroked his chin. And then something unexpected happened. A smile crept across his lips.

"Maybe I've misjudged you, Hailey."

At last! Zeke thought.

"Truly Sir, I am absolutely serious about this."

The smile spread.

"If this dreary occupation ever ends, we will work together. Perhaps I should have an open mind to your stories."

"Come on," hollered the other rebel. "I'm missing my tea break."

Zeke and Ariyabata both laughed. Zeke hurried out of the classroom. As he walked away the voices of Ariyabata and the soldiers echoed off the walls. They were arguing. Oh well, he thought, maybe he'd made a new friend.

The corridor went black. Bricks battered his body. An avalanche of plaster crashed down and buried him. Before his consciousness failed, he heard a roar approaching and then the boom.

Part Three

Chapter Twenty-Six
The Medical Facility

Zeke knew nothing. Lost in a dreamless sleep. Then, light seeped into the darkness. He reached out to it, like a diver struggling to the surface. But the tiredness was too much, and he sank back into the depths. The tide of consciousness flowed again, only to ebb. Flow and ebb. Flow and ebb. A sea of oblivion, slowly washing him ashore.

He awoke.

A familiar stink of disinfectant greeted him. He was in the school's medical facility, a cave deep within the canyon. Soft lighting, medicine cabinets, vials of nanomac gels lined up in rows. A white-coated blur came into focus. Doctor Chandrasar. She took his hand.

"Do you know where you are?" she asked.

Zeke nodded. His throat was too dry to speak. Still holding his hand, the doctor lifted a glass of water across for the bedside table.

"You've had a terrible shock," she said. "The nanomacs inside your body are doing their work, but take it easy."

Zeke gulped from the glass.

"I imagine you're in pain?"

Zeke started to sit up, winced, and lay back. "I ache all over, Doctor."

"I should think so. A cracked skull and three nasty fractures. And bruises from head to toe. Thanks to the wonders of nanotherapy, your injuries are nearly healed. But it's going to hurt like hell for a few hours."

Zeke stared into Chandrasar's eyes. Feline eyes. Worried eyes.

"It was a missile, Zeke. Landed directly on Teaching Block B.

Travelling faster than the speed of sound."

Images of falling concrete crashed into Zeke's memory. His heart beat faster. Chandrasar scanned him with her medical magnopad. She seemed satisfied with his vitals and continued. "You were buried under a ton of debris."

"How was I rescued?" he asked, perplexed.

Chandrasar smiled. "That's the good thing. Cusp ordered the teachers be released from their shackles. From the bio-metal. In seconds their powers came back. With their psychokinesis, they moved all the rubble, lump by lump. And they worked very fast. The emergency medimacs got to you in under twenty minutes. They brought you here and I saved your life."

"Thank you," Zeke mumbled.

"You're a lucky boy," she said, and stroked his forehead. "And try to hold onto the fact something good has come from this. Cusp had the bio-metal put back on. But it's as if the attack forced the two sides together. The rebels are a lot friendlier now. Another thirty students have sworn allegiance and been freed. The teachers won't. The Mariners' code of conduct won't allow that. But under their breath, I think even one or two of them are beginning to support the Unpro."

"But who fired the missile?"

Chandrasar shrugged. "Nobody claimed it. But it has to be the Martian State Brigade. The thugs. Does it matter who sends the bomb? The results are always the same."

Zeke felt a surge of alarm.

"Who else was in the building?"

"It was breaktime, wasn't it? Everyone had left the building. Three fifth years were in the lobby, furthest from the blast. They translocated out in the nick of time."

Zeke's muscles roared with pain as he wriggled up the bed.

"But Mariner Ariyabata, Miss?"

She looked down.

"Yes, the poor soul was at the epicentre. He and those two unfortunate rebels. They didn't make it, I'm afraid."

The room turned cold.

"But, Miss, surely, with nanotherapy?"

"The nanomacs need something to work with, Zeke. I'm very sorry to tell you this, but their bodies were obliterated."

He fell back onto his pillow. Nausea flooded his throat.

"I'd like to rest now."

sla the Incisor breezed into the Facility, dressed in combat fatigues, green eyes blazing and a sheen of ginger on her scalp.

"That doctor of yours is a tough customer. Adamant I couldn't see you. I had to threaten fisticuffs."

Zeke turned away and glared at the wall.

"Zeke?"

He said nothing.

Isla sighed and drew a chair up to his bedside.

"Don't blame me, it's—"

"It's you who invaded the school and is keeping us under lock and key!"

He slapped the circle of gold metal around his upper arm.

"Listen, kiddo. We're not playing soldiers here. It's war. The governor's going to kill us if he catches us."

Zeke swivelled round.

"I doubt that he'd be quite that bloodthirsty."

"People with his kind of power stop at nothing to keep it. He's the king of Mars. But without Earth backing him up, he's nothing. Independence would take it all away from him."

Zeke pushed out his bottom lip. True, there was something about the governor that made him uneasy. But to suggest he was a power-crazed murderer?

"And I suppose your precious Ptolemy is a saint?"

Isla looked hurt.

"You don't know him like I do, Zeke. He's a great and kind man who wants the best for Mars. It's just…"

"Just?"

"The pressure he's under. Leading a revolution. Occupying the school. People we've known for years getting killed. The stress—"

She erupted into tears. She threw her hands over her face and sobbed. Zeke stared at her, dumbfounded. Isla the Incisor, the most fearless warrior in Mariners Valley, crying?

Instinct took over. Zeke shuffled closer and put his arm around her shoulder.

"Oh Zeke, I never thought it would be like this. Tolly's become a stranger. The war's changing him."

"There, there," Zeke said gently. The same two words his mother used to say to him. (His mother, millions of miles away, on a planet-sized time bomb.)

Isla cried into her hands. Eventually the tears dried. She sniffed and composed herself.

"Zeke, whatever happens, I'm your friend. I hope you'll always be mine."

He nodded.

Her skin flushed from cream to pink.

She's quite beautiful, Zeke thought, and immediately felt embarrassed. Isla, meanwhile, seemed equally embarrassed by her emotional outburst. She sat up straight, so that Zeke's arm fell away.

"Well, I'm glad you're on the mend. That was my main worry."

"Thanks."

"You're such a good boy, Zeke." Isla went on. "Always so faithful and true."

Zeke shrugged, not sure he liked that description.

"Please remember, if you join the Unpro, that bio-metal comes off. And if you decide to go back to Tithonium, on a mission, I'm happy to go with you."

"Okay."

"Good," she replied, standing up. "I'm glad we've had this little chat."

Scuff put in an appearance the next day.

"Satsumas?" he said waving a bag in front of Zeke's nose. "Last ones on Mars, according to the vendomac."

Zeke glanced into the bag, at the nuggets of orange. The smell reminded him of Christmas, of turkey and walnuts and pulling crackers with his Mum. It seemed a lifetime ago.

"Thanks."

Scuff sat down beside the bed and absentmindedly peeled a satsuma.

"I was hoping someone else would be with you," Zeke remarked.

"Like old times?" Scuff replied and wolfed down the now-naked fruit.

"Yes."

"She was at the memorial service this morning. For Mariner Ariyabata. She was pretty choked up."

"How did it go?"

Scuff unpeeled another. "Gloomy, bro. Knimble led the service, Lutz still being out for the count."

Silence fell upon them while Scuff gobbled down the second satsuma.

"You heard the bad news?"

Zeke shook his head. "Worse than a fatality?"

"It's all over Mars Valley Radio. The governor's troops are advancing on the school."

"What?"

"He's going to rescue us from the Martian State Brigade and Unpro. He's ordered the rebels to retreat before the heavies arrive, or face death."

"I can't see Cusp giving in to threats."

"Then the Governor says there'll be the biggest battle Mars has ever seen. He's threatening to liberate the Chasm, come what may. Apparently, he's armed with bazookamacs, you know, those gun-toting robots."

Zeke's mouth ran dry. Images of bullets and corpses flitted through his mind.

"These are really sweet," Scuff said, ripping another satsuma in two and sucking out the juice.

"When will they get here?"

"They're coming in Brontos, and it's about seven hundred miles between Tithonium Central and the school, so three days."

"This is terrible," Zeke said.

Scuff shrugged.

"A lot of students are pretty stoked for a fight."

"Why?"

"Half the school have joined the rebellion. And more every day. They're out in the quad now flexing their psychic muscles. Isla's training them in basic combat."

The room swayed. Zeke couldn't believe it. The school was about to become a battleground?

"B-but, the Mariners are neutral. And the Chasm is under the protection of the Mariners' Institute."

Scuff tossed a satsuma in the air. "All that went out the window when war broke out."

"What about you?"

Scuff tapped his gold arm band.

"I don't do fisticuffs. I'll sit this one out."

Silence fell across the room, save for the sound of Scuff chewing satsumas.

"So, what's the plan?" he asked as length. Zeke hesitated. "Chandrasar is doing my check-up at eleven. If that's okay I can go. I feel absolutely fine, now."

They exchanged glances. "Physically," Zeke added.

"Didn't the doc give you nanomeds for post-traumatic thingy?"

"Yes," Zeke said. "That helps. But I can't stop thinking about Ariyabata. One moment I was talking with him and the next he was…gone."

Scuff pulled out a fourth satsuma. "That's life," he said, slicing the peel with his thumbnail.

"I mean…Makes you wonder what life's about," Zeke went on. "A bomb just fell from the sky and snuffed him out like a candle. It could happen to any of us."

Scuff finished off the satsuma.

"I know what life's about. Satsumas," he said. "The sweet moments of existence."

Zeke's belly rumbled. "Can I have one?" he asked.

"Sure, thing, bro." Scuff held the bag upside down. It was empty.

"Oops!" he said. "The last satsumas of Mars. All done now."

Chapter Twenty-Seven
The Cranny Cafeteria

Afternoon sun glinted off the panoramic window. The cafeteria was deserted, other than the 'macs clanking and clinking as they cleared up the lunchtime rush. Zeke drained the dregs of a moonshake but pushed the cheese toastie away. His appetite was gone.

Outside, the canyons threw huge shadows across the valley. The landscape was an endless desert of ochre and black. And somewhere out there, in the dusty distance, an army was getting closer.

Zeke still had the Psychometry teacher's diginoculars. He aimed them at the ground three miles below. The school was crawling with rebel soldiers and students. But it was becoming harder to tell the difference. Students marched up and down, past the ruins of Teaching Block B. Some practiced lifting heavy boulders with their minds. A small group of fourth years huddled in the quad, eyes firmly shut. Maybe they were remote viewing, looking out for the enemy.

Zeke aimed the diginoculars at the Grand Hall. Juanita Almera, one of his classmates, emerged and a soldier unlocked her armband. She stretched her arms as if waking up and fell into line with the marchers.

A week ago, the new term began with a party. Everyone was celebrating. Principle Lutz ruled over the school with her usual rod of iron. Funnily enough, Zeke would give anything to have her back at the helm. Anything to hear her bark in three languages that he was in detention. *Strange*, he thought, *how you can come to miss the things you hate*. Only, Lutz's strict regime didn't seem so hateful now.

Then a random series of events plunged Mars into crisis. The attack on the Televator. Lutz's collapse with future fever. The Unpro rebellion. The bomb attacks. Random events, and yet Zeke couldn't help feeling there was a plan to all this, some shadowy intelligence at work.

The auto-door swished open and Pin-mei Liang walked in. Zeke jumped to his feet. He quickly sat down again and tried to look cool.

"I was searching for you," she said, sitting at his table.

A drinksomac trundled over.

"A drink, Miss?"

She waved it away with her hand. Their eyes met. Zeke noticed her chin. Pin used to be moonfaced. But as she'd shot up, her face had grown a tad longer.

"I'm glad you're alright," she said. Her words were kind but distant. He shrugged.

"The wonders of nanotherapy. Mariner Ariyabata wasn't so lucky."

A tear formed in her eye.

"Anyway," she went on. "When you were lost in the rubble, it made me think."

"About?"

She gazed directly at him.

"You, Zeke."

"How awful for you." He meant to be jokey but it sounded caustic.

"If you'd died in there…." she trailed off.

"I didn't," he said, mustering as much bravado as he could.

"What I want to say is that we need to move forward. *I* need to."

Zeke said nothing. Butterflies fluttered in his stomach. Pin-mei looked out at the windbitten crags.

"It's terrible enough that Bartie's gone. If anything happened to you, too…"

Their eyes met again. Pin-mei's were dark and fathomless.

"I was wrong. It isn't your fault he got killed."

"It's nobody's."

"No, it is. It's mine. I got poor, sweet Bartie killed." And with that she choked up.

"Pin, no!" Zeke cried. "Blame Enki, blame the Particle Beast, blame the long-dead Hesperians. Don't blame yourself." But she broke out in sobs.

The air darkened and a figure formed. It was Trixie.

"You're wanted," she said to Zeke, and grabbed his arm.

"Not now!" he shouted. Trixie's eyes glowed faintly and the cafeteria melted away.

The principal's office was now a war room. A map covered her desk. Cusp and three of his subordinates were studying its contours, all lost in thought. Zeke recognised the men from Yuri-Gagarin Freetown and Edenville.

"Drink?" Isla asked, pushing a steamy mug of moffee into his hand. Moffee was a strain of the Coffea bush, engineered to grow in the barren Martian climate. It whiffed of furniture polish. But there was enough of a kick to make it popular with colonists. Before the war, the Chasm had real coffee imported. But not anymore.

Zeke took a few sips and tried not to wince.

"Thanks, needed a cuppa," he said, through gritted teeth. Isla laughed. "You'll get used to it, kiddo."

Cusp glanced over at Zeke and clicked his fingers.

"I'm not one of your soldiers," Zeke grumbled, but Cusp didn't seem to hear.

"You see the problem?" Cusp asked, tapping the map. Zeke looked closer and recognised the mushroom shape of Ophir Chasma.

"Not really, um, Sir." That last word stuck in his throat.

Cusp pressed his hands together, as though praying. A frown crept across his forehead.

"It's both a strength and weakness. The school is at the far end of the canyon. A dead end. No way out other than south, straight into the governor's troops."

"You could go up," Zeke ventured.

Cusp gave him a sideways glance. "You might be able to fly. My soldiers cannot."

Zeke stared at the map, at the cliffs, scarps, gullies and ridges. Two billion years of geology.

"So how is it a strength?"

Cusp broke into a cocky grin.

"It's a hell of a good defence position. The school is practically a fortress. And our enemies can only attack from the front."

"Yes, but they're coming with bazookamacs. Probably all sorts of other weapons."

Cusp's eyes gleamed. "And I've got Mariners. Psychics. I think I have the upper hand."

Zeke pushed out his bottom lip. Cusp had a point.

"So, what did you want me for?"

Cusp sank into Lutz's leather chair.

"You're my reserve. Plan B from Ophir Chasma."

"Electron's Blade?" Zeke asked, sitting down across from Cusp. The great leader nodded. "You can make all this go away."

Zeke stared at the map. All the contours and gradients flowing around the paper. He thought of his mother and the rest of humanity living on borrowed time. And all the students who were going to die in battle. And Pin-mei, Scuff, Isla, Doctor Chandrasar, even Justice. And all the colonists of Mars, attempting to build a better life, free of tyranny. Lastly, he thought of Mariner Ariyabata.

During his time on Mars, Zeke had faced some tough decisions. And even though this was the most difficult, it was also the easiest. His mind was made up in a nanosecond.

"I'll do it."

Chapter Twenty-Eight
Zeke's Room

Scuff found Zeke on his bed, face buried in his hands, with an open backpack at his side.

"Wazzup, bro?"

Zeke peered through his fingers as though they were the bars of a prison.

"It seemed so easy back in Cusp's office."

"I think you mean Lutz's office," Scuff remarked, picking at his nails.

Zeke said nothing.

"You've got a plan, I just know it. Are you going to tell me?"

"It has to be top secret. Understand?" Zeke replied, sitting up.

"Got it."

"Cusp thinks the governor has long-range cams aimed at the school. Spying."

"Obviously."

Zeke let out a deep breath.

"So, I'm going back to Tithonium. The idea is that I steal Electron's Blade. Translocate it back here before the troops arrive. Cusp can knock them all out and take them prisoners. Then armed with the Blade, he can win the war in a couple of days. Nobody has to die."

"Sounds good to me," Scuff said.

"But how do I get to my far-ship and save our families?"

"How do we even know the governor was serious about that?"

Zeke activated his magnopad and placed it on the duvet. A six-inch hologram of the governor arose from the screen.

"You sure drive a hard bargain, boy," the hologram began. "But to stop those bloodthirsty rebels, I'd walk on hot coals. It took a lot of favours, but I did it. Back on Earth, the old fleet of space balloons is being dusted down to replace the Televator. I've commandeered one for your mother and the Barnum clan. Now don't go adding to the passenger list, these balloons are small. However, your loved ones are promised a trip into orbit, high enough to rendezvous with your far-ship. I already sent word to your families. They'll be there. Now you get back here pretty darn pronto, boy. The deal won't be on the table forever."

The hologram fizzled out.

"But how will you steal this alien gizmo and still get us on board the ship?" Scuff asked.

Zeke shrugged. "There's the problem."

Minutes ticked away. Both boys stared at the carpet, lost in thought. After an age, Scuff stirred. "We have to take the Space Catapult to get into space. Twenty miles from Tithonium. Why don't we steal the Blade, deliver it to Cusp and translocate straight to the Catapult?"

"But surely the governor will try to stop us."

"We'll just have to be quick. Normals can't translocate. Even if he guesses what we're doing, it will take him hours to get soldiers there."

Zeke leant back against the wall, thinking.

"How do we operate the Catapult?"

"There's staff, the catapulters. I'll persuade them."

Zeke frowned. "How?"

Scuff pulled out a wad of Martian dollars. "What's the use of having a rich Daddy, if I can't bribe the odd official along the way?" he said with a huge grin.

Zeke stared at the cash. He didn't like the idea of Scuff forking out money. But they were fighting a war. And their families could die in Earth's destruction at any moment. Suddenly, anything seemed okay.

"How will we even know how to fly the far-ship?" Zeke went on.

Scuff laughed. "You'll figure it out. Don't forget you translocated out of another dimension. Fifty-five million miles to Earth will be nothing."

Zeke rolled his eyes. "Not much of a plan, but it's going to have to do."

"When do we leave?" Scuff asked, rubbing his palms together.

"You don't," Zeke replied firmly.

"What!"

"Cusp wants me to stage a fake escape. Convince the governor I'm on the up-and-up."

"So, we escape together."

Zeke put his hand on Scuff's shoulder.

"Best if I go alone. Really. Less chance of you getting hurt. And the Governor might use you as a hostage."

"Zeke!"

"No, Scuff."

Scuff jumped up and paced around the room. He stopped in midtrack and wheeled round to face Zeke. "You will come back for me, won't you?" His face was bright with fear.

"Of course, I'm coming back with the Blade. And anyway, we're mates. I wouldn't go without you."

"Cool. We'll go to Earth together. Bring our folks back here where it's safe. Hey, buddy, I might even go to Alpha Cephei with you."

Zeke laughed. "One step at a time."

And they high-fived.

"I'd never leave you behind, Scuff. Never."

This time it was Doctor Chandrasar who opened the door to Lutz's apartment. She was pale. Since the war, Zeke thought, everyone was looking like, well, *glsh-glsh*.

"She's expecting you," Chandrasar said.

Principal Lutz was in bed. Still in that awful pink nightie. But she looked even older. Like an apple withering in the sun. She gestured

feebly for him to sit beside her. As he drew up the chair, a wave of
déjà vu washed over him. An image of Lutz's predecessor popped
into his head. Lutz Four, lying on her deathbed.

"You've come to say *adieu*," she remarked. Her eyes were watery.

Zeke nodded, at a loss what to say.

"How are you feeling?"

"Better with this." She pulled back the duvet to show a golden
band around her upper arm. "It blocks out the visions. All those
terrible things to come."

She sighed.

"Like what?" Zeke asked.

She glared at him.

"Like what, Ma'am?" he added hastily.

"I forget now," she replied, and looked away.

"You said I was going to die."

"Did I?"

Zeke nodded. Was she going to be difficult?

"I need to know, Ma'am."

She turned back.

"There's going to be a huge attack. Maybe you can stop it. But you
won't be coming back. Happy now?"

Zeke shifted in his seat. That sounded slightly more positive than
her last divination. Although it also sounded unbelievable.

"That's what you saw?"

"Maybe."

Zeke forced back an urge to snap.

"So why did you say I was doomed?"

Lutz took a sip of water from the glass on her nightstand.

"Did I? The last few days are all a blank."

Zeke puffed out his chest. "Tell me what you saw, in detail, please."

She fixed him with a look that was both haughty and sad. "That
you will never return to the Chasm. No more than that."

Zeke pursed his lips. She was playing with him.

"Surely then, I'm going to die. It's the only thing that would stop me returning here."

Lutz clicked her tongue. "You seem very attached to a place you keep trying to leave."

"Well, it's my home."

Silence settled on the room. Zeke felt a lump in his throat. The Ophir Chasma School for Psychic Endeavour really was his home. And now that he was going, he realised how much he loved it. Memories flowed through him.

Lutz stirred.

"*Ach so.* Precognition is not an exact science. And I cannot tell you too much. There is the danger of a self-fulfilling prophecy."

"The what?"

A sly look crept across her face.

"Careful with that glass," she said.

"What glass?" Zeke asked, sitting back. His arm knocked the nightstand and the glass toppled off the edge. Water splashed onto his lap. He jumped up, wiping his trousers.

"Don't worry. It will soon dry off," she said, with a hint of her former ebullience.

Zeke sat down again, flushing. He grasped her point.

He glanced at his watch. The hour was growing late and he still had to stage his escape.

"There was something else," he said.

Lutz sighed. *She knows what you're going to ask*, whispered the inner voice at the back of Zeke's head.

"Principal Lutz, be honest with me. Why do the Mariners never come back from deep space?"

Tears welled up in her eyes, "Why do you think?"

Zeke straightened his back. He answered slowly, as if the words were burning. "Because they're all dead."

Lutz gave a little shrug.

"Nobody knows for sure. But it seems the only explanation. A century of galactic colonisation, and not one far-ship ever came back. Nor those who went in search of them, nor those in search of the search parties."

A numbness seeped into his body.

"Why?"

"Again, how could we know? Your father was supposed to solve that one. Then he didn't come back, either."

"My father isn't dead," Zeke said loudly.

"*Peut-être. Vielleicht.*"

Zeke said nothing. An anger simmered inside him. Anger at the Mariners. At Lutz for sending boys and girls to their death for a hundred years. An anger at the universe for allowing his father to die.

And yet, even as the anger boiled, Zeke remembered Van Hiss's testimony. The Earth was about to implode. Billions would be snuffed out in an instant. What choice did the Mariners have? For every life sacrificed, hundreds were saved. Would he have chosen any different?

And what of his father?

He clenched his fists. All the other Mariners might be dead, but not his dad. Zeke felt it in his bones. And didn't Lutz say nobody knew for sure? There could be another, less deadly explanation. Just they hadn't figured it out yet. His father lived and breathed on Alpha Cephei and he was going to get him. Rescue him. And yes, he'd find a way to cheat death too.

Through the open door, Zeke could hear the clock in the living room. Ticking. Ticking away the seconds of his life. Everyone's life. With tremendous effort, he pushed all these upsetting ideas from his mind. He had to focus on the here-and-now. War was coming to his beloved school and he, and he alone, was in a position to stop it.

"Gotta go," Zeke said. An impulse seized him and he leaned forward. Lutz grimaced as she realised his intent. But he did it anyway. He hugged her. Her body stiffened for a moment, then relaxed.

"Thank you, Principal Lutz."

That was all he could say. Because she was right about one thing. This was their last meeting.

She ruffled his hair.

"*Mein liebling,* you were always one of my favourites."

Yes, he thought, *I suppose I was.*

He pulled away and started to leave.

"Hailey, one more thing."

He hesitated in the doorway and looked back at the frail old woman in the bed, suddenly so old and weak. Her days of striking fear in the hearts of students were over.

"Don't hate me. It had to be done."

"I know." She'd helped kill hundreds of Mariners. And yet he couldn't bring himself to recriminate the old woman. Maybe, in her shoes, he'd have done the same.

"And look after dear Marjorie. She's going to be very useful one day."

"Oh? Right, sure," he replied and walked out of the principal's life.

Chapter Twenty-Nine
The School Grounds

Zeke slipped through the fire exit into the cold darkness. The night sky gleamed overhead, bursting with stars. But below, the canyons blotted out the starlight. It was as if he were standing at the centre of a black hole.

The courtyards made a ghostly world. Photon lamps in the gravel painted badminton nets and basketball hoops with an eerie luminance. A solitary guard patrolled the school wall. Desks and benches were piled up against the concrete. Cusp's defences for when the time came.

Zeke waited till the man was out of sight. Throwing his backpack over his shoulder, he ran over to the bicycle racks. He flicked the switch on Albie's handlebars. The bicycle frame glittered with lights. The headlamp beamed, a slice of daylight in the void.

"Stealth mode!" Zeke hissed.

Albie dowsed his glare.

"Sorry, Master Zeke," he apologised, his tinny voice at minimum volume.

Zeke undid the padlock and pushed the bike over to the ruined school gate. The only way across was to lift Albie up and over the rubble. Once on the far side, Zeke glanced back. The Grand Hall grew out from the cliff, all buttresses, arches and facades. The termite mounds of the accommodation blocks towered nearby. Tiny tongues of yellow flickered in windows, nightlights for those nervous of the dark.

Zeke's heart throbbed. It was no different to the night he first arrived, confused and scared. And now here was the last night. Time to say goodbye. Faces flitted through his mind's eye. Pin, Scuff, Chandrasar, Knimble, little Gary Aspeck, even Trixie Cutter. He supposed they were asleep now. And when they woke up he would be long gone. Then he thought of Jasper Snod, sleeping in the Spiral's belly, dead but not dead. Zeke shivered in the chill air. He focussed on the school he loved so much.

"Lutz is wrong, I'll be back," he muttered.

He turned to face the great ocean of emptiness.

"Albie, use night vision. And maximum pedal assistance."

A square of green light appeared above the handlebars. It was an electro-magnetic screen, illuminating a murky landscape of stones and shadows.

Zeke gritted his teeth, placed his right foot on the pedal, and pushed off hard. The scream of alarms shattered the stillness.

The vast curtain of the night covered the universe. The great, black silence where nothing lived. Zeke's calves strained as he pedalled at full pelt. His wheels scattered dust behind. Ahead of him, obstacles loomed from the darkness, visible through the bike's EM screen. Slabs of ancient basalt, resting in this wilderness for eons. They looked like limbless monsters thrusting from the ground. Zeke dodged left and right, his lungs heaving.

What was that? A noise!

It was barely audible, a mechanical putt-putt. He glanced back. Two fingers of light flickered in the distance. Glow worms! The star-light-powered scooters used by the teachers. Someone was in pursuit. The headlamps twisted as their riders steered through the assault course of rocks. Two feeble beams poking through the desolation.

SMASH!

Zeke felt the crash of stone against metal. He tumbled off and landed with a nasty bump. *That's what happen when you don't look where you're going,* remarked his inner voice angrily. He jumped up.

"Albie, are you okay?"

"Status report, Master. A small dent to front wheel. Repairing structural integrity."

Despair flowed through Zeke. He stared at the distant headlamps. Glow worms were not equipped with night vision, only Zeke had that advantage, thanks to Albie. Nor were they built for speed. But they weren't dependent on knee power. They were a slow but relentless enemy. How long could he stay ahead of them?

The bent wheel pinged as it snapped back into shape. Biting back the pain of a bruised elbow, Zeke mounted the saddle and started off.

He pedalled and pedalled and pedalled. Space and time seemed at a complete stop. However fast he cycled, he made no progress. The putt-putt of the two engines grew louder.

"Hailey. Come back!"

It was a man's voice. His words carried far on the crisp Martian air. The man sounded a few metres behind, although Zeke knew it more like a half a kilometre. He didn't recognise the voice but it had to be one of Cusp's men. Maybe Cusp should have let a few of his followers in on the secret. If Zeke was caught now, and taken back, everything would be ruined.

Zeke gritted his teeth and pushed harder.

"In the name of Ptolemy Cusp, I order you to stop," shouted a second voice.

How long had he been cycling? It felt like forever, but was only about thirty minutes. Zeke's legs were beginning to burn with muscle exhaustion. Still he travelled on.

"Stop or we shoot."

Were they serious? The rebels and the school were on the same side now. Would they really fire at him? Zeke cursed the metal band on his arm. If only Cusp had taken it off, then he'd be able to translocate away. But they'd left it on. Again, to make the escape all the more convincing. Conveniently removing the armband might look suspicious to the governor.

"We won't warn you again, boy."

On and on. On and on. Bumping over stones. Dodging boulders. Zeke's heartbeat thundered in his head. His legs burned.

A bullet winged past, low, aimed at the wheels. Then another. The rebels intended to damage his bike and force him into another crash. There was nothing he could do but keep pedalling.

Something whooshed past him from the opposite direction. From the soup of darkness up ahead. A gasp in the night.

The noise of crunching plastic echoed through the canyons. Then came swearing and shouting. Zeke glanced back. The light was so meagre it was hard to be sure. But the first glow worm had stopped abruptly, causing the second to collide. Zeke could smell smoke and burnt rubber.

Yes! He had an unknown ally.

He cycled on with renewed energy, his feet a blur. Forty metres, maybe fifty. The glow worms vanished, out of sight behind the forest of rocks. There was no way his pursuers could catch him now.

Zeke focussed on the EM screen. The last thing he needed was another accident. On and on.

It happened in a nanosecond. A boulder blocking the trail twisted. Stretched. Stood up. Zeke hit the brakes. Red pinpoint eyes glared at him. Arms reached out, encrusted with shards. Razor sharp crystal fragments.

The Craton!

It leapt, seizing Zeke as it arced above the bike. Zeke and the bike toppled. The creature held him in its jagged embrace, as they rolled in the dirt. The stink of dank chemicals was overpowering. Like a school chemistry lab.

Zeke had come too far to give up. As they tussled on the ground, he brought his knee up hard. The Craton shrieked and its grip weakened. Zeke broke free. He stumbled to his feet.

"*Slk yriwiw*" he cried. Hesperian for 'I am friend'.

He cast around in the blackness, seeking the creature. Where was it?

"I am on a mission. You must not stop me," he added, still speaking Hesperian.

Zeke knew only too well how deadly the Craton could be. First, there was its venomous bile. And if that wasn't enough, the Craton was psychic and moved heavy objects by will. Zeke slowly rotated, hands out, seeking his attacker. Its rasping breath seemed to come from all directions.

The dark rippled. Speckles of faint light crept towards him. Starlight reflected in the Craton's crystal disfigurements.

"I know you're there," Zeke said, trying to sound fearless. "You must let me go."

"Child-from-the third-world asks for *fthff*. Did it grant *fthff* to Craton? At the city of the hoomans?"

Zeke's subconscious was an imperfect dictionary. He could not translate every Hesperian word. Others took a little time to form meaning in his head. Ah okay, *fthff* meant liberty.

"That was not me. You know that," he cried.

He'd lost sight of it again. Was it there? No, he was seeing things. Shadows among shadows. Then he caught its glow, more the hint of a glow. It was pacing around him.

"There is much evil to come. I will keep child-from-the-third-world safe. In Craton's nest."

Zeke pictured its underground lair beneath the Beagle Research Station. But that was very far from Ophir Chasma. Why was it so far north?

"Hunting you, child," it said, reading his thoughts.

Zeke's pulses were racing. It was about to strike. He sensed it.

"Why me?"

"We speak the first words. The words from long ago. We are the last speakers. We are the same."

Zeke straightened up. Maybe he could appeal to its better nature. If it had one.

"We have more in common," he said in English. "We're both human."

"Hocgo," it hissed. Liar.

"No. Tell me your name." If only he knew its human identity. That would change everything.

A shape blotted out stars. The Craton had slipped out from the rocks into the open.

"I am Craton," it said in English.

The figure threw back its shoulders. Zeke dived to the left. An arc of bile gushed through the air, narrowly missing him. The foul liquid splattered a large stone, sizzling like acid.

"My name is buried," the monster cried, readying itself for another bile attack. Zeke crouched low, stuck between the monster and a spur of basalt. He was trapped.

But a red laser was dancing on the creature's chest. Something whistled out of the night. And then a thwack. The Craton screamed.

"Albie, headlamp on," Zeke shouted.

The bike was lying nearby. The headlamp threw a puddle of white onto the sand. Enough to light up the Craton's jagged, soot-coloured body. An arrow was lodged in its shoulder. Blue liquid spurted from the wound. The Craton staggered backwards.

"Craton will kill you," it screeched and melted into the starry sky.

Chapter Thirty
A Hole in the Ground

Zeke woke suddenly, from dreams of fire and falling. Falling upwards.

His throat tightened. Where on Mars was he? Some kind of pit? Then it all flooded back to him. Mariner Chinook saved him from the rebels and the Craton. How Chinook led him through the dead night, to a pothole under a huge basalt spur. Then, the two of them crawling down that hole into a pit.

"You went out like a light," the Mariner said, sitting nearby. His iBow rested at his feet, casting its faint blue glow across the cave.

Chinook glanced at its LED display.

"Five a.m. Sun up soon."

Zeke picked up the iBow and studied it from tip to tip.

"All these functions, it's really ace. Target locking, aim assistance, wind calculation. Gosh, it's even got a cam."

"As long the string is taut, and the aim is true, that's what matters," Chinook replied. He sounded blunt.

Zeke looked at him. The man was haggard.

"Sir, you've been out here for two days. I know you're the great hunter and all that, but—"

Chinook waved his hand.

"Yes, it's difficult. No water, no game. The only life I've found is oxygen moss. No nutrition in that. I might as well dine on dust and stones."

Zeke fished in his backpack and pulled out a bottle of water. Chinook grabbed it and gulped down every drop.

"Sir, don't you think it would be better to give up? While you still can?"

"Never! Cusp's a traitor." Chinook's voice was defiant.

"Well, the school and Unpro are on the same side now. After everything that happened."

"The Mariners never take sides. Our eyes must rest firmly on one goal alone. Saving humanity."

"You can't stay out here. It's not the forests of Earth. Even on Europa you could filter water from the ice."

Chinook stared at him. For a moment, the great oak of a man seemed confused, like a child.

"Mars is as dry as a bone. That is why I've come to a decision. I'm coming with you. To Tithonium"

Zeke shrugged. Why not?

"You know I'm on a mission, Sir."

"I will not help you, Hailey. It would break my Mariner's Oath. But I will not hinder you either. And I'll keep my own counsel."

Zeke threw him a blank look.

"My mouth stays shut," Chinook explained, with a ghost of a smile.

Zeke studied his magnopad. Still no reply from the governor. He checked the signal. It was fine.

"That creature," Chinook began. "What in heck was it?"

Zeke sighed. "A human being, Sir, like you or me."

"Not at all like you or me."

"A hundred and fifty-odd years ago, the first astronauts arrived on Mars. Can you imagine what it was like? Before the terra-forming."

Chinook nodded.

"No air, no respite from solar radiation. Those early visitors were pioneers. And this Craton was one of them?"

Zeke cleared his throat. "Yes, Sir. There was a team of British scientists. They set up the Beagle Research Station in Ius Chasma. One of them discovered a Hesperian orb. After that they all disappeared. Except the one who found the orb. Over many years, he or she morphed into the thing we saw tonight. Contaminated by Hesperian technology."

Chinook's eyes were wide.

"But how can you know this?"

"Because I found a book," Zeke said, pulling a leather-bound journal from his backpack. "I rescued it from the ruins of the Beagle Station."

He handed the book over to his teacher, who examined the cover.

"Beagle UK Research Station Logbook. Year 2090," Chinook read aloud, before flicking through the tattered pages.

"My theory is this, Sir. Remember humanity didn't know back then about psychic ability."

"The twenty-first century was a dark age."

"I think one of the crew was psychic. Obviously, they wouldn't know it. But leaving Earth and its magnetic field meant any psychic talent started waking up. The orbs are powered by brainwaves. So, the astronaut's ability triggered the orb, or the other way around. That person suddenly found they had super powers."

"That must have been bewildering," Chinook said, stroking his chin. "if you had no idea what it was."

"It gets weirder."

Chinook laughed. "Seriously?"

"The Craton forgot who it used to be. Maybe it doesn't want to remember. But it's told me enough. If I can find out which one of the crew it was, its human memory will return. And then we can find what it did with the others."

"Murdered them, would be a good guess."

"*Sharlyk erk gffth zhhh glrrk ztt hrfkii*"

"I get goose pimples when you do that," Chinook remarked.

"In English, 'give me my flesh name and I'll give you the vanished.'"

"They must be long dead, young Hailey."

"Must they? The Craton survived, why not them?"

"And you think this book has the clues?"

Zeke nodded. "I sense it."

"And you've read it?"

Zeke nodded again. "Yep, just haven't put all the pieces together yet."

Chinook stroked his cheek. "Does Craton mean anything in Martian? Might be a clue."

"Hesperian, Sir. But it's not a Hesperian word…" Zeke sat bolt upright, his eyes flaming. "…so, it can only be English."

"Never heard of it. Are you sure?"

Zeke sank back. "Um, think so, I'd better check in a dictionary."

"The governor's going to keep you a tad too busy for word-building."

"Guess so."

"And why bring it with you anyway?" Chinook asked with a frown.

Their eyes met. Chinook only knew parts of the plan. It seemed safer that way. Zeke was keeping the journal on him, so it wouldn't get left behind. And then, if he ever reached Alpha Cephei, he could read it at leisure. Hopefully, he could work out the Craton's identity, so that when he returned he could save the day. If he returned.

Zeke took back the journal. They sat quietly for a few minutes, each deep in thought. Zeke folded his arms and shivered. The pothole was dark and cold.

"How did you know of this place?" he asked.

"I gave up hunting after you saved that great mar-rat. Instead, I reconnoitred the region, mapping out dunes and rocks. I came across this hideaway on one of those trips."

More silence. There was something Zeke wanted to ask. Carefully, he put the words together in his head.

"Sir, you once said you'd tell me why you didn't go."

Chinook flashed him a razor-sharp look.

"Into deep space? Yes, I did."

"Mariner Chinook, I know the truth now. Lutz told me."

Chinook cocked an eyebrow. Zeke went on. "The deep space translocation is so great it kills the Mariner. That's the only logical explanation."

"And you think me so cowardly I backed out? Put my life before scores of colonists?"

Zeke stared at the dirt. "I'd understand if you did."

Chinook let out a deep sigh. "I served my Mariner's apprenticeship on Europa."

"I know, Jupiter's frozen moon."

A gleam burned in Chinook's eyes. "A world of two colours. Everything above the horizon black, everything below white."

"Sounds dull," Zeke remarked.

"Dull? That damn moon stole my heart. Glaciers colliding, soaring into the night like glass spires. The thrill of driving my buggy off ice dunes. The moment in mid-air. Then the crash and the crack as you land. The numb cheeks, the splash in the face."

"I suppose Jupiter was really impressive?"

"Never saw it. Not on the ground. One side of Europa always faces Jupiter. The colony was on the far side, turned to the cosmos. The entire moon acted as a buffer between us and Old Red Eye. And all the radiation he gave off."

"How do you cope with so much radiation?"

"A combi," Chinook explained. "Quadruple strength sun block. Magnetic deflectors—"

"Magnetic deflectors?"

Chinook raised an eyebrow. "What did they teach you at Earth school? A string of small satellites re-route Jupiter's magnetosphere around Europa, rather than through it. Each satellite is highly charged, so it attracts the magnetic flux away from the moon. That's why our psychic powers aren't cancelled out either."

"Oh, right. I knew that," Zeke replied in a not-very-convincing tone.

"So, sun block, magnetic deflectors, daily decon. Even then, radiation sickness was common among the colonists. Thank the Lord for nanotherapy. All those little nanomacs zapping our tumours before they got outta hand."

Chinook stared into space.

"I worked on the water desalination plant."

"Making the seawater drinkable?"

The Inuit nodded.

"One day there was an accident. Two engineers went out on an inspection trip, checking the filters. They were driving back in their buggy, when a corroded fuel cell exploded."

"Oh, no! Killed?"

"Not on my watch. I was in the control room, watching their cabin cam. The blast knocked them out. There was nothing for it but to use my powers. That's why the Mariners were there, after all."

Zeke sat up. This was getting interesting.

"I translocated to the buggy. About half a klick. Using psychokinesis, I was able to pull them free and translocate them to the medical unit. Saved their lives."

Zeke waited with baited breath. There had to be more, he could sense it. Chinook looked him straight in the eye.

"There was no time to rub on the sun block or slip into a safety suit."

"You went out into all that radiation unprotected?"

"Affirmative. Naturally, I took a decon course later and thought nothing of it."

"You were okay, then?"

"I served my apprenticeship. Six months later it was time to take a far-ship to the stars. I thought nothing of the medical exam. Until I failed it."

"Oh!"

"Long story short, I'd been exposed to vast levels of radiation. Every cell in my body was contaminated."

"But Sir, surely you're alright. The nanotherapy…"

Chinook's face was drawn, his eyes watery.

"Nanotherapy keeps me alive. Every day I take the maximum dose. Those mechanical varmints crawl through my body, zapping damage as it crops up. But my exposure was so radical, the nanomacs can only keep pace with it. If I stopped the meds for any reason, in a few short weeks I'd be dead."

Chinook fished in his pockets and pulled out a pill box.

"I always keep a month's supply on me. In case."

Zeke's eyes widened as the jigsaw came together in his mind.

"But if you went to a distant planet, well, there'd be no civilisation."

"And no medical industry to manufacture my pills."

Their eyes met.

"The Mariners Institute rejected me on health grounds. They can't send a Mariner on a mission if it risks his death. Rather ironic, if you think about it."

Zeke's heart sank.

"You must have been gutted."

The Mariner rolled his eyes. "You could say that."

"I'm sorry."

Chinook batted away Zeke's words with a wave of the hand.

"So, my life changed direction. I went into teaching. Ended up back at the Chasm, my old school. Principal Lutz was wonderful, very supportive. That's one heck of a kind lady."

Zeke frowned. That was hard to believe.

"And that's how I ended up in this hole in the ground." Chinook said. He beamed at Zeke. An attempt to mask the pain. The pain he felt every day of his life. This huge, lion of a man, barred from his destiny. He was supposed to be a hero, a pilot to the stars. Reduced to lesson plans and homework. It was all kind of tragic.

"Sir, how do you cope with it?"

"Shh!" Chinook snapped. Zeke threw him a bewildered look. Then he heard it too. The chop-chop of a gyrocopter. And it was getting nearer.

Chapter Thirty-One
The Ellipse Office

The plate of doughnuts was now a plate of crumbs. Zeke glanced around the empty room, rubbing his stuffed belly. He was alone. The security had separated him from Chinook shortly after arrival.

The door flew open and the governor stormed in, flanked by two guards. One had a ferromagnetic rifle over his shoulder.

"Well now, if it isn't our little ol' ally, Mister Hailey," The governor said, eyes twinkling.

Charm first, then come the guns, Zeke thought.

"Where's Mariner Chinook?" he asked.

"Enjoying the hospitality of the Ellipse," the governor answered, grinning like a monkey. He sat down in the sofa opposite Zeke.

"I think we need a summing up. So much has happened these last days. And I wouldn't want there to be any more misunderstandings." There was an edge of steel in the governor's voice.

Zeke forced a smile onto his lips. The most important thing was to play along. The governor's troops would arrive the following day at the Chasm. Zeke drew a deep breath.

"I'm going to translate the last few words of Hesperian. You'll use it peacefully to prevent any further bloodshed. I get a farship and translocate back to Earth to meet my mother. And Scuff's family."

"The perfect deal. Everyone gets something. And the balloons for your families are confirmed with UNAAC. I can't cancel that now, so don't you worry about a double cross." the governor said, relaxing back onto the cushions. "And your chain is removed?"

"Yes," Zeke said, and scratched his arm. The skin was still a little sore. Zeke spotted a chessboard on a cabinet in the corner. All thirty-two pieces were set out, ready to play. Time for a demonstration. Zeke focussed on the board. Slowly it lifted into the air, glided across the room and landed on the coffee table between them. At the last moment, a white pawn slid off.

The governor caught it and put it back in its square.

"Very impressive, Zeke. Do you play?"

Zeke shook his head. The governor moved the same pawn two squares. "The trick is to think a few steps ahead. Figure out what moves your opponent might make and plan for them."

"Sir, this far-ship?"

The governor flicked open his magnopad. It projected a small holocube above the table. Zeke saw the orange craters of Mars, from on high. The viewpoint shifted away from the planet into space. The conical shape of a far-ship soared into the cube. Far-ships were enormous, to accommodate as many colonists as possible. And yet he was getting one all to himself.

"I suggest you go onboard and get to know the controls. How that iron bird works. Before you tell us the translations."

Zeke's mouth dropped. It sounded too good to be true. There had to be a catch.

"You don't trust me, do you?" the governor smirked. For a non-psychic, he seemed pretty adept at reading minds. He pressed a button on the magnopad. The holocube changed scenes. Now they were looking through the lens of a surveillance camera, down into a small room.

Zeke gasped. Pin-mei and Trixie Cutter were sitting on the floor, looking glum.

"While you were pedalling through the wilderness, my command-oes sprang a surprise night raid on the school. Slip in, acquire the targets, slip out and Unpro's none the wiser."

Zeke glared at the governor, burning with hatred.

"You can't blame me for taking out some business insurance. In case our deal goes south."

Zeke screwed up his fists, but said nothing.

"And one more thing," the governor added, adjusting the holocube again. This time a schematic appeared. It was some kind of cannon, with an array of cylinders and tubes attached. The weapon rotated for a full three-dimensional view.

"My backroom boys came up with this beauty. A ferromagnetic blaster. One burst will soak the entire school in magnetic ions. Every psychic on the premises will find their abilities wiped out. Only for six hours, but my soldiers can blow the Chasm up in ten minutes."

Zeke felt hot tears in his eyes. Tears of anger.

"Of course, with Electron's Blade, we won't need the blaster. Put them all to sleep, and peacefully take them prisoner. It's up to you, my young friend."

Zeke leapt to his feet, in a pure rage. His eyes lit up, as every item of furniture started levitating off the ground. The governor clicked his fingers and the security man aimed and fired. Zeke felt as if a wet flannel was inside his skull, smothering his psychic faculties. The furniture thudded back onto the floor.

Zeke opened his mouth but no words came. The governor chuckled.

"Checkmate, don'tcha think?"

It was exactly as he had seen on his out-of-body wanderings. A tall blade of gleaming metal, the height of a man, and covered in etched symbols. Zeke was near enough to touch it, to steal it and translocate back to the Chasm. If only he still had his powers.

He studied the artefact closer. The symbols weren't Hesperian letters or numbers, Zeke knew that. So, what were they?

The blade was set in a rough basalt base, embedded with dials. Each of these were smooth and circular like pebbles. Zeke looked closer but could not see any writing.

He glanced around the small room. With the Governor, Enki and two guards, it felt claustrophobic. Enki had that inane grin plastered across his face. What was wrong with him? Zeke couldn't put his finger on it.

"You're wondering if there are any…accessories?" Enki said.

Zeke didn't reply.

Enki opened a drawer in the white wall and fished out a large ring. One side was jagged and the other smooth.

"This was found nearby," Enki added. He handed it to the governor, who slipped it over his head.

"It's a crown?" Zeke asked, wide-eyed.

"Tish," Enki replied. "A *quclxii*."

"A headset? Oh. For the Blade?"

"Clever boy," Enki replied and ruffled Zeke's hair. Zeke bit back an urge to slap him.

"I wear this, when you can figure how to switch the damn contraption on," the governor explained. He was flushed with a smug satisfaction. Clearly, he was looking forward to wearing the crown.

"There must be more…you know…instructions?" Zeke said.

This time, Enki pulled out a blue orb about the size of a large pomegranate. He held it in his hand. The thing was beautiful, with a glowing marble sheen. Darker shades of sapphire melted into ice blue. The orb called to Zeke. He reached out his fingers.

"Naughty, naughty," Enki said, hastily bundling it back into the drawer.

"The orb has the instructions?" Zeke asked.

Enki nodded. "Which I have written down. No need to activate it now."

Because you don't want to me to see the whole text, muttered the voice inside Zeke's head. Enki clicked on his magnopad. A stream of Hesperian text appeared in mid-air. Zeke skimmed through the alien symbols.

Put on the headset. Stand no more than four zugzugs from the Blade. Speak aloud the activation code.

Easy enough, Zeke thought. Mundane even. There was just the last sentence. Zeke studied it in detail. No English translation popped into his brain. That might indicate the words were a name or had no meaning in English.

"Found something?" Enki enquired, drooling with anticipation.

"The activation code, it's just meaningless syllables. All you can do is read them out and—"

"And?" The governor and Enki both asked together.

Zeke stared hard at Enki. "You don't know how to pronounce it, do you?"

Enki sniggered, like a toddler caught with a hand in the cookie jar. "You got me."

"But—but, the citadel. You said the words."

Enki nodded. "A Mariner died screaming that citadel password. That's how I knew. I've tried so hard to work out the phonetics from those few syllables. The job proved impossible. But you! Your entire brain is a dictionary."

"And that's why you need me. To translate just that sentence."

"And save lives," the Governor piped up.

Zeke chewed his thumb. The Governor slapped him on the back. "You don't trust me, I know. That's why I'm going to trust you."

"What?"

"Sometimes you have to invest in people. That's what I'm going to do with you."

Zeke gave him a blank look. The governor's eyes were twinkling brighter than diamonds.

"I'm putting all my faith in you, son. I'm sending you up to that farship of yours. You can even take the little ladies. Once onboard, you can check everything out, prime the engines or whatever Mariners do on those vessels, and you're good to go."

"You're setting me free?" Zeke asked, incredulous.

"Sure am," the governor continued. "You'll see this deal is genuine. Go get your father. Just remember to give us the password when you're up there. You see, I'm not asking for it while you here enjoying my hospitality. I know you have doubts. I know if I used force you might lie. So, I want you to give it to me in your own time."

Zeke's mind was racing. "I need to pick up my friend, Scuff."

"Son, there's no time. The battle for Ophir Chasma starts at dawn. If we're gonna avert bloodshed we need to act fast."

"But—"

"No buts, it's up to you. Stop the fighting and then you'll have all the time on Mars. As long as you want. Take every buddy you got.

Only we have to act this moment. The Space Catapult can have you on your ship before nightfall."

Zeke's fingers were running out of nails. It sounded too good to be true. He returned his gaze to the last line of the hologram. He began to work out the alien letters, one by one.

Sthath. That was the syllable 'sa'. Followed by *cthra* and *ffith* or cra and fie. So, it spelled sa-cra-fie. What next? *Sthath, sthoth, wgu, nthath, wgith, rrith, vah.* Zeke translated them and strung them together in his head.

Sa cra fie sa so wu na will lee va

"What does it say?" Enki squealed. Zeke ignored him and focused. He frowned. The syllables. They had a familiar ring. His gaze hardened.

The breath stuck in his chest.

"What is it, son?" the governor asked, clasping his hands.

Zeke couldn't speak. He collapsed into a chair. His skin was whiter than snow.

"Nothing, nothing," he said feebly. He loosened his collar.

And the Hesperian letters kept glowing. Saying the same thing for countless millennia. Only not in the ancient language of the Hesperians. The words spelled out a quite different language, written in the Hesperian alphabet. Yes, the odd syllable had been added, like the second *sthath* and the *nthath.* That was necessary. There must be human speech sounds beyond their alien mouths. So, the odd letter was necessary to approximate human phonetics. The final letters were a good example. As they couldn't say 'live', they said 'liv-va'.

Because it was the word 'live'. The entire sentence was English.

Sacrifice so one will live.

Chapter Thirty-Two
The Space Catapult

The blades merged into a blur, whipping dirt into the air. Everything was lost in a sand cloud. The Monarch lifted from the haze and slowly pulled away. Its deafening roar subsided. Dust drifted. Settled. Shapes emerged, blocks of concrete, structures.

Zeke, Pin-mei and Trixie stood like statues, waiting for the scene to clear. Two soldiers stood behind them, armed with rifles. Real ones that fired bullets. One prodded Trixie in the back.

"Oi, do you mind?" she snapped.

"Forward. The terminal," he barked, a huge swarthy man with a face as flat as an iron.

"Yeah, on the double," said the other, a smaller black man.

Pin-mei and Trixie took a step.

"Come on," Pin-mei said gently and tugged Zeke's sleeve.

"What's wrong with Boy Wonder?" Trixie asked.

"Nothing," Zeke mumbled, and picked up his feet.

The group crossed the courtyard.

"Goodness!" Pin-mei exclaimed, pointing to the overhead canyon. A cylinder ran up its side. All the way to the peak.

"You've never ridden the catapult?" Trixie asked.

"You have?" Pin-mei replied.

"I've been off-world a few times, on business trips."

"I never knew."

"My life doesn't revolve around you and Blue Boy, you know."

"Shut up," snarled the flat face.

"When my powers return, you are so dead," Trixie muttered darkly.

"Anyone here?" the soldier bellowed. His voice echoed off the concrete walls.

"War's so bad for trade," Trixie remarked. "Unless war *is* your trade," she added with a wink.

The auto-door in the dome-shaped reception swished open. A slightly-built man emerged and hurried over. He had a thick mop of black hair, a moustache and sunglasses.

A disguise! Zeke realised at once who it really was, from the build and gait, but said nothing. He no longer cared. His brain was as numb as ice.

"Alright, alright, show us your passes," said a voice that was gruff and squeaky at the same time.

"Passes? We don't need passes. The governor sent us," said Flat Face, but nonetheless searched his breast pocket.

Whack!

The stranger punched Flat Face on the nose. The man toppled like a falling oak, blood spurting and out cold. The black soldier desperately grabbed his rifle. Too late! The stranger somersaulted and as his feet landed, karate-chopped the soldier's neck. The black soldier staggered back but amazingly kept his balance. He grabbed the attacker. They grappled for a few seconds. Then somehow the stranger got behind, threw his arm around the soldier's throat and squeezed like a vice. The soldier struggled, violently attempting to break free. Blood flooded his face. The eyes glazed and his movements slowed. And then he slumped, eyes open but empty. The stranger whisked out a syringe and quickly injected both men.

"Knockout nanomacs," said a voice that was now much higher. The stranger yanked off the wig to reveal a scalp of strawberry stubble. Next, off came the false moustache and glasses.

"Isla the Incisor!" Pin-mei cried and clapped her hands in glee.

Isla flashed her pearly grin. They hugged.

"Oh, great, G.I Jane, all we need," Trixie remarked with a roll of the eyes.

"Delighted to see you too," Isla said with a good-natured laugh.

"Zeke, you look like you've seen a ghost."

He attempted a weak smile but it crashed and burned. How could he explain he'd had a message, in English, from two billion years ago?

"What on ruddy Mars are you doing here?" Trixie asked.

Isla nodded at Zeke.

"Keeping track of our prize asset. Ptolemy knew we'd need a back-up plan. His grasp of strategy is formidable."

Trixie gave a little mock yawn. "And what plan would that be?"

"How are your powers?" Isla asked, looking at Pin-mei.

"We're all ion blasted. I think another two hours before it wears off."

"Okay, we hang here, then Zeke translocates back to the Ellipse with me. We seize Electron's Blade and translocate it back to the Chasm. Hey presto, we've won."

Her eyes glittered like emeralds.

"What do you think, Zeke?" Pin-mei asked.

He shrugged. "It could work." The words came out as a mumble. Pin-mei and Isla exchanged looks.

"By the way, how did you get mixed up in this?" Isla asked Trixie. Zeke heard the sneer in her voice and remembered they both had feelings for Ptolemy Cusp. Isla was his lover but Trixie flirted with him at every chance.

"Hey, what's that?" Trixie cried.

Everyone followed her gaze, out across the sea of sand.

"What's what?" Isla asked, seizing one of the soldier's rifles.

Trixie hesitated. "Thought I saw something wriggling. Maybe I imagined it." The wind whistled from far away. The valley remained still.

"The desert plays tricks on the mind," Isla suggested. "Now to my question. What nefarious scheme are you up to this time, Trixie?"

The infamous bully nudged Pin-mei.

"Actually," Pin-mei said, "she was trying to save me from the commandoes. Back at the Chasm. So, the commandoes took her as well."

Isla raised her eyes, as if to say "Trixie doing a good deed, whatever next!" Instead, she said, "Once your powers are back, Trixie, you're free to go."

"Oh, I'm staying put. Any passing go-ship and I'm hitching a ride."

Isla's mouth dropped.

"This planet's going to the dogs. And war is havoc on my complexion. Time to find a new market," Trixie said, as way of an explanation.

"That's rich coming from you," Isla protested. "The Valley's number one arms dealer."

"Hey, I just sell them. I never thought people would actually use them."

Isla spat. "Talk about rats leaving the sinking ship."

"Whatever, but this ship *is* sinking. I can feel it."

"Feel?" Zeke piped up.

Trixie shivered and hugged herself.

"Dunno, exactly. Precognition isn't my strong point."

"But you sense something?"

Trixie nodded but said no more. Zeke thought of the 'future fever' that was sweeping the school, Lutz being the first victim. Something bad was coming, he had no doubt. But was it the war or something worse?

"SHOOT!"

Soldiers sprang from the ground in a flurry of sand. Camouflage netting dropped to their feet. Zeke counted four, all armed with neural disruptors. And the disruptors fired.

The humming screeched inside Zeke's skull like a dentist's drill. His eyelids weighed a ton. They cracked apart to reveal dazzling lights. He covered his face.

Where was he? He peered through his fingers, head pounding. The lights dimmed. He was somewhere dark. In front of him, buttons flashed and gauges shone. A virtual dashboard. And he was strapped to his seat. A Sycamore! He was inside a Sycamore, the tiny pods used for landing on Mars.

A girl groaned beside him. It was Pin-mei. Well, of course, Sycamores were built to carry two passengers.

"I think my head's going to pop," she said weakly.

"It'll pass soon. The after-effects of neural disruptors pass quickly."

The humming grew louder.

"That noise," Pin-mei began to say. "Are we in a Sycamore?"

"'Fraid so, and loaded into the Space Catapult."

"No!" Pin-mei cried. She tried to force up the padded bar across their legs.

"The hatch will be sealed for lift-off, no way we'll open it," Zeke said.

"But surely, there must be an abort button on the dashboard?"

They both scanned the controls in front of them.

"Disabled," Zeke said.

"You're taking this all very calmly," Pin-mei snapped. She clearly wasn't. Zeke sighed. He didn't care about anything much at the moment.

"How does this work, anyway?" he asked.

"Remember how Scuff adapted his grav-scooter? Same principle."

"Remind me," Zeke said, lacking Pin-mei and Scuff's talent for science.

"Basically, the Catapult's collider is blasting us with anti-gravitons. The Sycamore is clamped in place. When we reach maximum power, the clamp springs open. The Sycamore shoots up the tunnel like a bullet."

"So...in the weaker Martian gravity, we achieve escape velocity?"

Pin-mei nodded. "Plus, a rocket strapped to the Sycamore for one last push as we exit the Catapult. That then drops off."

"Easy-peasy," Zeke remarked.

They fell quiet, as the humming steadily increased.

Pin-mei's hand clasped his. Her skin was cold.

"So, the old team's back together again?" she said.

"Seems that way," he replied, unsure if she thought that a good thing or not.

"I'm sorry, Zeke."

"What for?"

She paused. "Blaming you for Bartie's death."

"Pin—"

She squeezed his fingers. "And you were right, it's not my fault either. It was Enki first and last for putting Bartie in harm's way. I get it now."

"You—you loved Bartie?"

"Not like that, not how you mean. Bartie and I were friends. We could talk and joke and share stuff. He got how girls feel. Not many boys do. But, wonderful as he was, he wasn't you."

Zeke wasn't sure if it was the cabin or his collar that was heating up. And the hum was deafening.

"I miss you more than sunlight, Zeke. Can we be friends again?"

Zeke stared into her small, beautiful face, bathed in the glow from the dashboard. Electric reds and greens and yellows and blues. Her eyes shone like opals, iridescent with colour. A spasm clawed at Zeke's chest, as if something was lodged in his heart. Who cared about the prophecies of the long-dead Martians? Pin-mei mattered and nothing else.

His tongue was paralysed. *Speak up, you idiot!*

"N-never stopped."

The Catapult chose that exact moment to detonate. Acceleration punched Zeke's stomach harder than a hundred fists. They were hurtling into space.

Chapter Thirty-Three
The Far-Ship

The Sycamore began to slow. It coasted noiselessly, high above the red craters.

"Target aligned," Albie said through the far-ship computer.

"Do your stuff," Zeke replied, sitting in the pilot's chair.

A circle opened in the base of the far-ship. A metallic grip fired out, grabbed the Sycamore and retracted. It disappeared inside and the circle closed.

"They're fine. Bringing them up," came Pin-mei's voice over the intercom.

Zeke leaned back, pleased that the docking went well. Through the observation window he could see the surface of Mars. A sandstorm was brewing over Noachis Terra, like wisps of smoke. To the north-west lay the Tharsis Region, with its three extinct volcanoes. Ascraeus Mons was the northernmost and largest. He peered closer, hoping for a gold twinkle, a reflection from the Perspicillum. But nothing, the distance was too great.

A memory flashed through his head. The Failsafe's final words before it exploded in the belly of that very volcano.

'You must leave someone behind, when this world is ending. A friend'.

Goosebumps tickled his neck.

Isla the Incisor stomped through the auto-door, her gravity boots banging on the metallic floor. Everyone wore gravity boots. The far-ship was in orbit and conditions were weightless. Pin-mei and Trixie were closely behind.

"Get me back to the surface at once!" she snapped.

Zeke shrugged.

"The relaunch programme's blocked. Luckily I never leave home without Albie" Zeke pulled a DVD from his chest pocket. "I've installed him onto the mainframe. He's rerouting the software so the Sycamores can take off, but it's going to take a good hour."

"What is the governor playing at?" Isla exclaimed, plonking herself into the chair beside Zeke. "Why not kill me? I'm public enemy number two, as far as he's concerned. Why catapult me into orbit along with you lot?"

"Who cares?" Trixie said, running he finger along the control panel. "I'm feeling a lot better now we're off the planet. Let's pop back to Earth, I can see Daddy, I do miss him."

Zeke stared at Trixie's face, expecting her usual sarcastic expression. Instead, he saw one of genuine longing. Even the school bully loved someone.

"This stinks of a trap," Isla muttered darkly. "Where's the Mariner who piloted the ship here?"

Zeke shrugged. "You tell me. The ship's deserted. All those floors you passed on the way up, enough for five hundred colonists. Empty."

"Okay, give me a status update."

"Albie's done a thorough scan," Zeke said. "The far-ship is in complete working order. Theoretically, we can translocate to Earth. I've got a rendezvous planned with Mum."

Zeke pushed a swarm of troubling thoughts to the back of his mind. What about Scuff's family? Maybe Zeke could pick them up too. But if Pin and Isla and Trixie found out that the Earth was doomed, they'd want their families saved as well. That would take time. The governor had said these space balloons were very small. The plan began falling apart. He had to focus on the main goal, saving Mum, and not worry about his friends' relatives.

Is this what Ptolemy means about being a great man?

Pin-mei stirred. "Zeke! I know translocation is your thing. But shift a huge spaceship millions of miles? You're not that strong. Nobody is without years of training."

"I translocated between dimensions. A first for the human race."

"And I was second. You're not the only gifted kid around here," Trixie butted in. "Have you seen it yet?" she added.

Zeke nodded and beckoned them with his finger. He crossed the bridge and activated an auto-door. They piled onto the balcony on the other side and looked down.

Isla gasped.

Trixie cooed.

Pin-mei attempted a whistle that failed miserably.

The balcony overlooked a transparent, cube-shaped container the size of a house. A shimmering balloon floated inside, submersed in clear liquid.

"What on Mars is that thing?" Isla asked, her cheeks a little green.

"Something beautiful," was Zeke's reply.

The cellular creature was almost as big as the container. Little shudders and ripples passed through its outer membrane. Its interior was all fluid, with a dark-orange nucleus at the centre. Countless tiny ovals and stars and ribbons rotated around the nucleus. As these objects wriggled, their movements triggered a kaleidoscope of colours. Purples, greens, yellows and blues flowed and merged, like an overgrown soap bubble.

"That's what they make at the protoplasm farms on Europa," Trixie explained.

Isla stared at her, mouth gaping. "You mean, actual, giant..."

Trixie smirked.

"Yup, giant protoplasms. Single cell animals. Cultivated from blank DNA and nurtured to the size you see before you."

"But, why?"

"There are limits to the human brain, even for a genius like me," Trixie began. "The average Mariner is bright enough to translocate around the solar system. An immense distance. But to travel to the heart of the galaxy? To cross scores of light years in seconds? Light takes four years just to get from the Sun to the nearest star. And decades to reach the nearest habitable planets. No human has the brainpower for that."

"So where does that thing come in?" Isla asked.

"The protoplasm acts as a kind of echo chamber," Zeke said. "First, a Mariner's DNA is copied onto its DNA helix. Genetically, they're the same life form. Then the Mariner bonds with it telepathically. When the Mariner translocates deep space, the protoplasm magnifies his brainwaves."

Isla hugged herself. "Creepy. With a capital C."

Pin-mei took Zeke's hand. "You can't be serious. After all that we know now."

Zeke shrugged. "That the deep space jump kills the Mariner? It's still not proven. Anyway, maybe that's my fate. First get my Mum. Then find my father, or die trying."

Pin-mei opened her mouth, about to protest.

"You're a bit ahead of yourself, aren't you?" Trixie butted in. "Until you're bonded, you're not going anywhere, and that takes days."

Now it was Zeke's turn to smirk. "Not if the far-ship is programmed with the smartest transport app ever invented."

"Not your precious Albie again?" Trixie replied.

"He's already uploaded my DNA signature. That mega-microbe you're looking at is a bit of me. All we have to do now is the telepathic link. And Albie thinks he can get that down to a few minutes. He's reshaped the algorithm to carry ten times more data."

"Hang on, you're not taking me on a joyride to Alpha Cephei," Trixie said with a snarl.

Zeke raised his hands to calm her. "Earth will be the first port of call. Give me a chance to warm up." He stared at Pin-mei.

"I'm staying right here," she said. "Mars needs me. The school needs me. And, frankly speaking, they need you. In fact—" her voice wavered, "— so do I."

For some reason, Trixie guffawed with laughter.

"Another fifty minutes, roughly, and the Sycamores will be online again," Zeke replied.

"Zeke, surely you're not walking away when the Chasm needs you most?" Pin-mei pleaded, her eyes suddenly wet.

"What difference would it make? I can't win a war."

Pin-mei clenched her fists. "It's not about winning, it's about being there."

She doesn't know what you know, whispered that little voice at the back of Zeke's head.

They stared at each other, friends again, no more bad feelings, but still divided.

The intercom beeped. Albie's voice crackled through the speaker.

"Master Zeke, we have an incoming transmission from the governor of Mars."

"Something tells me it won't be good news," Isla remarked, and followed the others back onto the bridge.

Chapter Thirty-Four
The Far-Ship Bridge

"Howdy, folks," the governor said from the large plasma-screen over the controls. He was sitting in the Ellipse Office, with a small leather case on the desk in front of him.

A crocodile's leer plastered his face.

"What's going on?" Isla bellowed at the screen, her cheeks redder than her hair. The governor laughed.

"War. That's what's going on."

"But why have you put us up here? Even me?" Isla continued.

"I'm coming to that. I'm trying to give Mister Hailey here a little incentive to be nice." The governor paused, as if expecting a reply from Zeke. But Zeke just stared at him, lost in thought.

"I've got something to show you. I think it's going to motivate you all to be a tad more cooperative."

Zeke took a couple of steps towards the screen and asked, "Where's Mariner Chinook?" The governor glanced away. "Oh, he's gone. Said he was needed at the school."

"He left without me?" Zeke replied. It seemed incredulous that Chinook would up and go without him.

The governor thumped the desk with his fist. "I think we've got more important things to talk about than one misplaced teacher. Your precious school is about to be blasted out of existence."

Pin-mei gasped.

"By your troops, I suppose?" Zeke asked.

The governor said nothing, nodding to someone off-camera. The transmission crackled. A sky-high view appeared, looking down onto mud-coloured spire-tops. The Ophir Chasm School for Psychic Endeavour.

"Must be a helimac," Pin said. "A flying drone."

The cam on the helimac zoomed in. Dots turned into circles turned into faces. The school wall was now a battlement lined with ninjas. There were only ninjas now. Any distinction between school student and rebel had melted away. Everyone wore the same black hoods and outfits.

The cam panned along the faces, each etched with a steely frown. Zeke knew many of them. There was a guard from Yuri-Gagarin Freetown. Next to him, Zeke recognised Edenville's blacksmith. There were the teachers, Zoe Kepler and Alistair Knimble among them. And of course, Zeke's classmates. Dedy, Juanita, Aku… Zeke peered for a glimpse of Scuff, but he was nowhere to be seen.

"Oh," he remarked sadly. It was little Gary Aspeck. He had a big determined frown on his face, but it wasn't very convincing. His fear was plain to see.

The helimac's cam circled round, till it was facing south, away from the school. The Valley was crowded with Brontos, special tanks rigged out for the Martian environment. In the foreground, three rows of soldiers stood ready. Every one of them armed, not with a neural disruptor, but deadly bullet-firing rifles. Zeke spied three of the soldiers from the journey on the Monarch. He and they had survived the missile attack together. Despite their fierce expressions, Zeke could not hate them. Two sides were about to fight to the death. And yet, they were all the same stuff. Flesh, bone and thumping hearts. Rebel and soldier. Human versus human. No villains. Not here. The villain was a thousand miles away, sipping posh coffee and eating doughnuts.

The cam zoomed through the ranks of soldiers and lingered on a large canon. Then more crackling and the screen returned to the governor's face.

"Yes Zeke, that's the ferromagnetic canon. Every Mariner in the school is now no more psychic than my dumbest grunt. My army are trained killers. Your fellow students and teachers are anything but. My men will plough through them."

Zeke screwed his hands into fists, but kept silent.

"Give me the code, Zeke. Give it to me and bloodshed can be avoided. I'll put them all to sleep with Electron's Blade. My men will remove the rebels, but leave the school folk as they are. Not enough prisons for everyone. And you? You can walk away. Skedaddle off to the stars and your precious daddy."

"Do it, Zeke. For God's sake, do it." It was Trixie, with what looked like tears in her eyes.

"She's right, Zeke. Sometimes even you can't save the day," Pin-mei said. Zeke gazed at her.

"I thought you were all for fighting. Back at the school—"

"That was then," she replied. "But we've lost. Do it before anyone dies."

Isla gently touched Zeke's arm.

"Never thought I'd be saying this, but I agree. Better to lose the battle and live to fight another day."

"Don't you all see?" Zeke said, flushing with anger. "The Governor's lying. I don't know what Electron's Blade does, but it's not that. This whole thing is one great lie, a charade of mega-proportions. All to get that password."

"Then give it to him," Trixie shouted and stamped her foot.

Zeke turned back to the screen.

"The answer, Sir, is no."

For a second, storms raged behind those cool grey eyes. Then the Governor chuckled and shook his head. He opened the leather case on the desk. Inside was a red button and a timer.

"Checkmate, boy," he said, and pressed the button.

Moments ticked away. Zeke and his friends exchanged glances. What now?

"Master Zeke," Albie said over the ship's radio system. There was an edge of alarm in his voice. That was a first. "I detect a missile launch on the surface. A missile on a trajectory to collide with this ship."

Trixie shrieked. Isla ran to the ship's controls.

"Fly it! How do we fly this tin can?"

"Oh, the ship's manual flight is in off-mode," the Governor said. "My techies made sure of that. Until you get your powers back, you ain't going anywhere."

Trixie let rip a stream of foul-mouthed insults.

The Governor didn't bat an eyelid.

"By the way, kiddies," he said. "That missile has a warhead that will blow you out of the sky."

Zeke went from hot to cold. It was the shock of realisation. The last piece in a jigsaw. He stepped nearer to the screen.

"A missile? An awful lot of missiles have been fired recently."

The Governor chuckled.

"First the Televator," Zeke said. "That was your excuse to go to war. Then the one used on the Monarch, and the one that killed Mariner Aryabhata. And there was that bomb back at the bar."

The Governor gave a bow.

"I knew you'd work it out. The so-called Martian State Brigade never existed. Pure fabrication. Make the people afraid of bogeymen and they'll let you get away with murder. Mass murder. AKA war."

"You don't want to be governor. You want to be king," Isla snarled.

The governor shrugged. "Why not, I'll be great."

"You—you started the war as a way of seizing control?" Pin-mei asked, wide-eyed.

"What better way to wipe out my rivals and justify absolute power?" the governor replied, with such a smirk Zeke wanted to punch him.

"As for you, Hailey, I used the attacks to make you hostile to the Unpro, and more sympathetic to me. You were never in any real danger. Both the Monarch missile and the Tithonium bomb were set up to avoid any casualties. But they didn't seem to be working on you. So, I upped the stakes. Timed a missile to hit your classroom after the lesson finished."

"So, it missed me by a whisker. But it didn't miss Mariner Ariyabata."

"You see, boy? You see what damage your stubborn will has done?"

"Well, you failed to win me over," Zeke replied, glaring at the Governor. "And so, you lied to lure me back. Don't tell me, there

216

never were any space balloons. Our families aren't going anywhere."

"Tell a person what they want to hear and they'll make themselves believe it," The Governor replied with an evil grin.

Zeke ground his teeth, too furious to speak.

"Why didn't you just put a gun to Zeke's head," Isla bellowed. "Why go to these lengths?"

The Governor leaned forward. "And he'd let me shoot him, wouldn't he? But now I've got him and his buddies trapped. He won't let his buddies die. Or will you boy?"

"Master Zeke, four minutes to collision," Albie interrupted.

"Options?"

"None, Sir."

Albie was right. Their powers were erased, the Sycamores were offline, and the ship's engines shut down. They were sitting space ducks.

"Do something," Trixie yelled.

"Wait, don't these ships have star diving suits?" Isla asked.

Pin-mei nodded. "I saw some, in the arrival bay."

"Are you nuts?" Trixie bellowed in Isla's face. "Jump out the airlock with no training? Enter the atmosphere at re-entry speed? You'll either burn up or crash into the planet head-first."

"I can see the missile," Pin-mei wailed, pale as ice.

Zeke joined her at the window. Something was hurtling towards them. The missile was a speck against the red landscape, but the vapour trail was clear. They locked hands.

The governor called from the screen.

"What's it to be, Zekey boy? You got three minutes. Spill the beans and I'll blow the missile up. Promise. You have my word as a Texan. Tell the truth and you can go. If not, I'll fire off another. And I sure got a load of missiles."

The missile was visible now, a tiny toothpick, a shadow over the craters. A rocket full of death.

Zeke looked around the bridge. Pin-mei, so beautiful and clever and kind and unique. One day she might change the universe. Brave, formidable Isla. The best kind of soldier, tough but with a heart of gold. She only fought for the right cause. And those beautiful green eyes. Even Trixie, he couldn't bear the idea of her dying so pointlessly.

Panic was rising in his chest. Images flashed though his mind. The school, Scuff, his father, his mother back on Earth, waiting for the day she'd see her only son again. What was the right thing to do? What was it! He didn't know, it was all down to guesses and gut instincts.

"Two minutes, Master Zeke," Albie chimed.

His mind came back to Pin-mei. He'd only just realised he loved her. Was he going to lose her now, forever? Let her flame of life get snuffed out? Those eyes, deep and wise beyond her years. The easy smile, that always made things better. Her cute, upturned nose.

"Zeke!" Trixie cried, pleading for salvation.

"It's your call," Isla said. She was trying to look brave, but wasn't making a good job of it.

Pin-mei gripped his hand harder. "I don't want to die, Zeke." There were tears in those deep, wise eyes.

"Neither do I," Zeke admitted.

Sacrifice so one will live. It was beginning to make sense. He didn't know how, and never would now, but it was a message for him. The primordial universe was sending him a warning. Pin-mei had to live.

"Okay, okay," he shouted at the plasma screen. "If I tell you, do you promise?"

"On my darling mama's grave," the governor said, his eyes twinkling.

"The runes, they're pronounced *sa cra fie sa so wu na will lee va*, got that? *Sa cra fie sa so wu na will lee va?*"

The plasma screen went blank. Zeke and Pin glanced at each other, then through the window. The missile was hurtling towards them, a pillar of destruction. Nearer and nearer and...a fireball! An eruption of yellows and oranges. The far-ship rocked. Trixie slipped and landed on her butt.

The governor's ugly, leering face reappeared. "Enki says it could just be. I hope for your sake you're telling the truth. Next time I might not be so merciful." And then he was gone again.

"What's happening?" Pin-mei asked.

"They're going to try out the password. They have to keep me alive till they know for sure." Zeke said.

"And were you telling the truth?" Isla asked.

Zeke nodded.

"Then the Governor no longer needs you," she went on.

Zeke nodded again and cried, "Quick, wire me up!"

"What?" Pin-mei asked, eyes wide.

Zeke drew a deep breath. "We're leaving."

Chapter Thirty-Five

The Astral Plane

It was rather like watching a holo-movie. Zeke was looking down from the ceiling, as Pin-mei and Trixie strapped his body onto the T-shaped motherboard, adjusted the safety harness and fixed electrodes to the skull. He remembered doing the same for Edward Dayo, the day he left Earth. Dear, dead Edward. And soon it would be his turn to die.

"He's unconscious," Isla said, stepping back from the others.

"Yes," Pin-mei answered. "The computer is connecting him to the protoplasm. Creates a shock brainwave. He'll be fine."

"Didn't you say the Mariners died when they translocated a ship?" Isla went on, as pale as milk.

"We think so, for the deep space trips," Pin-mei replied. "But we're going to Earth, so no problem. Except Zeke has never done this before."

"He'll do it," Trixie said.

"How can you be so sure?" Isla asked.

"Because I know him," Trixie replied.

If Zeke had been in his body, he would have blushed.

"Well, you have to get me back first. I'm not leaving," Isla said, balling her hands into fists.

"The Sycamores should be online soon. I'll be coming with you," Pin-mei said in a grim voice.

"So, it's just Blue Boy and me," Trixie remarked, and fastened the last of the straps.

Wasting time, this isn't what you want to see, said Zeke's inner voice.

Zeke passed through the hull, into the vacuum of space. Instinct prompted him to gasp for air, but of course his lungs were breathing away back inside. Mars was far below, a tapestry of reds and ochres. And in the south a tinge of green, the oxygen moss plantations.

'Down,' he thought.

He began to drop, faster and faster. A solid object would heat up with friction from the atmosphere, burn, even explode. But Zeke was pure thought. He felt nothing.

Cracks turned into ravines. Bumps expanded into mountains and canyons. The ride was exhilarating. If only Ariyabata was alive to see Zeke's achievement.

Zeke aimed for Mariners Valley. The eight-kilometre-high cliffs hurtled up to meet him. He dropped to two miles above ground level and sped westwards. The desert rushed beneath him. He spared a thought for Scuff. Down there, somewhere. A tinge of guilt tweaked at his heart. But there was nothing he could do in his astral form. He had no more substance than a ghost. All he could do now was watch. Witness.

The white blocks of Tithonium Central came into view. They grew rapidly, from toytown blocks to real buildings. There was the Ellipse.

Zeke slowed. And in seconds he was coasting through corridors. Which way led to the room with Electron's Blade?

The sound of voices echoed off the walls. Two or more people were approaching. Zeke's first thought was to hide somewhere. Then he cursed his stupidity. He was on the astral plane and therefore invisible.

Two bulky security men appeared out of the gloom. They were carrying something big, one at the front and one at the rear. But what, exactly? Zeke lifted to the ceiling as they passed underneath. Their burden was a black plastic sack. Something man-sized was inside.

"Weighs a ton, this one," the man at the front remarked, struggling to hold on. The one at the back laughed. "Not for much longer."

"Quite right, Charlie," his colleague said. "Nothing cuts a man down to size than cremating his bones."

"Ay, lad. Pity he couldn't have a proper send-off. Didn't seem a bad sort."

"Charlie! War's war. There's going to be a lot more people shot in the back before all's said and done."

It was a body bag. The shock hit Zeke like a hammer to the face. These goons were transporting a corpse. But who?

The answer dawned on him with sickening dread. His mind wanted to throw up, but his body was too far away.

The men turned a corner, still struggling.

"What was he anyway? An American Indian?" the rear man asked.

"Nah, one of them Eskimos," Charlie answered.

"What's the difference, then?"

"Dunno, really. None, I suppose, now he's a goner."

They vanished from sight.

Zeke found the room with the Governor, Enki and Electron's Blade. He floated in a corner, glaring at them. A cold fury raged inside of him. An anger, a hatred, a pain. Zeke had never known a feeling like this. If only he'd had hands, he would have throttled the Governor to death. As it was, he was impotent, a disembodied spirit, condemned to watch.

"You're sure the little rat wasn't lying?" the Governor asked, scowling.

Enki gazed away. "We won't know till we try. If he is, the next missile gets closer. He won't put his little playmates at risk." He giggled. "Come, put it on and sit here."

He gestured to a seat positioned in front of the Blade. The Governor hesitated.

"You are sure there's no risk?"

Enki stared at his shoes.

"Absolutely. The Blade will tune in to your brainwaves. It will feel a tad hot. That will pass."

The Governor looked plagued with doubt. "Maybe we should test it on a guinea pig. One of the prisoners?"

"Tish, tish," Enki replied. "In a few minutes you're going to kill every enemy you have on Mars. Just as we've always said."

A slow, wicked smile stole across the Governor's face.

"Victory," he said, more to himself. "Tell me once more."

Enki gave him a strange look. "Simply focus. Say to yourself that you want everyone who hates you dead. Electron's Blade will scan every intelligent brain on the planet. In a thousandth of a second. And every brain harbouring aggression to you gets shut down. Permanently."

"Beautiful," the Governor said, awestruck.

"It will be quite instantaneous." Enki added. "Across Mars, every rebel, every opponent, even those with secret grudges against you, all will drop dead."

"And I'll be king. King of Mars."

"Quite so," Enki said softly, gesturing again to the seat.

The Governor sat down, and placed the *quclxii* on his head. It was indeed his crown.

Zeke watched on, incensed yet powerless. If only he had corporeal form, so he could use his fists, or his psychokinesis. Anything to attack these evil men. But his anger subsided into fear. Something worse than mass slaughter was about to happen. Hadn't he always sensed it? He hovered closer to Enki. The way the man moved, like a doll or a puppet... Somehow changed since their encounter in the pocket universe.

Enki moved to the other side of the Blade and threw his arms out.

"Oh, sweet moment," he muttered. "The Rupture begins." And then in a booming voice, "*sa cra fie sa so wunna will lee va.*" And then again and again. He had no idea that the words were English. That did not matter to him. His only interest was their use, not their meaning.

As Enki recited the words over and over, the Blade started to hum. A high-pitched whine, steadily gaining volume. The blade glowed. Veins of brilliant light appeared in the rocky base.

"Sa cra fie sa so wunna will lee va. Sa cra fie sa so wunna will lee va."

"Okay, there's that warmth you mentioned," the governor piped up. Enki ignored him, chanting the password like a man possessed.

"Enki, is it supposed to be this hot?" the governor shouted, sweat pouring from his scalp. "Enki!"

"Sa cra fie sa so wunna will lee va."

The governor shifted in his seat. The light from the Blade was intensifying. "It's burning," the governor suddenly cried, pulling at the crown with both hands. It did not budge. He tried harder. Nothing. He jumped up, wrestling with the device. It was welded to his skin.

"Help me," he cried, staggering towards Enki. His face was red. Blood-red. And then he screamed. The stench of seared flesh filled the air. He fell to his knees, weeping tears of agony.

A tiny, tiny part of Zeke felt pleased.

"Sa cra fie sa so wunna will lee va."

The Governor made one last effort to stand, still struggling with the death trap on his head. He shrieked like an animal, tumbled over and no longer moved. A beam of light shot up from the Blade, smashing the ceiling to shreds. Zeke caught a glimpse of Enki through the glare. The man was melting. Almost dead, yet with his mouth still gibbering the syllables. A puppet to the last.

Zeke watched on, half hypnotised by the fierce light. He'd failed and knew it. Enki had lied. He'd fooled the governor, and everyone. The Blade didn't read minds or dish out death from a distance. Its purpose was quite different. What else could the words electron and blade mean, coupled together? The machine had a way of cutting through atomic particles, into those extra dimensions hidden away on the quantum level. Every atom in existence was an intersection to other universes. Nearby, but forever out of reach at the same time. As solid as this universe, but invisible, intangible. Everywhere and nowhere at the same time.

Until the Hesperians came up with their technology. They built Electron's Blade. *Why* was anyone's guess. All the Blade needed was mental energy and someone to say the activation code. The governor unwittingly supplied the energy. Even his non-psychic brain was enough. Zeke wondered why the Hesperians built a machine that destroyed its own power source. Perhaps it didn't work like that, all those eons ago. Anyway, the Hesperians must have used it and let in a monster from the other side. Somehow, they stopped it. Imprisoned it in the Infinity Trap. Zeke had no idea how.

And now, two billion years later, it was happening again. That's why the Spiral warned him against using Electron's Blade. A double bluff. It seemed so obvious now.

He thought of Scuff, left behind. Zeke could do nothing to help him. Scuff, and everyone, was doomed. Mars would fall, and then Earth.

The glare exploded into a starburst of blinding white. The room shattered and the foundations shook.

Chapter Thirty-Six
Tithonium Central

"What on sweet Mars is that?" a woman asked. She was standing on Stephen Hawking Boulevard. A man stopped and followed her gaze. A few more gathered around them.

An intense beam soared through the ruptured roof of the Ellipse Building. It zoomed high into the tawny sky, disappearing into a fireball.

A fork of lightning blasted the ground. The woman gasped. Workers hurried out from shiny cube-shape offices, crowding around the cool palms. Everyone stared up at the spectacle, shielding their eyes from the brightness, but unable to look away.

"Never seen anything like it," the man said to nobody in particular.

More lightning bolts erupted, shooting in all directions. A roar filled their eardrums. And then a deafening crack. The ground shuddered.

"There's something dark, inside the fire," the woman said.

"I see it, like a hole," the man replied.

"Ew, what's that thing?" the woman squealed.

A tentacle unfurled from the dark epicentre of the fireball. Then more. Something was squeezing itself through a gap in the sky.

"Oh, isn't that a beak?" the man added, dumbfounded. The woman didn't answer.

The Spiral was now floating high over Tithonium. His tentacles began to rotate around his huge mouth. They formed patterns, spirals within spirals, drawing the eye of the onlookers into the drooling jaws.

"It's rather pretty, whatever it is," the woman remarked. She sounded calmer.

"Do you hear that?" the man asked.

"Yes, he's calling us."

"No, I hear singing," the man gently disagreed.

People around them murmured happily. No one could break their gaze, but no one wanted to. The woman raised both hands.

"Take me, Master Spiral."

"Me too," the man said. Across the city, more people were reaching up.

"I am hungry," a voice boomed from the heavens. Deep and echoing.

"Eat me then, please," the woman said.

"I will."

The woman's feet levitated off the pavement. For a few seconds she bobbed above the others, before rocketing upwards. A cheer rippled through the masses. But there were also cries of terror. A few turned and fled. Most stayed their ground.

"Me, don't forget me," the man shouted. As if in reward, he too floated upwards, slowly at first, then faster. Everywhere, people were rising into the air. They went smiling, waving to those around them. Those running away, those too clever to be hypnotised, were no luckier. They were snatched up, and disappeared into the sky, screaming for mercy. Blood rained.

Fitch Crawley was in his cell, shaving his head. Tufts of dirty blond hair surrounded him. He switched of the iShaver and rubbed his smooth scalp. His forefinger traced the red X on his head. The scar left behind by the surgeon's laser. The lobotomy forced on him by the Mariners to rob him of his psychic powers.

A thunderous noise shook the Mental Health Facility. One long deep roar, like the boom of a mountain horn.

"About time," Fitch muttered.

The walls shook, fractured and fell. The entire Facility collapsed, outwards, like a house of cards. Freedom. Fitch stepped over the ruins, until he reached the lawn. A few of the medical staff were grouped there, gazing at the phenomenon high overhead. They were oblivious to the destruction of their workplace, or even the escape of their most dangerous prisoner.

Instead, they cooed and pointed at the twirling folds of the Spiral. Among them, Fitch spied the two burly orderlies. How many times had they restrained him? Taunted him? The doctors and nurses levitated off the grass. Some of them laughed, but one older woman whimpered. She stared at Fitch with terror in her eyes.

"Bye-bye," he said, and gave a little wave. Every one of them whooshed skywards.

"Master, not the two who hurt me," Fitch said.

The two orderlies were already as high as a skyscraper when the Spiral let them go. They hurtled down, shrieking, and landing in a bloody splat at Fitch's feet.

Before his could enjoy a good cackle, a bolt of electricity struck him. Fitch threw back his arms and his body glowed. He cried out with ecstasy as brain tissue deep in his skull grew back. Tears of joy flowed down his cheeks. The feeling, oh that feeling! The tingling of psychic powers. The Master's reward. Resurrection.

"I'm back, Hailey, I'm back."

Josiah Cain was in mid-sermon when a distant rumbling disturbed the Marmish chapel. The congregation stirred.

Cain glared at them. The patience he once had for his flock, dried up when his son died.

"Brethren. Do not be distracted from the word of Our Lord. I will continue with today's reading from the Book of Revelations."

He cleared his throat.

"And I saw an angel standing in the sun, who cried in a loud voice to all the birds flying in the air, 'Come, gather together for the great supper of our Master, so that you may eat the flesh of kings, generals, of horses and their riders, and the flesh of all people, free and slave, great and small.' For this was the devil's false promise."

"I don't get it," piped up a little girl on the front row. "You said an angel, not a demon."

Cain drew himself to his full height.

"Daughter, sometimes a demon masquerades as an angel. But let me finish, this next bit is good.

"I saw heaven standing open and there before me was a white horse, whose rider is called Faithful and True. He wages war for justice. His eyes are of blazing fire, and on his head are many crowns. His robe is dipped in blood, and his name is the Word of God. The army of the skies followed him, riding white horses and dressed in white and clean linen. Coming out of his mouth is a sword sharp enough to strike down nations."

The girl nudged her brother. "That'll be the hero."

Cain banged his fist down on the pulpit. "The beast was captured!" he cried in a crescendo. "And with it the false prophet who performed its signs. The two of them were thrown alive into the fiery lake of burning sulphur."

"See," the girl said, "I love a happy ending."

"Everyone come and see!"

The words echoed through the chapel. Barnabas, one of the farmers, was standing in the doorway, panting like a racehorse.

"Outside...in the sky," he added, struggling to breathe.

At once, everyone rushed out from the chapel.

"Come back, I'm not done," Josiah bellowed, furious with his wayward flock. He followed them into the harsh Martian daylight.

"Ain't it pretty?" someone said. High in the sky, easily a hundred miles away, was the weirdest thing. Spirals. Spirals within spirals. A gigantic, glowing pattern. Cain rubbed his eyes. Was he hallucinating?

"Is it the *End of Times*?" an old woman asked. "When we'll be carried up to heaven?"

Cain's stomach turned to ice. He stared harder. Not spirals, but tentacles. The tall tales of those damned children, Hailey and Liang, flashed through his memory. How monsters lurked in other dimensions, always seeking a way in.

The Marmish started singing a hymn, *Shall We Gather at the River?*

They linked hands and swayed, their lips smiling, their eyes empty.

"Stop it!" Cain shouted, shaking those nearest. But they no longer saw him. One by one, their feet lifted from the ground. Each lingered a few seconds, and then shot up into the haze. Cain desperately seized his wife by her coattails. It was useless. She was sucked away, lost in a happy trance.

Cain threw himself through the chapel doors and limped back up the aisle. Perhaps the altar would save him?

"Cain, Cain, why do you persecute me?"

Cain wheeled around wildly. Where was the voice coming from? "Don't you know Bartie is waiting for you?"

"What!" Cain cried. The mention of his son brought tears to his eyes.

"All you have to do is want it," the voice said, "and I will bring you to your son."

Cain hesitantly retraced his steps to the door. Could it be true? The chance to see Bartie again was worth any risk. Even a deal with the devil. He stopped on the threshold, staring up at the slimy tentacles. And in a split second, he was flying.

"What in tarnation is it?" Justice asked. Professor Van Hiss stood next to him, staring through the eye-piece of his super-telescope.

A cloud was visible through the glass of the observation dome. It was far away, somewhere over Mariners' Valley. From this distance, it was tiny, a smudge of white against red sky. A shudder shook Justice to the core. A dark foreboding.

"This is being very strange," Van Hiss remarked, still glued to the eyepiece.

"What do you see?" Justice snapped.

"Most beautiful. This phenomenon is most beautiful."

Justice poked his employer, desperate to know more.

"The teeth are as big as houses. And radiant as pearls. The way they interlock in a circular movement is fascinating."

"What?" Justice cried.

"Be looking yourself, *ja*?" Hiss said, stepping back from the huge barrel of the telescope.

Were those spirals in Hiss's eyes? Justice blinked. No, the Professor was quite normal. Justice leaned over the telescope and peered through the eyepiece.

For a second, he could not make sense of what he saw. The telescope was focussed on a huge, snapping beak. Inside were grinding plates of daggers. Oh, not daggers, teeth. The beak was sucking in a constant flow of bodies. Justice thought of a food blender, and gulped back his revulsion.

He tried to look away. But the sight held his attention. It was too hideous. Too horrible. Too bloody. Too compelling. Too intricate. Too marvellous. Too happy.

Justice smiled, "You know, Mister Professor, Sir. Methinks we need a looksee at this darn peculiarity."

Van Hiss nodded. "I am thinking this is a singularity, not a peculiarity."

"Whatever. Let's get all up close and personal."

"It would take us days to be getting there."

Justice chuckled. "Unless we take the quick way."

Van Hiss clicked his fingers. "*Ja, Natuurlijk!*"

"Isn't there that emergency release panel in the dome?"

Van Hiss clapped Justice on the shoulder.

"Excellent, *mijn vriend!* In case of fire. The switch is on the telescope dashboard. I must be triggering it and—poof—a panel flies out."

"And the air whooshes into the vacuum?" Justice asked eagerly.

"*Ja, ja,* and us with it."

"And the singularity will take over, I just know it. We'll fly to Mariners Valley like a pair of chickadees heading south for the winter."

Hiss put his finger on a large red button. Before he could press it, the computer activated a high-pitched alarm.

"What the heck is that?" Justice cried, annoyed by the delay.

Van Hiss frowned, an expression of confusion on his brown face.

"Ach, the genesis particle alarm. The telescope must have found some." He glanced at a gauge. "Lots, apparently."

"Does it matter, Mister Professor, Sir?"

"Not any longer," Van Hiss beamed, flicking a switch and ending the alarm. "We are having better things to do." He reached for the button.

"What are you doing!"

It was Bobbi, standing on the gravity pedestal. His voice was on full volume and every one of his bulbs was flashing red.

Justice gave him a frosty look. "Joining a singular peculiarity."

"Or a peculiar singularity," Hiss added. Both guffawed with laughter.

"You'll be killed!" Bobbi shouted.

"*Nee, nee,*" Hiss began, as though speaking to a small child. "We will be merging our atomic signatures with a trans-dimensional phenomenon. It will be the liberating experience."

A robot can do many things simultaneously. And a robotoid even more. The tiny cloud was too far off for Bobbi to analyse. Instead, he scanned his masters. They were saturated in cosmic microwave background radiation. This electromagnetic radiation was a leftover from the Big Bang and found everywhere in the universe. But never to such dangerous levels. Electric pulses, invisible to the human eye, crackled around their heads. Bobbi guessed these were thought waves, but not from any human. Something was projecting its brain activity from afar. The men's speech was slurred, an indication that their own brains were impaired. Their heart rates were slowed, their breathing deeper, their muscles relaxed.

"You're…in a trance," Bobbi said, his voice synthesiser crackling with fear.

"Nonsense," Hiss snapped, and pressed the button. There came a pop, followed by a cyclone of howling air. And Bobbi was alone.

Chapter Thirty-Seven
The Far-Ship Bridge

Shapes clustered around Zeke. His eyes focussed. It was the three girls, all with expressions of concern.

"Thank goodness," Pin-Mei said. "We couldn't wake you."

Zeke tried to move, then remembered he was strapped onto the motherboard, arms outstretched.

"What's the plan?" Isla asked.

Zeke didn't answer. Something was wrong. He was…different. Bigger. His brain felt so alive, so strong.

"That's the feedback loop with the protoplasm. All your cerebral functions are boosted," Pin-mei explained.

"You're reading my mind, naughty," Zeke replied with a half-hearted smile.

She nodded. "My powers are returning."

"Look out the observation window," he said.

Pin-mei lifted from the deck and floated over to the window. She gasped. Trixie and Isla joined her. Trixie floating, Isla on foot.

"What do you see?" Zeke asked.

The words stuck in Pin-mei's throat. "The-the Spiral. Over Mariners Valley."

Trixie stepped back, falling into a seat. Her face was ashen.

"What's going on?" Isla asked. "Is it a raincloud? That grey curtain falling down from the spirals, it can't be rain, can it?"

"It's not falling down, it's falling up," Zeke said in a low voice.

"Come again?" Isla asked, a frown growing across her smooth forehead.

Zeke shifted within the safety harness, averting his gaze.

"That greyness you see, it's people."

"Don't talk rubbish," Isla snapped.

"The Spiral is sucking everyone on Mars up into his belly. He's eating them."

"Just like he ate Jasper Snod," Trixie muttered, more to herself.

"That's impossible," Isla replied, her voice booming.

Pin-mei touched Isla's forearm.

"I'm afraid not. The Spiral can move objects by thought, just like we can. Only on an immense scale. And he hypnotises them, so they go willingly."

There was a silence while Isla struggled to take it all in.

"You mean—Tolly!"

"He can't be saved, Isla," Zeke said, still looking away.

"Of course he can! I won't leave him."

Zeke turned to face her. "You will. You're coming with us. And we're leaving."

For a split second she returned his gaze, her face on fire with rage. Then she bolted for the door.

"Let G.I. Jane go. Who needs her?" Trixie said, standing up and taking a deep breath.

"We can't walk out on the school. Our friends," Pin-mei said.

"No choice," Zeke mumbled.

"Zeke!" She cried, hands on hips. "We've got to rescue Scuff, at least."

He stared at the ground. Pin-mei stamped her foot. "He's—he's like family. For pity's sake, Zeke, he's your best friend."

"You think I don't know that!" Zeke was shouting. "But Scuff is dead. They all are. He's either been ripped apart in the Spiral's jaws or is about to be. If we try to find him, we'll be eaten too."

"I can't believe I'm hearing this. You're leaving Scuff behind? You two were like brothers."

"Yes! The nearest to a brother I've ever had. My only brother.

And I'll never have a brother again. And I'm deserting him. Got it?" His voice was hoarse with emotion. Tears filled his eyes. "I've failed him. But I'm not failing you."

"Zeke—" Pin began to say.

"Shut it, sister, Blue Boy's right," Trixie said, putting her forefinger to Pin-mei's lips. "The sooner we save our bacon and translocate to Earth, the better."

"We're not going to Earth."

"Not your damn daddy again. He's not a priority," Trixie said.

"It's not about him anymore," Zeke replied. "We need a safe haven."

"Zeke?" Pin-mei said, "What about your mother? My parents?"

Zeke's voice trembled as he answered. "We can't save them either. We can only save ourselves."

"Nonsense," Trixie snarled. "I have a mum and dad too, you know. And I'm not completely hostile to them."

Zeke's whole body was shaking.

"I'm sorry. The Spiral will reach Earth in days. He's fast. But not light speed fast. We have to go somewhere light years away, where we can live out our lives."

Pin-mei swallowed.

"One thing we've established is that a jump to deep space will kill you, Zeke."

Zeke was about to answer when he realised Pin-mei was shimmering. No, not shimmering. Her entire body was made up from tiny, spinning spirals. Trixie too. The walls, floor, the dashboard, the ship controls, everything was a picture made of coloured spirals. They began to move, swell. Swiftly, they merged into one great spiral. *The Spiral.* As large as a house, floating in space, and laughing in triumph.

The emptiness of space sucked the air out in a heartbeat. Isla unhooked herself and walked up to the gaping doorway. The weight of the black star-suit made each step slow and clunky. As soon as

Isla put the suit on, it merged into a one-piece, making an airtight seal. She looked like a frogman, minus the flippers. Oxygen cannisters and a parachute slipped over her shoulders. A golden visor fed signals inside the suit, enabling the wearer to see.

Isla peered down at the mosaic of craters. A sudden wave of nausea forced her back. Maybe Zeke was right. Better to stay onboard and escape. He was a smart kid. When she was his age…a memory surfaced. Being a teenager.

Declaring herself a rebel. She did this to annoy her father as much as anything. Running away from the Swedish Embassy. What a damn foolhardy thing to do. She planned to trek across the wasteland to Yuri-Gagarin Freetown. Throw her lot in with the rebels. Within a couple of days, she was hopelessly lost. The water ran out. She collapsed on the sands, and waited to die.

Isla stepped up to the brink again. From this altitude, the tectonic fractures of Candor Chasma looked like gigantic scallop shells.

That's where she'd lain, frozen, starved, dehydrated. Delirious. On the edge of death. Until a hand reached out and grasped hers. A strong hand. Yes, it was Ptolemy, he found her. He saved her. And she'd loved him ever since.

Isla took a deep breath and jumped.

Seconds seemed like hours. Falling silently. She could see the table top of Candor Mensa and the jumbled terrain of the Chaos. As though she were dropping into a map.

The absence of any sound was eerie. Everything was rocky red. Isla's head spun.

"Keep it together, Tolly needs you."

The landscape spawned details, shadows, ridges, dust flumes. And the star-suit was warming up. Isla bit back an urge to panic. The rubberised nanotubes that made up the suit, were heat-retardant. She wouldn't burn. The danger was more that she might bungle the landing. Figures flashed on the visor's interior. She'd reached terminal velocity, at nine hundred and sixty kilometres per hour. The suit's exterior was a mere seventy degrees Celsius.

And still she was falling.

"Show rear view." But the far-ship was gone, already too small to be seen. Just the blanket of stars, coldly twinkling.

"Front view again."

There, to the west, the dark smudge of the Free Town. Her home. And that misty grey, rising up into the sky…Could it really be her fellow citizens?

She focussed on the visor screen. Numbers danced as the distance to the ground shrank. She was five miles high. Four point nine, eight, seven…

What was that!

A shape flashed by her. Something crossing her path at an angle. No, *someone*! A man zooming up out of nowhere and disappearing overhead. Too quick for her to make out the face, but beyond doubt a person. But at this height, anyone without a spacesuit would be dead. There was no oxygen.

No!

This time she saw them hurtling upwards. A man, a woman, and a small child. They flew past her in an instant. There was barely time to register their grinning faces before they were out of sight. Grinning faces? Isla felt ice-cold. Zeke had been right all along.

Her mind raced. This spiral creature was real and on Mars. But she would fight it. She'd stand side by side with Ptolemy. They'd defeat this vile monster or die trying.

What was happening? The visor's speedometer was slowing. The rate of descent likewise. But that was impossible. What about gravity? She could feel it, the deceleration. Four miles high and she was falling at the speed of a brisk stroll. And now a snail's pace.

Her heart was in her mouth. This couldn't happen. Not to her.

She stopped, frozen in space, the canyons of Mariners Valley below her but out of reach.

"You'll be happier with us. Tolly will soon be here and you wouldn't want him to be alone."

The words passed through her brain. Deep and comforting. Her razor-sharp fear eased a little. A smile crept across her lips. For a few more seconds she hung in the sky. Then, as if grabbed by an invisible hand, she started flying upwards, at the same angle as the others. She turned her head and saw the twisting circles of the Spiral.

Chapter Thirty-Eight
Principal Lutz's Apartment

The south-facing window gave a staggering view of Ophir Chasma. Towering cliffs tumbled into the distance. Basalt columns punctuated the valley, eroded over the millennia into precarious shapes. They teetered and tottered, as if on the brink of collapse.

Principle Lutz had seen this vista every day for over a century. But on this day, there was something new. A shape floated in the sky, way over to the west. Beyond Ophir Chasma, in the direction of the capital, Tithonium Central. The object was pale and spherical, like a moon. But with her diginoculars, Lutz could make out writhing tentacles and a snapping beak. It was feasting, she saw that as well, and her elderly heart trembled.

"My visions were correct," she said to the empty room. So too were the images she'd glimpsed inside the heads of Hailey, Liang and Cutter, when they returned from their first little jaunt. Hailey was so hard to read, the boy must have some kind of subconscious block. The other two were easier. But Lutz had hoped it was all in their wild imaginations. Now she knew better.

Principle Lutz drained her sherry glass, licked her lips, and began searching her handbag. It was in there the last time she looked.

Poor Hailey. He had quite exceptional talent. She had seen it from day one, at her lecture for the freshers. Even his father was never that strong. And there was Hailey junior, believing he was a non-psychic! But now the poor boy was going to die. *Quel tragique!*

The 'moon' was getting bigger.

She'd seen it in the psychic fits. Those idiots at the Ellipse Building triggering a crack in the universe. Some primeval monster slithering in. Everyone dying. No, worse than dying, trapped inside the monster forever, disembodied but not dead. And Zeke Hailey sacrificing his life so his friends could survive. But not the chubby one, too bad he got left behind.

The 'moon' was trying to speak to her, by telepathy. It would never get her. Not Principle Lutz. She would escape the only way she could. She would set the example.

"Ach, there you are!" Her hand grasped something cold inside the bag.

Her only regret was not saying goodbye to Marjorie. Funny, how fond you could become of a machine.

She pulled the iPistol from the bag and drew a deep breath.

Chapter Thirty-Nine
The School Battlements

It began with the soldiers. They all laughed and waved as they rose into the air.

"We won't need these anymore," said one, dropping his gun. The others copied him. Rifles clattered down onto the rocks. The soldiers whooshed off at an angle, towards the distant spiral.

"What the hell is this?" Cusp demanded of Mariner Knimble. But the Mariner was speechless. He gaped at the spinning tentacles in the sky. This was the end. He sensed it in his bones. He glanced around him, at the students and ninjas along the battlements, at the reserves gathered in the courtyards below. They were all about to die.

"Run!!!" he screamed at the top of his voice.

Panic broke out. People running in all directions. Up on the battlements, the rebels crowded around the steps in a desperate effort to get down. Pushing, shoving. Some lost their footing and fell. Among them was Mariner Kepler, who cracked her head on a stone and didn't get up.

All Knimble could think of was Doctor Chandrasar. She was stationed in the Medical Facility in the caves, waiting for casualties. He had to get to her. Be with her. For their final moments.

A voice was speaking in his head, but with tremendous will he ignored it. He must get to Chandrasar. To tell her with his last words, all the feelings he'd bottled up.

And then suddenly he was flying. The ground vanished and the cold Martian sky surrounded him. He was not alone. Bodies were all around, like a flock of birds ascending to the sun. He recognised teachers, students, rebels. There was little Gary Aspeck with a bewildered expression, Cusp was over there, still fighting it, kicking and punching. And, well, everyone. Knimble felt his muscles relax. Everything was going to be okay.

Chapter Forty
Nowhere

"My special, special boy," said the Spiral. He and Zeke were both back on the great bronze disc. The Milky Way flowed around them, like a river of luminous foam. Zeke looked down. The floor was etched with symbols. Neither human nor Hesperian, a compendium of alien writing. Was he in a dream? Could it be a real place? Maybe he was standing on some portal between galaxies? Between universes?

Whatever.

He drew himself up to his full height and eyed the Spiral.

"There's nothing to say. I want to wake up this instant. You've won. You've got Earth and Mars. But you're not getting us."

The Spiral rotated gently. It spoke through its fetid beak, green and drooling as it was.

"There is so much to say, Zeke. I want you to stay."

"Not going to happen."

Zeke got it now. After all these months and adventures. Some grand history was playing out. The end of the human race, just like the Hesperians two billion years before. He had merely delayed the inevitable. But now he had to escape, with Pin and Trixie. Refugees from the apocalypse. He would deliver the girls to his father, who'd know what to do. Sure, Zeke would die in the attempt, but better that than becoming a snack for the Spiral.

"You're very wrong, Zeke." The Spiral's voice was gentle, almost...fatherly. "I don't kill. I preserve. Everyone I digest will go on forever, part of a greater whole. They're all still in here. In my belly. Who would you like to talk to? Justice? Mariner Knimble? Oh, I know, the Hesperians? They can tell you what really happened all those centuries ago."

Zeke swallowed. He couldn't stop himself asking.

"Scuff? Is he in there?"

The Spiral spun a little faster.

"He's on his way."

Zeke clenched his fists and tried to wake up.

"But Zeke, I'm not going to eat you. I need you with Fitch, ruling over this galaxy. I'll give you immortality. You two boys, you're special. You can ride comets."

Zeke frowned. What did that mean? The Spiral had mentioned comets once before. It seemed obsessed with them. Or was it simply distracting him, buying time while back in the real world it crept nearer to the far-ship.

"Wake up, wake up, wake up," he muttered, squeezing his fists.

"Truly Zeke, we will be partners. Think of the power I can give you. And we can reach your father and rescue him."

Don't listen, it's a trick. It's always a trick.

"I am offering you my friendship, Zeke Hailey. This is your only chance to survive."

"You speak Hesperian?" Zeke asked.

"High and low dialects. You only know the basics. What they needed you to know. I can teach you more."

"What they needed me to know?"

"Do you think the orb came to you by chance? There's more to your story, more than you can guess. Stay with me and find out."

No, no, no! He mustn't fall for the Spiral's lies. It would say anything to tempt him to linger. And then he and the girls would end up in its belly.

"I ask, because I wanted to say this."

Zeke erupted with foul insults, shouting every nasty Hesperian word he could remember. The Spiral recoiled. Zeke permitted himself a slight smirk. The spell was broken. He woke up.

Chapter Forty-One
Scuff's Room

Scuff rocked to and forth on the floor, biting chunks from his nails. *Where was Zeke?* He checked his defences. The bed and desk were piled up against the door. How long would they last?

He'd held back from the battle. Even after Cusp ordered every armband be removed, so no student could be caught defenceless by the invading army. After all, wasn't Scuff a lover, not a fighter? Sheesh, an egghead at any rate. Brains too precious to be spilt in a knuckle fest. From the vantage point of the fifth floor, he'd watched as soldiers, teachers, rebels and students were sucked into the sky. Then he'd pushed his wardrobe across the window. To block the horrifying view as much as to protect himself.

But he could still hear them in his head. His acute telepathic skills tuned in to their hysterical laughter and desperate screams. He got it. Some were hypnotised and some were not. Their cries were diminishing now, as one by one, they vanished into the sky-hole.

And he could hear that too. Not so much hear as feel. An incredibly strong mental force. A mind. Alien and ancient, radiating power across Mars. He pushed it from his head, jumped up and paced the room. Where was his buddy? Surely Zeke would translocate in at any moment and save him. Zeke wouldn't let him down. Zeke wouldn't leave him to die.

He would, whispered a voice.

Scuff stomped his foot. "You're lying!"

At that moment, his room filled with a bright yellow light.

"What the—"

The orb! That useless big black orb in the corner! It was beaming fingers of light like a glitter ball. The hairs on Scuff's neck tingled. The orb rolled out onto the rug.

"Go, now!"

The voice came from the orb. Crackly and distant, and…familiar.

"Listen to me, go, before the Spiral gets you."

Scuff's brain raced. What was happening? The orb was speaking to him, in English. How was that even possible? A joke? A trick?

"Who the heck are you?" Scuff shouted.

"No time, just go."

"How! One foot outside and the Spiral gets me."

"Don't be dense, dummy. Translocate!"

"I can't, I'm only a second year," Scuff wailed.

"You're a Mariner. You can. Even if it kills you, better than ending up inside the Spiral."

Something in the hallway thumped against his door. Something big. The architrave splintered. Scuff wrung his hands.

"Zeke, is that you?"

The lights from the orb grew brighter.

"Translocate to the Infinity Trap," said the voice. "It's the only place you'll be safe."

"Are you nuts? Not only is it sealed shut, but the Spiral's inside," Scuff replied frantically.

"Then who's that at your door?"

Scuff bit his lip. The orb had a point. If the Spiral was here, did that mean it had escaped from the Trap?

A second blow. The auto-door cracked.

"Go! Trust in yourself. Someone's at the Trap to help you."

The orb whined. Its lights died and it crumbled to dust.

Scuff's heart pounded inside his ribcage. Wait here for Zeke to save him or take the advice of some alien gizmo? Oh, what the heck…he closed his eyes and thought with all his strength.

"The Cave of Wonders, the Cave of Wonders."

He opened his eyes. Still in his room. Still about to die.

One final bang shook the room. The door crumpled. A shockwave knocked Scuff off his feet. He tumbled backwards, one thought echoing through his synapses.

Leave!

He was rolling through the void. His lungs gasped for oxygen. A deafening noise rang in his ears, the sound of a trillion chimes.

"Ouch." He landed on his butt. Sunlight blinded him for a second. Faraway canyon walls boxed in the land. He was in the Valley somewhere, surrounded by rubble. High in the northern sky, the Spiral twisted around and around.

"Come to me," boomed its voice, speaking telepathically.

"Never," Scuff shouted back.

"You won't get away."

"Go to hell," Scuff bellowed. He scanned the landscape, hoping for somewhere to hide. But the plain was pancake flat, there was nowhere.

"I won't betray you, not like your friend."

Scuff took a deep breath. The Spiral was trying to distract him, lull him into a trance. Hypnotise him. He shook a chubby fist at the monster.

"Whatever happened, he didn't betray me." Scuff wouldn't let that happen, he wouldn't allow the Spiral to drive a wedge between him and his best bud.

"Then why are you alone?" it asked.

Scuff squealed. He was floating six inches off the ground! He shut his eyes as tightly as possible and with every fibre of his being pictured the Cave of Wonders. A flash of darkness, then cold stone smacked his rump.

Oh, my aching butt! he thought, jumping up. Writhing, snakelike rocks surrounded him, barely visible in the ghostly light. The Cave of Wonders. He'd made it! The brief elation subsided as he turned to see the Dust Devil. The human shape glowed within the funnel of moaning, spinning sand. That's where the light was coming from.

"You don't have long," it said. The voice sounded like Jimmy Swallow. Scuff peered closer. The creature even had Jimmy's face, the high-brow, long nose and full lips.

"What's going on? Why are you here?"

The Devil shuddered, its eyeless face looking right through Scuff.

"The sweep of galaxies comes full circle. The stars are back to where they started."

"Pardon me?" The last thing Scuff needed was some Hesperian mumbo-jumbo.

It hissed. "He's coming. Quick, imagine somewhere good."

Scuff remembered the previous encounter at the Infinity Trap. "But we need at least five psychic minds. Hey, I might be a genius, but even I'm not that good."

"The last time I was forced. The Professor needed power to overcome me. This time I'm willing."

"But why? Why me?"

"Young Barnum, where are you?"

It was the Spiral's voice, booming inside Scuff's skull. An urge arose inside him to answer. No! He steeled himself against its hypnotic power.

Scuff placed his hands over his ears. There was no time to think it through. Act now or die. Somewhere good? Sheesh, that was easy. Glass doors formed out of thin air. It was the way in to his favourite fast food joint, Baron Von Burgers, back in his home town of Lakeville.

"Barnum, wait!"

A tentacle slithered in through the mouth of the cave. Scuff shrieked even louder.

"I'm coming in!" he screamed, and dived through the glass doors, the Devil on his heels. The plastic seats and tables were deserted. Glass walls looked out onto blankness. Scuff stared up at the menu above the counter.

Wonder if I've got time for a double spitfire? His beloved dish, a beef patty barbecued with chilli sauce.

"Keep going!" cried the Dust Devil, its voice straining.

The creature was throwing its weight against the entrance, shoulder up against the glass. On the other side, the coiled tentacle pushed back.

"I don't understand," Scuff said.

The living whirlwind shifted its position. "I cannot allow the Spiral to capture the Trap and myself. With my knowledge, my programming, he would have a shortcut to everywhere. All times, all places, all universes."

The tentacle shoved hard. The door wobbled, but the Devil remained firm.

"It's the one thing that must never happen. I've triggered the auto-destruct. The Trap will implode to the size of an atom."

"Wh-a-a-at!" Scuff screamed.

"Eight seconds."

Scuff scrambled towards the far exit, leg muscles trembling like jelly. He burst through those doors and tumbled into oblivion.

Scuff choked. Water was bubbling down his throat. He kicked wildly. The surface broke and he gasped air down into his lungs. He sucked in a few more deep breaths, treading water. A sea. He had splash-landed into a sea. The salty water was warm. So too was the breeze. The sky shone around him like a dome of solid sapphire.

His heart leapt. He'd done it. Escaped the Spiral. Landed back on Earth. And now he was back, he could warn humanity. Maybe they could nuke Mars?

A shoal of red triangles darted around his submerged body. Glinting ruby-red fish. The sea was so still and glassy clear he could make them out easily. One bumped into him, its snout as hard as metal.

Strange fish, must be some tropical species.

Scuff spotted the shoreline a few hundred metres away and began swimming. The sand was white, like a line of sugar. Wherever he was, it was pretty. His feet found the bottom and he waded the remaining distance. More triangle-fish swarmed around him. The coast was coming into view. No buildings, just the powdered dunes, dotted with palm trees. Jagged fronds swayed against candy cotton clouds.

He stumbled ashore and collapsed onto his knees. Maybe he should kiss the ground? In this position, he noticed a rock in the sky. A moon.

Oh no!

It was totally the wrong shape and size. Tiny and egg-shaped, not spherical. It was Phobos, one of the two Martian moons! His heartbeat accelerated into overdrive, as he tried to take it all in. Before he could gather his wits, a nearby pink boulder rattled. A boulder. A boulder. Surely, it was a boulder? Only, it wasn't a boulder. The thing sprouted legs, lots of them, and stood. Scuff found himself staring into protruding, crablike eyes. Into an inhuman face. Mandibles began clicking.

Scuff froze. It felt as if the universe was shrinking, from its unimaginable vastness into this tiny little scrap of existence.

He was still on Mars. But there was life. This meant one thing. The Infinity Trap had hurled him back in time two billion years. He was lost, alone and among aliens.

Chapter Forty-Two
The Far-Ship

Zeke opened his eyes. The girls were strapped into their seats. "Now, Hailey, now! It's getting into my brain," Trixie screamed, rubbing her eyes raw.

"Me too, Zeke, he's calling to me," Pin-mei cried with a contorted face.

"Albie, begin the pulse. Translocation in twenty seconds," Zeke shouted.

"Affirmative, Master Zeke," the software replied.

A hum began deep in the ship's structure. It grew louder. His head throbbed as a horrible feeling flowed through his body, an intensity. This was the feedback wave, bouncing between Zeke and the protoplasm. The gigantic cell was magnifying Zeke's brainwaves.

"Albie, monitor and record my vitals," Zeke screamed above the deafening roar. He stared at his hand, his veins were swelling. His heart raced. Spasms racked his limbs. Only the strappings of the motherboard prevented him from falling. His brain strained against the shell of his skull. Forks of pain stabbed his forehead. Was he going to explode?

So, this was the end. There was no time to think it over. To grieve. But he had no doubt this was better. He had no desire to end up in the Spiral's belly. And at least this way, Pin-mei lived. And Trixie too, he was glad about that. But Scuff? He mustn't think of Scuff…

Zeke fixed his attention on Pin-mei. He wanted her to be the last thing he saw. But her beautiful Chinese face was contorted, as she struggled against the Spiral's hypnosis.

Zeke closed his eyes and gritted his teeth. Despite the pain, he summoned up an image of Alpha Cephei. A gigantic star burning white in the inky blackness of space.

"Zero," Albie said.

The last amplified brainwave slammed into Zeke's synapses. His spine arched, throwing his head back with a cry of agony. His mind latched onto a blue and purple moon, orbiting the yellow gas giant.

There! Go there!

Zeke felt every atom of his body, every atom of the bridge, every atom of the far-ship slide out of reality. His brain, and then the rest of the ship, floated in the realm of nothingness.

His heart popped. The blood vessels in his brain ruptured, flooding his cortex. Lights flashed before him. Scenes. His mother brewing a pot of tea in their kitchen. The Spiral chewing on screaming people. Pin-mei. Scuff. The Televator. The school. And then the lights faded to reveal a face. Only it wasn't human. Green-skinned, with dark brooding eyes and a long, baboon-like snout instead of a nose. A shock of turquoise hair topped the head and the creature had a lopsided smile.

And with that face before him, Zeke died.

Epilogue

A breeze flitted through purple treetops. Branches stirred, as though the trees were waking from a long sleep. Zamdro crept out from the undergrowth, into a glade, spear poised, ready to strike. A baby hornleafer slurped water at the edge of a river-thread. It hadn't noticed him. Zamdro scanned the animal's scaly legs and rump, licking his lips. Enough meat to make a suitable meal for Volka. Maybe even appease that terrible temper.

Zamdro carefully stepped nearer, through banks of puff-grass. Despite his efforts to be stealthy, the seed bellies of the grass cracked. Pink spores flooded the air. Still, the hornleafer drank, unaware of its doom.

He was just four breaths away. As quiet as a stone-bug, he stopped and aimed.

Wait, wait, wait till the moment is right. Feel it in the soul, own the destiny.

And Zamdro threw! His spear flew, quick and sharp, and—missed! It splashed into the river-thread. The hornleafer squeaked and bolted into mauve bushes.

"*Cruimsquat!*" Zamdro cursed, kicking a moss-husk which turned out to be rock hard.

"Ow" he squealed, now hopping from foot to foot. Failed again. He was useless.

Completely useless. No wonder Volka hated him. Zamdro wanted to cry.

He knelt down, on the edge of the river-thread, and stared at his reflection. At that crop of turquoise hair, the colour of sky petals. The one thing that separated him from the rest of the tribe. That made him special. He stroked it lovingly.

But turquoise hair wasn't enough to make Volka proud of him. Zamdro knew he was a disappointment.

Every muscle in his body tensed.

What was that?

Zamdro gazed up into the blueness of the sky. Nothing. The air was still and silent. But surely...? His scalp tingled. The spirit-senses were whispering. The voices that never speak, the eyes that never see. They were whispering in his mind. Sharing their secrets of foresight, as real as the river-thread was wet. Something had changed. Somewhere had come to an end. Someone was coming.

"Volka!" he cried. He must tell Volka. And with that, Zamdro bounded back into the dark undergrowth of the forest.

Mars is a planet of secrets. Uncover the truth at Zeke's web site: www.zekehailey.com.

And Zeke Hailey's final adventure will continue in
The Paradox War.